"Where are you?" Wezhardt demanded. "We heard gunfire."

"I'm inside the clinic proper, bottled up in a shower room," Mack Bolan replied.

A sudden crash of static drowned out most of Wezhardt's response. Beyond the double doors the Executioner heard noises of action—hurried footfalls, whispering voices and the squeaking of wheels.

"You've got to get out of there fast," Wezhardt finally said over the static. "Now! The radiation detector has just registered a strong signal. They've powered up one of their microwave emitters, probably the Gunn oscillator!"

Bolan glanced toward the doors. The squeaking stopped.

A low hum sounded, and the rest of Wezhardt's words dissolved in a blur of static.

MACK BOLAN ®
The Executioner

DON PENDLETON'S
THE EXECUTIONER®
DEVIL'S GUARD

A GOLD EAGLE BOOK FROM
W❂RLDWIDE®

TORONTO • NEW YORK • LONDON
AMSTERDAM • PARIS • SYDNEY • HAMBURG
STOCKHOLM • ATHENS • TOKYO • MILAN
MADRID • WARSAW • BUDAPEST • AUCKLAND

First edition December 1998
ISBN 0-373-64240-7

Special thanks and acknowledgment to
Mark Ellis for his contribution to this work.

DEVIL'S GUARD

Printed in U.S.A.

Some things are secret because they are hard to know, and some because they are not fit to utter.

—Francis Bacon

When a democratic government practices stealth and secrecy against its own citizens, everyone in that democracy is divorced from any understanding of circumstances affecting their own lives. If that's the standard, then there is no government. All you have is a conspiracy.

—Mack Bolan

THE
MACK BOLAN®
LEGEND

Nothing less than a war could have fashioned the destiny of the man called Mack Bolan. Bolan earned the Executioner title in the jungle hell of Vietnam.

But this soldier also wore another name—Sergeant Mercy. He was so tagged because of the compassion he showed to wounded comrades-in-arms and Vietnamese civilians.

Mack Bolan's second tour of duty ended prematurely when he was given emergency leave to return home and bury his family, victims of the Mob. Then he declared a one-man war against the Mafia.

He confronted the Families head-on from coast to coast, and soon a hope of victory began to appear. But Bolan had broken society's every rule. That same society started gunning for this elusive warrior—to no avail.

So Bolan was offered amnesty to work within the system against terrorism. This time, as an employee of Uncle Sam, Bolan became Colonel John Phoenix. With a command center at Stony Man Farm in Virginia, he and his new allies—Able Team and Phoenix Force—waged relentless war on a new adversary: the KGB.

But when his one true love, April Rose, died at the hands of the Soviet terror machine, Bolan severed all ties with Establishment authority.

Now, after a lengthy lone-wolf struggle and much soul-searching, the Executioner has agreed to enter an "arm's-length" alliance with his government once more, reserving the right to pursue personal missions in his Everlasting War.

PROLOGUE

May 2, the Zittertal Alpen, Austria

The steady sound of steel driving into ice had stopped. The setting sun threw shadows across the frozen surface of the titanic glacier that crept down from the Hochfeiler peak.

Three men shivered at the foot of the frozen flow, their breaths pluming before their faces. Though they were bundled up in heavy overcoats, they were still cold. Winter stayed a very long time at nine thousand feet above sea level.

The three men represented three generations of age, divided by time and experience, but united for the moment by a single purpose.

Helmur Ganth was sixty-three years old and of medium height. He was thick of feature and body, his gray eyes masked by dark sunglasses. Garth was president of Wust and Wimmer, a prestigious brokerage firm based in Berlin, with branch offices in nine European metropolitan centers.

Heinrich Heine's thin, ninety-four-year-old body was hunched over in a wheelchair, his lower face protected from the cold by a woolen scarf. His naked, blue-veined head trembled slightly. His face was withered and crisscrossed with a network of wrinkles, seams and lines. His eyes burned as hot and as blue as the sky high above the Alps.

Lieutenant-Colonel Aubrey Lesnick, U.S. Army, stood slightly behind Heine's wheelchair. His dark blond hair was cut in a severe military style. He was forty-three, and his unlined face was all sharp angles and planes. His brown eyes squinted against the sun's glitter from the ice field.

The three were watching as two men, a hundred yards into the base of the glacier, hacked and chopped at the ice with axes and hammers. They were young, barely out of their teens. Their heads were shaved. One had removed his heavy gloves, and blue tattoos stood out sharply against his pale skin. His right hand bore a crude likeness of a swastika, and the other a stylized iron cross.

His companion took off his scarf and wiped bits of ice from his face. The word *Herrenvolk* was stenciled in crude Gothic script across his acne-spotted forehead. A close inspection of the word would have revealed a successful, if painful, experiment with a red-hot needle.

The gloveless man inserted two fingers into his mouth and whistled piercingly, then shouted, "Almost have it, Mr. Ganth!"

Heine grimaced. "Does that animal think he's on a street corner in Dusseldorf?"

Ganth shrugged. "They are useful."

Heine spit onto the snow, then squinted at the pair of young men as they bent over the hole chopped in the ice and struggled with something within it.

"They can be trusted?" he asked.

"Of course not," Ganth replied. "They believe with all their hearts in the Aryan struggle—this week. Next week, they could be just as passionate about cross-country skiing."

After a long moment of grunting and cursing, the two men dragged a long rectangular box out of the hole. It was made of lead and shaped like a casket.

Heine leaned forward, his fierce eyes gazing raptorially at the dark, metallic surface of the thing. A half century of ice clung to it.

The pair of youths carried it, sliding and stumbling across the base of the glacier to Ganth, and they dropped it carelessly at his feet. They panted, and despite the cold, they were perspiring.

"Hard work," said the one with *Herrenvolk* stenciled across his forehead. "I think you owe us another few hundred marks."

The man with the tattooed hands gestured to the casket. "You want us to open it for you, sir?"

Heine's toothless mouth opened. Spittle strings clung between his gums. "What lies within is not for the eyes of swine," he snarled.

Herrenvolk glared at the old man. "Go to hell, old man. We don't work for you."

He turned to Ganth. "When do we get paid?"

Before Ganth could respond, Heine said, "Immediately."

One clawlike hand dived inside his coat and came out gripping a Walther P-38, the official service pistol of the German forces during the war. Heine didn't seem to aim; he squeezed the double-action trigger, and two flat cracks shattered the still, frosty air.

The first 9 mm slug took the youth with the tattooed hands directly through the heart. The second bullet inscribed a perfect circle on the other man's forehead. The two shots had come so fast they sounded like a single report.

Ganth and Lesnick regarded the two corpses lying in the snow with dispassionate eyes. Steam arose from the blood streaming from their bodies.

"Your eye is as keen as my father told me," Ganth said wryly.

Heine shoved the pistol back inside his coat. "Before we leave, you must plant that trash in the hole they've dug. Maybe in another fifty years someone may wait for them to surface. I can't imagine who."

He laughed, a dry crackling sound. One gnarled finger pointed to the casket. "Open it, Helmur."

Ganth's eyebrows rose. "Here?"

"Why not?"

"I assumed you would wish a ceremony of some sort—"

Heine laughed again, and this time it held a bitter, humorless edge. "You engage two street pigs to dig it out of the ice, and you think I want a ceremony? Rituals can wait, Helmur."

Ganth thought it over a moment, then shrugged. "As you wish, sir."

Taking a chisel from the tool belt around Herrenvolk's waist, Ganth attacked the solder holding the lid in place. As he worked, Heine glanced up into Lesnick's expressionless face.

"You stand in the presence of history, Colonel," he said sardonically in English. "Does that not send a chill up your spine?"

"I am honored, sir," was Lesnick's flat reply.

"I thought as much."

Ganth removed half-century-old solder in sections, chunks and the occasional strip. On his knees, he worked his way around the casket. Far from being offended that Heine had assigned him this manual labor rather than the American, he was trembling with awe. His father had never told him exactly what lay within the leaden container. He said only that the contents were treasures beyond compare.

Ganth was the only child of Oberführer Eric Ganth, a man who had distinguished himself in the service of the Brandenberg Division, the Third Reich's elite commando force. The elder Ganth had been one of the less notorious Schutzstaffel alumni, and he had never been invited to testify at the Nuremberg War Crimes Tribunal. Eric Ganth had died in Bavaria nineteen years before, his excesses with his former fraternity known to only a few.

One of the few was Heinrich Heine. Standartenführer Heine, like Oberführer Ganth, had served the Reich faithfully as fortress commandant of Castle Wewelsburg, the SS monastery and repository of artifacts.

Heine, Eric Ganth and one other man had met for the last time in the castle in the predawn hours of May 2, 1945, and sworn an oath. Later that day, the three men had stood on the Hochfeiler glacier and watched, as with great ceremony, SS troopers buried a three-by-four-foot leaden casket in the ice.

All the troopers knew was that the contents of the casket couldn't fall into the hands of the Allies. Hitler had died less than forty-eight hours before and the war, for all intents and purposes, was over.

Eric Ganth had performed mathematical measurements and calculated that the casket would be in position for recovery fifty years hence. Ganth, Heine and one other man promised to meet at the glacier on that day, a half century in the future.

Of the three, only Heine had kept the promise. Helmur Ganth represented his father, and the third member of the triad hadn't appeared. Lieutenant-Colonel Aubrey Lesnick had stepped into the vacancy.

Whether the casket held gold bars or priceless art objects looted from European museums, Helmur Ganth didn't care. The casket and its contents were legacies from a glorious era of blood, honor and iron resolve.

The final piece of solder came away in his hands. He rose stiffly to his feet and stood at attention beside the casket. On impulse, he raised his right arm and slashed the cold air with the flat of his hand. "It is done. *Seig Heil*."

"Oh, shut up," Heine growled. "Don't befoul the atmosphere with memories of that maniac. He has nothing to do with this."

Ganth dropped his arm, feeling humbled and foolish.

Heine wheeled his chair close to the box and bent over, his long-nailed fingers gripping the edge of the lid. Taking a deep breath, he closed his eyes. A thin smile touched his lips, and he heaved the lid up and over onto the red-streaked snow. Ganth leaned forward, eyes wide. Lesnick moved closer, inclining his head a fraction of an inch.

Ganth wasn't sure of what he was looking at. Oilcloth-wrapped objects of varying shapes and sizes were packed tightly and neatly into the casket. For all the awe the contents evoked in Ganth, he might as well have been peering into the hope chest of a spinster.

"Sir," Ganth asked softly, "do you know what these things are?"

"Of course I do," Heine snapped. "I inventoried them myself in a crypt beneath Castle Wewelsburg. Teudt was responsible for the actual packing, and he packed them in the order I listed."

Mouth open and shining wetly, Heine began to carefully remove items from the casket, unwrapping the oilcloth coverings reverentially. Ganth and Lesnick stood by silently and watched as the old man identified each piece in a breathless voice.

The first object was a brown, grinning human skull, the cranium encircled by a discolored golden diadem.

"The skull of Heinrich der Vogler, the leader of the First Reich, a thousand years ago...."

Next came a large package containing a battered shield and a pair of three-foot-long swords. The hilts were inlaid with gems.

"The shield and swords of Emperor Charlemagne, one of the greatest of Aryan monarchs..."

Inside a small package was the head of an ancient-looking spear, the metal dull and notched. Leather thongs affixed it to a broken wooden haft.

"The Holy Lance, with which the German centurion Longinus pierced Christ's side as he hung on the cross...."

After Heine unwrapped the items and inspected them briefly, he placed them on the snow beside his wheelchair. He reached into the casket for a fourth time, then he paused. His eyes slitted.

"Something is wrong," he hissed. "It should be the next piece. It's not here."

Heine pawed through the casket, pushing the contents from one end to the other. He kept up a steady refrain of "It's not here—it's not here!" His frantic breath clouded before his face like steam escaping from a cracked boiler.

Ganth laid a hesitant hand on Heine's bony shoulder. "Sir, what is missing?"

Heine flung off the hand. His raging blue eyes bored into the lenses of Ganth's sunglasses with such ferocity that the younger man took an involuntary step backward.

Crooking his fingers like the talons of a hawk, Heine snarled, "The Dag! Teudt stole the Dag!" Spittle flecked his lips.

Ganth cleared his throat and asked calmly, "You mean a knife, sir?"

Heine struck at Ganth's arm. "Don't speak to me like I'm one of your senile investors!"

Straightening in the wheelchair, Heine mimicked, "'You mean a knife, sir?'" He took several deep breaths.

"The Dag," he said in an even voice, "is an emblem of my office in the Order. It dates back to 772 A.D. It was ceded to me by Himmler himself, in the Great Hall of the castle. It represents the number of original knights who formed the Order. It is a holy object. Sacred not only to myself, but to our society."

Hesitantly Ganth said, "But surely the lack of this...artifact cannot cause us harm. After all, it has been buried for fifty years, and we have only grown stronger."

Heine's lips compressed in a tight white line. His voice was low, deadly, as cold as the glacier looming over them. "The Order can survive without it. But it cannot survive thieves and traitors."

Eyeing the butt of the Walther protruding from the old man's coat, Ganth asked, "To whom do you refer, sir?"

Heine's fingers dug into the wooden arms of the wheelchair. "Himmler assigned three of us tasks for the burial detail. Your father saw to the construction of the container. I collected and inventoried all the artifacts. Teudt packed them and sealed the container. Of the three, Teudt is not represented here."

"So you suspect that over fifty years ago Teudt stole the Dag?" The note of outrage in Ganth's voice wasn't forced. "For what purpose?"

"The Dag represents an important link in the chain of a tradition dating back a thousand years. Without that link, our chain is broken. And there is very little you can do with a broken chain."

Ganth cast a fearful glance into Lesnick's expressionless face. "But our undertaking...it is too late to abort it. The colonel has been prepared, the timetable is set, the window of opportunity is narrow—"

Heine interrupted Ganth with a savage gesture. "Stop babbling. The undertaking will continue on schedule. I will concern myself with finding Teudt. He has violated the most fundamental pledge of the Order—Honor Is Loyalty."

Heine's voice dropped to a gloating croon. "He has had fifty years to forget that pledge. I will take a great deal of pleasure in jogging his memory."

May 30, the Upper Amazon Basin, Brazil

In the village, only shadows moved.

The grass-roofed huts were empty, and the cook fires long extinguished, but the Tupi-Gurani people were still there. The thirty-seven inhabitants—men, women and children—were scattered on the ground where merciless autofire had hammered them. The bodies lay in silent, bullet-slashed heaps. The bare earth had soaked up their blood like a sponge, turning the ground into crimson-stained sludge.

Mack Bolan emerged from the bushes at the perimeter of the village and watched and listened. A half moon shone on the jungle like a brightly polished medal. He moved through the brush in a wide circle, his figure sliding in and out of the shadows, blending with the shifting pattern of moonlight and dark.

He kept the Desert Eagle leathered snugly in the holster on his hip, but a foot-long combat knife was in his right hand. He used it to push aside hanging lianas and foliage in his path.

Bolan peered closely at the ground and saw the marks of many booted feet, and places where twigs had been stepped on and broken. Once he bent and picked up a small brass object. More by feel than sight, he identified it as a 7.62 mm cartridge case from an assault rifle.

In the heavy jungle growth on the north side of the village, his silent circuit completed, he stopped and bent again. He studied a small residue of viscous liquid on the grass. He touched it, smelled it, then stood. It was gun oil, and judging by the three widely separated indentations in the grass, the oil had dripped from a tripod-mounted machine gun. Whoever had attacked the villagers had intended nothing less than a massacre. The attackers had been fairly efficient in policing the killzone, but they had neglected to collect a few calling cards. This had been a military-style operation from start to finish, with an emphasis on anonymity.

Bolan froze and sank to one knee, the Desert Eagle slipping quietly into his hand. Two men in khaki were moving fast through the village. They carried Gewehr 3-A3 West German army assault rifles, and walkie-talkies were slung over their shoulders by straps. Though they passed too far away to see their faces, Bolan heard them speaking in German.

The pair vanished into the jungle on the southward edge of the village. Bolan returned the pistol to its holster and glided through the brush again, reevaluating his first suspicion that he had stumbled onto one of Brazil's indigenous tragedies.

It was no secret that the Indian inhabitants of the Amazon Basin were being methodically exterminated on orders of the authorities. No one bothered to negotiate with the Indians for the lumber rights to their land; they were simply shot on sight and had no choice but to retreat farther into the rapidly shrinking forest.

This massacre didn't seem to be the work of the Brazilian military or hired mercenaries. Though Bolan wasn't fluent in the German language, he had understood the two men well enough.

The pair of Germans were searching for someone, and Bolan was pretty sure he knew who it was.

The hospital and research station was at the edge of the village. It was much larger than the huts and had a covered veranda. The veranda leaned, and a palm-frond wall lay fallen-in by the fury of automatic-weapons fire. Bolan crept up the sagging steps and entered the main room of the building.

By the light of a pencil flash, he saw that chairs had been smashed, the walls themselves torn down, tables broken, bottles and vials of medicine shattered on the floor. Bolan found the small radio transceiver in a far corner. It had been blasted into a twisted mass of metal, plastic and broken glass.

The examination room and laboratory looked as though grenades had been lobbed into them. Everything had been shot, smashed and torn, and there was nowhere for anyone to hide.

Bolan returned to the examination room. By the narrow beam of the small flashlight, he saw a small trace of blood on the littered floor. It was dark, but it was still tacky to the touch.

Placing the pencil flash between his teeth, Bolan covered the room inch by inch on his hands and knees. He saw nothing but debris. At the far corner, he turned to retrace his steps, then stopped. His trained hearing had detected a faint difference of sound when he had moved into the corner. Bending low, he lightly rapped the floorboards and heard an unmistakable hollow sound.

Bolan cleared away the debris from the corner as quietly as he could. He saw nothing but bare floorboards at first, then the light of the flash showed him the thread-thin outline of the trapdoor.

Jamming the long steel blade of the combat knife into the tiny space between the edge of the door and the floor, Bolan tried to pry it open. It refused to budge, held fast by a catch on the underside. Bolan put his back against the wall and launched a straight-leg kick at the knife's handle. There was a sharp snap of metal as the catch broke, and a three-by-three square of flooring popped up.

He returned the knife to its ankle sheath, unholstered the Desert Eagle and swung down onto a narrow ladder. There was a small, dark room only ten feet below.

The dirt walls were reinforced by plywood panels. The room was empty, but it had been used recently. There were footprints on the hard-packed dirt floor and a spotting of blood. The footprints led to an earth wall, the only one not shored up by wood paneling.

Bolan's fingers found a break low near the floor. At a tug, a small section of the wall came away and revealed a passage just big enough for a medium-sized man to crawl through. The passageway was hidden by sheet metal covered with dark paint and glued-on dirt to match the wall and floor.

The soldier squeezed into the small opening. It was an exceptionally tight fit. He struggled for twenty feet, then saw a dim light and heard a low roaring sound, the rush of the Madeira River, a tributary of the Amazon.

The passage opened into a chamber ten feet wide by seven high. Diffused moonlight was peeping through another opening, on the far side of the chamber.

Over the rush of the river, Bolan heard the rasp of labored breathing and the faint rustle of cloth. He shone the pencil flash around. The man leaning against the wall stared into the light without blinking.

"Honor Is Loyalty.... Honor Is Loyalty...."

The man repeated the phrase in German, staring at the light without really seeing it. He was an elderly man with thin white hair topping an equally thin face. His eyes were surrounded by dark rings of suffering, sunk deep back in their sockets. His face was encrusted with dirt.

His exposed left leg was covered in dark purple patches that shone moistly in the gloom. A small bullet hole was visible midway on his thigh. The exit wound was farther down on the inside of his leg, a raw, fist-sized crater surrounded by a discolored ring of proud flesh. A length of rubber hose was knotted tightly around his leg above the wounds.

Bolan could smell the odor of putrefaction. The man had tied on the tourniquet to stop the bleeding, but had evidently neglected to loosen it. Gangrene had settled in the leg, and only amputation would save his life.

Bolan kneeled beside him. "Dr. Tohrbach?"

The man continued to mutter.

Bolan pressed a hand against the man's seamed forehead. He was burning up with fever.

The man shrieked at the touch. Glassy eyes gleaming, his mouth convulsed, starting another scream. Bolan clamped a hand over Tohrbach's mouth and holstered his automatic. With his free hand, he quickly unsnapped a pouch on his web belt and took from it a small squeeze hypodermic. It contained a stimulant developed by the medics at Stony Man Farm. Whether it would reverse Tohrbach's delirium, Bolan had no way of knowing, but he injected the ampoule's contents into the man's inner arm just the same.

Tohrbach's scream turned into a moan, and Bolan released him. The man's head lolled, and he banged it back against the wall. His eyes closed and his body sagged.

Bolan shone the flash around the room. There was nothing in it but a padlocked metal strongbox. It bore a curious symbol on the lid, both familiar and strange at the same time. In faded gold paint was a triangle, which was bisected by a stylized lightning bolt. The bolt resembled one of the twin lightning strikes the SS had chosen as both its initials and its insignia.

Looking at it, Bolan couldn't help but wonder what kind of hellzone Hal Brognola had sent him into. He recalled the big Fed's initial overtures for the present mission.

The day before, Brognola had contacted Barbara Price, the Farm's mission controller on the secured line from his office in the Department of Justice building. He told her that a "conduit" in Interpol had passed along a radio message to the State Department, which in turn had passed it along to him. Bolan had been at the Farm at the time, and the big Fed had contacted him there.

"You ever heard of Dr. Gerald Tohrbach, Mack?"

"Should I have?" The use of his first name rather than "Striker" made him instantly suspicious.

"Not unless you keep up with advances in biochemistry. He's a German-born scientist, but a naturalized American citizen. He's on the board of the World Health Organization."

Brognola described Tohrbach as a dedicated medical man, a man who had spent all his life trying to help the less fortunate of the world both spiritually and with more practical aid. For the past twenty years he had operated a research center and hospital in a small Indian village in the Upper Amazon Basin.

That very morning, a voice message had been transmitted from Tohrbach's village to an Interpol office in São Paulo.

"It was only a few words," Brognola said. "Evidently he didn't have time for more. He said, 'Village under attack. Der Orden—'"

"Sound more like a concern for the local authorities or the United Nations, Hal."

"That's what I said. But the State Department contacted the

President, who was very clear on this. They want someone with no traceable governmental-agency ties to go down there and look around.''

"What's Interpol's interest in this? Why don't they send an investigator?''

"That's all I'm at liberty to divulge. What do you say, Mack?''

Bolan had hesitated. The arm's-length relationship he had with the federal government was uncertain even when he chose to accept missions from the Feds, but Brognola had acted as a buffer between him and other law-enforcement agencies frequently in the past, so Bolan had said yes. And he was once more walking a hellfire trail.

TOHRBACH'S EYES FLEW open, and they were no longer so bright and wild. He said in slightly accented English, "I expected you yesterday. After I made the call.''

"I'm not from Interpol,'' Bolan said. "Who did this to you, to the people?''

Tohrbach focused on something behind Bolan, as though he were trying to view the past. "I should've known. I missed the reunion. I knew Ganth had died, and didn't figure after fifty years anyone would be there. I mean, I was only a boy when I took the oath. A frightened boy whose entire world was in flames.''

Tohrbach shifted position and grunted in pain. "They came on us suddenly at dawn and killed everyone.''

"Who did?''

Tohrbach covered his face with his hands and a great, shuddery sob broke from his chest. "Killed them all. The children—''

"Dr. Tohrbach—'' Bolan began.

The man dropped his hands. His face was contorted in such a mask of self-loathing and rage.

"Don't call me that!'' he half shouted. "Not anymore! My name is Teudt! Karl Gustav Teudt! Lieutenant Teudt of the Reichssicherheitshouptampt!''

It took Bolan a moment to recognize that ear-filling conglomeration of consonants.

The man was referring to the Reich Main Security Office, the foreign-espionage bureau of the SS. Now he knew why Brognola had hedged about giving him the full picture, and why Interpol was involved. For years, Interpol's administrators had favored veterans of the Reich Main Security Office as both field men and contract agents. The Nazis had filled most of that agency's staff positions with party members from the early thirties through the end of the war.

Tohrbach-Teudt had obviously used Interpol's influence to get a new identity and a new citizenship. Though Bolan bore the average German soldier of that conflict no particular animosity, SS and Gestapo members were a different breed. They had pledged their loyalty to their organization, not to their country.

Bolan shook Teudt by the shoulder. "Turn off the waterworks. Who attacked the village?"

Teudt took a great breath. "The Order."

"The Order of what?"

"Of Thule."

That was a new one on Bolan. "What's the Order of Thule?"

"The source of Nazism, the fundamental wellspring of the National Socialist Party, the true power behind the rise of Adolf Hitler."

"I never heard of it."

"That is its greatest defense. A political party can be smashed, but not the power behind it. The Third Reich was shattered into a hundred pieces. But the Order exists unchanged and unchanging to this day, as it has for nearly a thousand years."

Afraid the old man was ranting in a delirium again, Bolan changed the subject. "What did they want?"

Teudt gestured to the strongbox. "That. It was supposed to have been buried with the other sacred relics, but I kept it back. I didn't think they would ever know it was missing. I didn't want the chain to be forged again. We buried the most sacred relics of the Order in a glacier fifty years ago this month. The three of us vowed to return to the glacier this month on a prescribed day. Or if we were unable to attend, we were to arrange for representatives to attend in our place."

"And you," Bolan said, "broke the vow."

"Ganth is dead. Heinrich is well past ninety. I've had no contact with them for a half century. I have a new identity, a new life. How could they have found me after all this time?"

"Through the same agency that arranged for your new identity and new life," Bolan said grimly.

Teudt's eyes widened in horrified realization.

"The old firm never lets you retire," Bolan said. "Especially if they think you owe them something. Tell me, if you didn't expect them to track you down, why the escape tunnels?"

"I successfully appealed to the Ministry of the Interior to stop a logging operation nearby." Teudt's voice was hoarse and weak. "I had the tunnels constructed in case the mercenaries came after me."

Bolan looked around quickly. "I've got transportation not too far away. We can make it while it's still dark, but we've got to move fast. Patrols are looking for you."

"*Ja,*" Teudt murmured. "I have heard them. And a helicopter."

When Bolan went to pick him up, he struggled, pushing his hands away. "Leave me. I'm dying. You know it and I know it."

Bolan hesitated, looking into the man's face, then at the discolored, suppurating leg. Teudt was right.

The old man gestured weakly to the strongbox. "Take that thing with you. Sink it into the Madeira. Make sure they never get their hands on it again."

Teudt's eyelids drooped, and his head fell forward. Bolan watched as his entire body was racked by terrible shudders. Then, as if his bones were suddenly liquid, he flowed to the floor. His final exhalation was a prolonged hiss.

Bolan arranged the man's body, folding his hands on his chest. Though the smell of necrotic tissue was strong, he doubted that blood poisoning or blood loss had killed him. Teudt had simply given up.

He picked up the strongbox, which seemed to weigh less than ten pounds. Tucking it under one arm, he went through the far passageway. Emerging from a screen of thick-leaved bushes, he saw the river less than a hundred feet away. A narrow path led from the concealed opening to the riverbank.

He followed it, deciding to walk the river's edge rather than backtrack around the village. He had parked his Land Rover downriver a mile to the south.

Engine noise muffled by the sound of the rushing current, Bolan didn't hear the boat until it had slid from the shadowed overhang of a heavy-boughed hardwood tree. The boat was sharp keeled, outfitted with an outboard motor and a mounted searchlight.

A brilliant blade of light stabbed out and impaled Bolan.

2

"Don't let him get away!" someone shouted in German.

The voice, distorted by the electronic amplifier, had an unearthly sound. Bolan dropped flat, beneath the light, and rolled to one side. The searchlight swung to follow him. He saw three khaki-clad men aboard the boat, all armed with Heckler & Koch #94 autocarbines. Two of the three men fired.

Staccato bursts shattered the stillness of the jungle, birds screeching as a steel-jacketed rain ripped through the foliage.

Bolan rolled back into the underbrush, showered with sheared leaves and twigs. The brilliant beam of light swung back and forth, probing the darkness for him.

The autofire suddenly ceased, the magazines of the weapons exhausted. Bolan heard metallic clickings as the empty magazines were ejected and new ones rammed home.

Swiftly Bolan got to his knees, the Desert Eagle gripped in both hands. He brought the searchlight into the pistol's sights and squeezed the trigger only once. As the heavy, deep-throated boom of the big gun sounded, a .44-caliber round shattered the searchlight in an eye-dazzling blaze of blue sparks.

The men on the boat cursed viciously, and all three opened up with their weapons. Tracer slugs cut threads of fire through the night. Bolan knew better than to dig in and try to return triple streams of autofire. He crawled through the underbrush, changing direction twice, heedless of the thorns that scratched him and the vines that tried to snare him.

The men continued to fire wildly into the darkness. If they were angry or dedicated or stupid enough to come ashore and try to track him, they would receive the final surprise of their lives.

Though the rain forests of South America were far removed by time and distance from the tangled green hell of Southeast Asia, Bolan hadn't forgotten a single trick of jungle warfare.

He figured the men on the boat would stay put and radio the patrol he'd seen in the village. Even if they had heard the gunfire and were racing to its source, he doubted he would encounter them.

A little over a mile downriver, Bolan emerged from the jungle onto a narrow dirt road. In a copse of jungle pines, covered by camouflage netting, was his open-topped Land Rover. It was an old model, and somewhat battered, but it was the best Brognola could arrange on short notice.

Yanking the netting away, the Executioner got in and started the engine. Though the sound of the engine turning over and catching wasn't particularly loud, in the quiet of the night it sounded like a band striking up a fanfare.

Putting the strongbox on the passenger's seat, Bolan pressed the accelerator and the vehicle moved fast along the road. He didn't turn on the headlights, relying on his memory to guide him around obstacles and curves. He kept checking his backtrack in the rearview mirror.

One of those checks showed a small flash of reflected light, bright against the sky. A helicopter was diving from the sky, silhouetted against the glow of the moon. Safety lights flashed red and green.

Bolan's hands tightened on the steering wheel, and he floored the gas pedal. Rather than radio the jungle patrol, the men on the boat had called in their aerial reconnaissance.

The Land Rover roared along the road that twisted between tall jungle walls. Bolan hadn't been able to identify the make of the chopper, but he was positive that if it wasn't armed, the men aboard it were.

He heard the vanes whipping the air and the engine sounds growing louder with every passing second. He risked another backward glance. The helicopter was barely one hundred feet behind him, perhaps only twenty-five feet above the treetops.

Fortunately the road that cut through the jungle was too narrow to allow the aircraft to descend to a lower altitude.

Flickering spear points of yellow flame danced briefly just beneath the chopper's undercarriage, and .50-caliber bullets dug up great gouts of earth behind the Land Rover, throwing them into the air. Bolan jerked the wheel and swerved back and forth.

Bullets slammed into the tailgate, one shattering the windshield to the left of Bolan's shoulder. He steered the vehicle beneath an arch formed by the intertwining boughs of tall, leafy trees, and was temporarily hidden from the crew of the chopper. He heard the strong thrum of the engines and whirling blades as the helicopter hovered over the arch, then moved on.

The soldier eased off the gas and braked, putting the Land Rover in neutral while he weighed his options. He would run out of road in another mile or so. The dirt path opened up into a vast, treeless tract where the logging operation Teudt had mentioned had been under way only a few months before.

The timber company was gone, leaving behind barren ground and an almost limitless sea of tree stumps. The loggers had built this road through the jungle to the river, and though Bolan was grateful for that, he damned them for removing all spots of cover for five square miles.

If he drove slowly and carefully, it was possible to navigate around and sometimes over the tree stumps, as he'd done on his arrival. Now, slowly and carefully would be tantamount to painting a bull's-eye on his head.

Ditching the Land Rover and hiding out in the jungle would buy him time, but it would also give his pursuers the chance to call in reinforcements. They would cover the river, the village and every way out of the jungle. Bolan didn't have the inclination to play a prolonged game of hide-and-seek.

He made a quick decision, grabbed his war bag from the back of the Land Rover and shoved the strongbox into it. He got out, and after a brief search, found a twenty-pound lump of sandstone on the roadside.

From his bag, he removed a coil of thin nylon rope with a collapsible grappling hook attached to one end. He measured out a three-foot length, cut it with his combat knife and looped the remainder over his right shoulder.

He got back in and wrapped the rope around the steering wheel and the column, but he didn't tie it. He put the Land Rover into gear and drove down the road at barely 10 mph, holding both ends of the rope in his left hand.

At the demarcation point between the jungle and the tract, Bolan saw the helicopter waiting for him. It hovered fifty feet over the treeless expanse, and he recognized the two counter-revolving sets of blades of a Messerschmitt. It was an old model, but it appeared to be in excellent condition. A red cross was emblazoned on the fuselage.

Bolan's lips quirked in a mirthless smile. It was a good disguise, since the aircraft of medical-aid organizations constantly buzzed to and fro over the Amazon Basin.

A long gun pod was mounted beneath the craft, containing a .50-caliber machine gun with a 200-round magazine. Though the gun pod packed devastating firepower, Bolan knew it was a "bolt-on" weapon, and therefore less accurate than an internal gun.

Its operation required a gunner, and he was forced to rely on the pilot to bring a target into the stream of slugs.

Bolan put the Land Rover in neutral, then lashed the wheel tight to the column so it would follow a straight course. He slid out of the driver's seat, slinging his war bag over his right shoulder.

With the door open, he stood beside the vehicle, hefted the stone and jammed it down over the gas pedal. As the engine roared, Bolan carefully pressed down on the clutch and engaged the third gear.

The Land Rover leaped forward, and Bolan flung himself away from it, the rear tires barely missing the toe of his boots. He crouched in the shadows bordering the edge of the jungle.

He watched as the pilot of the Messerschmitt caught sight of the Land Rover rocketing from beneath the trees, plumes of dust spurting from the tires.

The helicopter whirled, descended and zoomed in, its landing skids barely ten feet above the barren ground. The snout of the

M-3 protruding from the end of the pod flickered with fire, .50-caliber slugs punching a cross-stitch pattern in the dirt in front of and to the left of the vehicle.

The Land Rover kept going, avoiding direct hits. The lines of impact scampered across the dirt, chewing up a tree stump and flinging wood chips and splinters in all directions.

With the rear of the chopper facing him, Bolan began to run, skirting the edge of the tract. He went in the opposite direction of the pursuit, hoping to put considerable distance between himself and the helicopter before its crew realized no one was driving the vehicle.

With the amount of dust swirling in the air, churned up by the chopper's rotors, the Land Rover's tires and bullets pounding the ground, he felt there was at least a fifty-fifty chance the diversion would work long enough for him to disappear into the shadows.

At the sound of the crash, Bolan adjusted the odds. He looked behind him, then stopped and went to one knee.

The Land Rover had plowed into a tree stump, one wheel going over its smoothly sawed top. It tipped to the right. Its momentum might have carried it on over, but a storm of bullets striking the bodywork caused it to list, tilt, then crash over on its side, wheels spinning.

The helicopter hung over it like a bird of prey, strafing the body with steady bursts. One burst punctured the gas tank, and its contents went up in a brilliant fireball.

The Messerschmitt wheeled away from the licking flames, and for an instant the entire area was illuminated by the orange-yellow flare. In that instant, the tinted, bubble-enclosed cockpit of the helicopter was facing Bolan.

Caught in the glare, Bolan unleathered the Desert Eagle and began running again, along the jungle's edge.

The aircraft did a figure eight from east to west and made a roaring pass, driving down from the rear. Bullets exploded dirt all around him. Bolan flung a shot up and behind him, but he didn't pause to see what effect it had.

He dug in his heels and skidded to a sudden stop, dropping flat just as the chopper roared overhead. It came so close to the jungle perimeter that it banked sharply to port, the vanes slashing through the tips of tree limbs.

Rolling over onto his back, Bolan squeezed off three shots as the chopper ascended, correcting for the decreasing range. The helicopter was either armored, or the motion of the aircraft threw his aim off, because his shots seemed to have no effect.

Leaping to his feet, Bolan ran broken-field style across the tract. He changed direction and raced away from the jungle, crossing a flat, bare space, heading for a drainage ditch dug by the loggers.

The helicopter's pilot managed to straighten out and level off, but by then Bolan was nearly to the ditch. The gun pod spit lead, and bullets kicked up dirt in waist-high fountains two yards behind him.

Bolan dived headlong into the ditch.

The helicopter roared overhead, its skids scraping the edges of the ditch and causing several shovel loads of dirt to collapse onto Bolan. Springing to his feet, the Desert Eagle in his hands, he squeezed off three rounds.

Two of the bullets drilled through the rear tail assembly, and the third twisted the struts of the right landing rail out of shape.

The helicopter veered wildly up and away. The pilot maneuvered the craft in a high, wide circle above the stump-dotted tract. Standing knee-deep in mud, Bolan watched it describe the circle, then hang in the sky, well out of the two-hundred-meter range of his handgun.

He knew what would happen next: the crew of the chopper would call for ground support. They would hover and report on his movements and position and cut off any attempt to return to the jungle until more troops arrived. They would make no more passes at him unless he tried to escape the killzone. He was bottled up in a muddy ditch, with no adequate cover to make a stand, and they could afford to be patient.

Bolan removed an apple-sized and shaped grenade from his war bag, then unslung the coil of rope and attached the grappling hook to the triggering ring of the grenade.

Holstering the Desert Eagle, he climbed out of the ditch, holding the grenade in one hand and the rope's slack in the other.

He stood at the edge of the ditch and stared up at the hovering chopper, a direct challenge.

The grenade was an M-68 fragmentation type, equipped with an impact fuse. The detonation mechanism was armed electrically three seconds after making a hard contact.

Objectively three seconds was a very fast fuse, but subjectively it was another matter. Three seconds was an eternity in which Bolan would be completely vulnerable to .50-caliber autofire.

The Executioner and the helicopter faced off. The aircraft didn't move, except to list slightly from side to side. The crew obviously suspected he was luring them in. So Bolan slowly turned his back on the chopper and began to deliberately walk toward the edge of the jungle. It was barely one hundred yards away.

He kept walking, senses alert for any change in sound from the chopper's position. There was a whining, high-pitched roar, and he spun.

The Messerschmitt dropped suddenly from where it had hung poised in the sky. It swooped down, head-on. The pilot kicked it into a steep dive, then banked so the gun pod would be aligned with Bolan's right side.

The soldier stood his ground, a dark and dirt-streaked figure. He whirled the rope with its grenade-weighted end over his head, gauging distance vertically and horizontally.

When the helicopter was only thirty feet away, and less than twenty in altitude, he gave the lariat a final, humming spin and launched it at the aircraft's rotors. At the same time, the machine gun opened up. Autofire sowed the ground with .50-caliber seeds.

Bolan flung himself ahead of the dancing eruptions of dirt in a controlled somersault back toward the ditch. He kept rolling until he felt solid ground give way beneath him, and he splatted down into the ditch's muddy bottom. The stream of bullets didn't intersect with his body, but they chewed up the edge of the ditch.

Even as he rolled, the rope wrapped itself around the main rotor shaft of the Messerschmitt. The grenade banged loudly on the canopy, and the pilot pulled back on the stick.

The helicopter reared, seeming to stand on its tail.

Facedown in the ditch, Bolan heard the heavy bass note of the explosion. Flame, smoke and shrapnel bloomed in a hellfire flower atop the aircraft.

The rotor blades went pinwheeling off in opposite directions. The helicopter keeled over, and the bubble-enclosed cockpit cannonaded into the ground. The fuel tank ruptured, then went up in an eardrum-slamming explosion.

Bolan got to his feet. Black smoke rolled over him in low clouds. The Messerschmitt had made its one-point landing barely thirty feet away and lay crumpled and burning on its starboard side. There was no movement from behind the shattered canopy.

The heat was searing and the billowing smoke made him cough, so Bolan climbed out of the ditch and put distance between himself and the wreckage. He surveyed the scene.

It was like an impressionistic painting of Hell. Two blackened shapes burned steadily in a barren expanse of dirt and tree stumps, and the licking flames cast an eerie, shifting light. By the light, Bolan glimpsed movement at the end of the road leading out to the tract. A burst of autofire sounded, and bullets kicked up dirt several dozen yards in front of him.

The two-man patrol he had seen in the village was racing toward him, firing their weapons as they did so. They were too angry to take their time to aim properly, and too far away for a stray shot to tag him.

Bolan unleathered the Desert Eagle, checked it to make sure the slide mechanism wasn't fouled by mud or dirt, brought the fore blade and rear combat sights into target acquisition, adjusted for elevation and windage and squeezed the trigger twice, shifting the barrel slightly from left to right.

It was a long shot for a handgun, but the two men went down. One rocked to an arm-flailing halt and went over onto his back. The other jackknifed at the waist, and his head reversed positions with his feet.

Bolan didn't bother to check the accuracy of his shots. He knew he'd hit them, and even if they were still alive, they were in no condition to crawl after him.

Shouldering the war bag, Bolan began to walk across the tract. He wasn't concerned about the hike in front of him. He was thinking about Teudt and the murdered Indians. He didn't know why a former German intelligence officer was worth slaughtering a village or sacrificing manpower and ordnance for, but he knew where he could find the answers.

And when he found those answers, he knew what he would do next.

The Executioner would give as good as he got.

3

May 31, the Federal Republic of Germany

For more than thirty years, a concrete wall topped with rolls of barbed and razor wire divided East and West Germany and dominated that country's character. In central Berlin, nearly all traces of the Wall had been removed. Even Checkpoint Charlie was no more than a nondescript kiosk in need of a fresh coat of paint. Nonetheless, to travel from former West Germany to former East Germany was to cross a wide chasm not measured in miles.

The West possessed the memory of fifty years of relative prosperity. The East still suffered the wounds inflicted by sixty years of a brutal dictatorship.

Reunification was conceived as a way to heal the wounds. The concrete wall and barricades were down, but *Die Mauer im Kopf,* "the Wall in the head," was as strong as ever. The principal effect of reunification had been insecurity. As insecurity grew, so did intolerance toward foreigners, especially refugees.

The Republic of Germany's constitution mandated that anyone at a border seeking asylum be allowed to stay, pending an immigration hearing. There were well over a million refugees in Germany, fleeing from Afghanistan, Iran and Bosnia.

In the reunited Germany, refugees and foreigners became the scapegoats of the nation's traumas.

According to Germany's secret service, there were about forty thousand extremists belonging to at least eighty neo-Nazi organizations. For the most part, the extremists were young men who called themselves skinheads. They brandished the emblems and shouted the slogans of the fascist regime that had ruled most of

Europe a half century before. Some of them carried baseball bats studded with nails, they listened to blaring heavy metal rock music with racist lyrics and they greeted each other with the straight-arm Nazi salute and shouts of *"Seig Heil!"*

They also tended to get drunk, then storm into the streets to attack anyone who didn't meet their standards of racial purity, American servicemen included. They proudly claimed responsibility for scores of arsons, assaults and murders. Only a handful of the perpetrators had ever been prosecuted, and fewer still had been sentenced to jail terms longer than three years.

The deficit between crimes and convictions had been noticed by human-rights groups in Europe. They argued convincingly that the republic's failure to forcefully prosecute members of neo-Nazi organizations only encouraged more outbreaks of violence. Some civil-rights advocates in the government made graver charges; they accused some of their fellow members of deliberately looking the other way, of following the orders of shadowy figures moving in shadowy ways.

Though there was no sign of a new führer, the time was ripe for one. Followers were already in place, waiting for him to appear and make a Germany for Germans.

Other countries also contended with the problems posed by unified Germany, the least of which were geo-economic. The end of the cold war placed the spectrum of old politics and loyalties in a colorless limbo.

The former Soviet Union, the United States and NATO struggled with the question of what to do about the many nuclear missile silos, sites and weapons stockpiles dotting the landscape inside both East and West Germany.

American military and NATO bases were easy to find in Western Europe, especially in Germany. They were surrounded by fences and posted with signs declaring the areas to be military reservations and therefore inaccessible to the average German citizen.

However, the average German citizen was aware that although the bases possessed strategic and tactical missiles, the "big guns," the missiles with nuclear warheads, were hidden all over Germany in camouflaged sites.

One site, inside a fortified bunker covered with turf, in the middle of a cow pasture, was designated as Site 611 by the Department of Defense, SAC and NATO. Less than half an hour outside of Berlin, near Potsdam, it contained six Pershing II missiles.

The Pershings possessed warheads of 400 kilotons and were launched from massive twelve-wheeled tractor trailers. Their terminal guidance systems were based on radar area-correlation systems: the onboard computers compare images of the targets "seen" by the missile with images previously programmed into them. The range of the Pershings was limited, approximately seventy-five miles, but perfect for striking targets in East Germany.

The problem was that there were no longer any targets in East Germany, but the Pershings were still scattered all over Western Europe. Some had been dismantled and sold, some disarmed, but most were waiting for either to happen.

At Site 611, the one dozen United States Army personnel stationed there were among those waiting. Technical duties consisted primarily of running checks on the fuel payloads of the missiles, detecting and correcting leaks, running system diagnostics on the ground and onboard targeting computers, making sure the satellite uplink frequencies to Cheyenne Mountain in Wyoming and NATO bases in the Mediterranean continued to signal all clear, and in general acting as high-tech nursemaids and hall monitors.

The nontechnical personnel serviced the trailers that held the missiles, checking the air in the tires, turning the engines over every twelve hours and acting like a janitorial staff.

No one was too concerned about maintaining the camouflage; every farmer within twenty square miles knew they were there. Great squares of turf had fallen from the bunker, revealing the concrete beneath, but they were rarely patched up. Even the security guards patrolling the perimeter were relaxed.

It was light duty to pull, and though a top secret clearance was required just to get inside the foyer, no one was fixated on every security detail. The standard protocols were still observed, however.

At 0800 hours on Wednesday morning, when Lieutenant-Colonel Aubrey Lesnick triggered the metal detector, not even Corporal Turnbull, who held the sensor wand, became unduly excited.

The helmeted MP waved the silver rod in front of Lesnick's face, and the squeal from the sensor came again. He looked at Lesnick questioningly.

"Sir, I'm getting a—"

"I know what you're getting, Corporal," Lesnick said impatiently. "I had some dental work done yesterday, remember? That's why I left early."

"Yes, sir, I remember." Turnbull's questioning look didn't go away.

"Bridgework, boy. New bridgework."

Turnbull nodded. "Yes, sir. But if I might ask you to open your mouth?"

Lesnick groaned. "Oh, for Christ's sake."

He took off his uniform cap and tilted his head back, opening his mouth wide.

Turnbull bent down and peered up inside Lesnick's mouth.

"Don't even *think* about sticking your fingers in there," Lesnick snapped.

"Yes, sir. I mean, no, sir."

Not having bridgework himself, or knowing anyone who did, the MP wasn't sure of what he was looking for. He saw gleaming steel affixed to back molars and a saliva-damp pink arch adhering to the roof of the mouth.

"Can you pop it out, sir, and we'll try again?"

Lesnick shut his mouth with a snap and pulled himself up to his full height. Glaring down directly into Turnbull's face, he said, "No, I cannot 'pop it out.' The standard procedure is to recalibrate the sensor. If you're unable to do that, I'll relieve you of duty and do it myself."

Turnbull backed away, speaking very quickly. "No, sir, of course I can do that. But I'll have to log this in—see, every time the detector is triggered, a record is made, and I have to reconcile my log with the record and explain why I allowed entry into the facility."

"Corporal, I'm one of the men who drafted the security procedures at this site. You don't have to explain them to me."

Cap tucked beneath an arm, Lesnick marched past the security station. Turnbull heaved a whistling sigh, then muttered, "Asshole."

Lesnick walked down a short corridor, turned left, returned the salute of an MP standing there and entered the operations center.

The technical staff of the day shift—three men and two women—were conducting the first of three diagnostics performed in a twenty-four hour period. They were seated before computer consoles, wearing headsets, tapping keyboards and gazing at the machine talk scrolling across their monitor screens.

Lesnick stood and watched and listened. He didn't go to his desk in the corner or take off his jacket or hang up his cap. All he did was consult his wristwatch.

The technical staff had their attentions focused on the diagnostic. Lieutenant Kinnard, the shift supervisor, asked questions in a monotone and received equally flat responses from the staff.

"Infrared cross tie?"

"Enabled."

"Guidance system nexus?"

"Standby."

"Rear payload-constriction flange?"

"Green."

"Tracking and control radars?"

"Enabled."

"Thermal-imaging signature-recognition systems?"

"Standby."

The droning conversation went on, then one of the women stiffened in her chair. "Good Lord!"

Her monitor screen fluttered briefly. The words and images scrolling across her screen tore up in a jagged pattern of multicolored pixels. All over the operations center, the staff swore and slapped keyboards.

"What's going on?" Kinnard shouted.

He swiveled his chair and caught sight of Lesnick for the first time. "Sir—"

Lieutenant-Colonel Aubrey Lesnick turned slightly toward

him, then collapsed into a loose-limbed heap on the floor, his head striking the concrete with a sharp crack.

Kinnard shouted for the MP, who came in at a run. He kneeled beside Lesnick and attended to him while Kinnard tried to restore order to both the operations center and the system.

He went from station to station, tapping keys on each board. "Shit," he said. "I've never seen the effects of an electromagnetic pulse, but this sure seems like one."

"No way," one of the women said. "All the power would be out."

Another technician called out to Kinnard. He was pressing the earpiece of his headset against the side of his head. "We're still linked to the NORAD mainframe in Cheyenne Mountain. This is a localized failure."

Kinnard surveyed the blank, amber glowing screens then snarled, "Well, get *on* this, people! Boot up our backup systems! Every goddamn technodweeb between Greece and Wyoming will be blaming us for pushing the wrong button or some such shit if we're not back on-line *stat!*"

Kinnard took a small silver key from his pocket and went to a file cabinet at the rear wall. To do so, he had to step over Lesnick's body. The MP was checking his pulse.

"How is he?" Kinnard asked.

"His pulse and heartbeat are irregular, his breathing is shallow. He's also very warm, like he's running a high fever."

The MP peeled back one of Lesnick's eyelids, and both he and Kinnard cursed.

Lesnick's eye bore a milky glaze, like the membrane of an egg.

"Get him to the hospital," Kinnard ordered.

While Kinnard spun the dial of the cabinet's combination lock, then removed and unlocked the case of backup diskettes with the key, Lesnick was carried out of the operations center by the MP and a technician.

Lesnick was rushed by ambulance to the General George S. Patton Military Hospital in what was once called the American sector of Berlin. He died en route, thirty minutes before the wail-

ing ambulance reached the emergency room, and less than ten
after he collapsed.

While the chain of command was notified, Lesnick's dog tags
taken and preparations made to break the news to his next of
kin, an autopsy was ordered by the chief of staff at the hospital.

A report to the German authorities was mandatory, in case
Lesnick had died from something contagious.

The doctor assigned to the autopsy was forty-one-year-old
Captain William Radfort. Postmortems didn't disturb him; he had
performed hundreds of them during his civilian employment by
the Los Angeles County Medical Examiner's Office. He'd only
had to perform eight in the fourteen years he'd served in the
armed forces, and usually the cause of death among military
personnel was easy to determine—drug overdoses, car crashes,
training accidents and the occasional suicide.

The body of Lieutenant-Colonel Aubrey Lesnick posed a severe problem. When Radfort took a temperature reading of the
liver, it was at least five degrees warmer than it should have
been. He duly noted the anomaly into his tape recorder.

When Radfort opened up the abdominal cavity, his eyes
bugged out.

There was almost no moisture inside Lesnick's body. The organs were all where they should have been, but they weren't
glistening with blood or any other bodily fluid. The liver, the
storage depot for the circulatory system, contained some blood,
but it was in the form of dark, gummy, congealed splotches.

Radfort spoke rapidly into the recorder. "The subject's abdominal cavity shows very little moisture, indicating that the
cause of death was extreme dehydration. I cannot explain this
condition."

The captain picked up the circular bone saw, plugged it in and
applied the whirling, razor-sharp edge of the blade to the top of
Lesnick's skull. Deftly he cut away the top of the cranium, put
it to one side and inspected the condition of the brain.

He grunted in disbelief. The brain should have been glistening
with cerebrospinal fluid. It wasn't. The organ was dry, and rather
than being a whitish gray in color, it was a pale beige, almost
as if it had been seared briefly by an extraordinarily hot flame.

Radfort poked the brain with one rubber-sheathed finger. It was hard. Not rock solid, but far harder than any human's brain could possibly be outside of a mummy's.

Radfort had never seen anything remotely like this in a human body barely three hours dead. But he dredged up a memory from his past, over twenty years before during his second semester at Florida State University's medical school.

One of his fellow students had engaged in a sadistic impulse by covering it with the cloak of scientific experimentation. The guy had taken one of the lab rats and tossed it inside a microwave oven in the student lounge. Contrary to his expectations—and to his great disappointment—the unfortunate rat hadn't exploded; it had simply stiffened and died.

Out of curiosity, Radfort had taken the rat and dissected it. The major organs had burst, then hardened to a stonelike consistency; almost every trace of fluid in the rodent's body had boiled away. Though the condition of Lesnick's organs wasn't as extreme, the similarities were frightening.

Radfort examined Lesnick's head. Both eyes were covered by a gelatinous film, as though the liquid within them had evaporated. He propped the man's head back and forced open his mouth so he could take a look at the tongue and the softer mouth tissues. What he saw brought a burst of profanity from Radfort's lips.

Lesnick's tongue was like a shriveled piece of fruit. His teeth, the ones containing metal fillings, were shattered. Extreme heat would have caused the fillings to swell and fracture them.

Adhering to the roof of Lesnick's mouth was a mass of semimelted plastic and metal.

Radfort couldn't guess at its purpose, though it resembled dental bridgework. He studied it silently for nearly a minute, trying to make up his mind what to do. The standard procedure would be to remove it, tag it and continue with the autopsy. He was baffled and a little angered by this unexpected problem that interfered with what should have been a perfectly routine postmortem and a golf game he had scheduled for the afternoon.

Radfort turned off the recorder, went to the telephone and called the chief of staff, who, after listening to Radfort's expletive-littered report, called the officer of the day, who in turn called an intelligence officer posted to the G-2 department on base.

Major Hyams dropped by within the hour and stood by patiently as Radfort, with a pair of forceps and a scalpel, removed the wad of metal and plastic from Lesnick's mouth, taking a goodly portion of desiccated tissue with it.

The intelligence people played it safe and took the material to Ostara Development, a private solid-state-physics lab and electronics firm near the Tegel airfield.

The researchers tried only a few tests before determining that the mass was made of plastic and metal. They also determined that it was bridgework subjected to a short burst of HPM, a high-power microwave. The burst was probably not more than two seconds in duration, and was potent enough to interfere with sophisticated electronic equipment.

The people from G-2 were aware of the incident at Site 611, but they said nothing to the researchers or their supervisor, Dr. Ilona Wezhardt. They did want to know where the HPM had originated.

"From this," Wezhardt said, pointing to the smears of melted circuitry inside the plastic portion of the bridgework.

She told them that the bridgework was a highly advanced, almost unbelievable masterpiece of miniaturization. It was a microwave transmitter, set and timed to let loose with a HPM burst at a predetermined time and place.

Of course, the burst had literally cooked Lieutenant-Colonel Aubrey Lesnick, but Wezhardt doubted it was affixed to the roof of his mouth for the purpose of assassination. A gun, a knife or even a car bomb would have been simpler and far less expensive.

Wezhardt theorized that such a powerful transmitter built on such a scale would cost upward of three hundred thousand dollars.

The G-2 officers knew that various scientists, both in and out of the employ of the U.S. government, had managed to produce some miniature HPM transmitter prototypes not much bigger than a bread box, but nobody had ever made one as small or as powerful as this one.

The G-2 officers and Wezhardt were in complete agreement on one point—not only was the thing extremely dangerous, but also the implications of how and where it had been found were terrifying.

Lesnick's dentist was located and interrogated. He denied having any knowledge of the bridgework, and he angrily swore he would take a polygraph to that effect.

The G-2 officers took him up on his promise and administrated the test. He passed.

Simultaneously another group of intelligence officers investigated all of Lesnick's civilian and military contacts in Germany. The day's duty log and personnel roster of Site 611 were requisitioned and studied. The systems at the site were back on-line, due to the quick rebooting of Lieutenant Kinnard. He reported no further problems.

Within an hour of receiving this information, there was a great deal of covert activity among military officials. They moved to pass the word—and the buck—at once.

There were international calls over scrambler circuits from Germany to all military bases in Europe, then the intel went across the sea.

Fourteen hours after Radfort found the mass of metal and plastic in Lesnick's mouth, a message was sent to the American Joint Chiefs of Staff via a back channel.

The back channel under the control of the JCS was the Digital Information Relay Center in the Pentagon basement. Operated under a twenty-four-hour guard, and open only to those with the highest clearances, the center was linked to military commanders and installations worldwide.

It allowed senior officers to communicate in single-copy messages that weren't filed or recorded. At banks of code machines, computer terminals and satellite uplink stations, technicians deciphered incoming messages and routed them through secured telephone lines to the proper people within the Pentagon.

The report from G-2 regarding the system failure at Site 611, the manner of Lesnick's death and what it could mean, was so chilling that the technician who had received it sat stunned for a long moment. He pulled himself together long enough to send the data via modem to a five-star general several floors above him.

The general looked it over, phoned the technician in the basement and ordered him to transmit the same data to compatible equipment located in the West Wing basement of the White House.

A National Security Agency officer manning the equipment took the data up to the Oval Office. The President looked it over and groaned.

"This is scary stuff," he said hoarsely, then dismissed the officer and picked up the telephone.

He called a private number that rang a secured line in the Justice Department building. A man named Hal Brognola answered.

The hunting horn had sounded.

4

June 1, Stony Man Farm, Virginia

The knife incorporated three blades in one, spreading out from the stone hilt like a W, with the center blade being the longest. The metal was dull and tarnished, the edges notched. The haft carried a sunburst design in gold, and within the burst was inscribed a letter or Roman numeral—*V*. It looked very old.

Aaron Kurtzman turned the object over in his pawlike hands and said, "It's called a Dag."

Mack Bolan sat at a table in the first-floor computer room. A steaming cup of black coffee was gripped in his right hand, but he was more interested in the item held in Kurtzman's hands.

"The Dag," Kurtzman went on, "is an emblem of the Geheimgericht, the Silent Tribunal, a sort of a medieval vigilante group that ran roughshod over Germany in the sixth century. The *V* symbolizes the number of knights who formed the first tribunal under Charlemagne."

"Is it worth anything?"

Kurtzman heaved his broad shoulders in a shrug. "To antiquarians, maybe."

"The hardmen in Brazil weren't antique collectors," Bolan replied. He had told Kurtzman about the killing fields in South America upon his return to the Farm less than three hours earlier. "They thought it was worth slaughtering a village of Indians."

"Teudt never should have gone through Interpol," Kurtzman said. "If one of the Nazi brotherhoods, say the Odessa, was hunting for him, it was like phoning in an appointment for your own hit with the Mob. The agency has been rotten with Nazis since the thirties. Hell, one of its presidents ended up at the end of an executioner's rope in Nuremberg Prison. It's been a joke ever since, regardless of their PR.''

Kurtzman returned the knife to the strongbox. As he shut the lid, he studied the symbol painted on it.

"Doesn't look like any Nazi insignia I'm familiar with," he said. "And the history of World War II is one of my passions."

"It's the emblem of something Teudt called the Order of Thule," Bolan replied. "Mean anything?"

The horizontal crease in Kurtzman's forehead deepened. "There's an island off the coast of Greenland with that name. The Navy has a base there."

"I doubt that was what he was referring to," Bolan said wryly.

"There was a secret society in Germany, back before World War I, called the Thulegesellschaft. It was sort of an elite social club for industrialists and the very rich. Some historians believe it was the direct forerunner to the Nazi party."

Kurtzman wheeled his chair to the nearest computer terminal and began tapping the keyboard. "Let's see if we can find another reference to it somewhere."

Aaron Kurtzman was one of the most gifted computer geniuses in the world. His personally designed system at Stony Man Farm was networked with hundreds of governmental agencies, universities and international think tanks. Bolan couldn't remember a time when Kurtzman hadn't been able to dredge up a bit of important data, no matter how obscure.

As Kurtzman tapped the keys and manipulated the mouse, he asked, "Have you told Hal you're back?"

"Barb put in a call to his office. He hasn't gotten back to me."

As if on cue, the intercom beeped and Barbara Price's voice asked, "Mack, Aaron, are you there?"

"Yeah," said Kurtzman. "Both of us."

"Hal's waiting for you in the War Room. He arrived about five minutes ago."

Kurtzman tapped in the commands to continue the data search and download the findings to the computer system in the War Room.

The two men took the elevator to the basement level. The doors slid open on a big room whose main feature was a big conference table. At the head of the table sat Brognola, tapping his fingers impatiently on a stack of file folders. A stub of an unlit cigar was clamped between his jaws.

Bolan noticed that several of the files were marked with the insignia of the U.S. Army, and several more with the symbol of the State Department. Brognola looked at him and said, "We've got a bad one, Striker."

Kurtzman wheeled his chair to the computer terminal built into the table. "Am I a part of this?"

Brognola nodded. "One of the reasons the Man dropped this in our laps was the Farm's top-notch intel-gathering resources."

Bolan took a seat. "The Man is involved?"

"I've just come from a meeting he arranged with the JCS. This is a top-priority, high-risk situation."

"What's its nature?"

"Fatman."

"Shit," Kurtzman said softly.

"Fatman" was the current code word for a nuclear crisis in Europe.

"For a number of reasons," Brognola stated, "it was decided the Farm would handle this—or rather *you*, Striker, as this situation calls for your particular approach."

Thinking of the dead Indians in Brazil, Bolan asked calmly, "What if I have something else to occupy my energies?"

He was tweaking Brognola. It never hurt to remind the big Fed that his alliance with the government was at his sole discretion.

"If you do," Brognola replied, "then you may be dooming a good portion of Europe to a nuclear hell on earth."

Brognola wasn't being melodramatic. Bolan saw genuine fear in his eyes. He nodded and said, "Go."

The Justice man carefully recounted everything that had happened in Germany from the moment Lieutenant-Colonel Lesnick had entered Site 611. Opening an Army file, he fanned out four faxed photographs of the gadget found inside Lesnick's mouth.

"I wish I could produce the actual device for our people here to study, but it's being held in Germany pending a final determination."

"So nobody knows how or why this thing got inside of Lesnick?" Bolan asked.

"Or how many other of these devices may be in other mouths right now," Brognola said grimly.

Kurtzman was listening to the briefing while his computer terminal scanned several files at once. "I may be able to offer a possible why. Microwaves operate on the fringe line between infrared and lower frequencies. A by-product is an electromagnetic pulse that fouls up communications and electronic systems. That's why people with pacemakers aren't allowed near microwave ovens."

"The G-2 people already thought of that," Brognola said. "The computer systems at the site came back on-line. They ran a diagnostic, and everything checked out."

"What level diagnostic?"

Frowning, Brognola consulted a sheet of paper from a folder. "A Lieutenant Kinnard ordered a level one and two."

Kurtzman grunted. "Yeah, that's what I thought. I'm familiar with the systems used at those sites. Levels one and two are routine automated procedures to verify system performance. He needs to run a level four, which is the most comprehensive type of diagnostic. That requires techs to physically verify operations of mechanisms and linkups. With a level four, you can guard against possible malfunctions in self-testing software. Trouble is, it takes a while, and the system has to be taken off-line."

"That's probably why he didn't conduct it," Brognola said. "After the failure, I'm sure he was worried about a reprimand. I'll memo the G-2 officer in charge so arrangements can be made."

In one of the Army files, Bolan came across a photograph of a woman. It was a head-and-shoulders shot, and she looked to be in her late twenties or early thirties. Her black hair hung in ringlets past her shoulders, and she wore a pair of wire-rimmed eyeglasses. She was obviously posing for an ID badge shot.

"Who's this?" he asked.

"Our German expert on solid-state physics. Ilona Wezhardt,

Ph.D. She's head of the research department of Ostara Development, a private electronics firm that acts as a NATO consultant from time to time. According to G-2, she's been exceptionally helpful to them. She'll be your contact in Berlin. We can't tell her who you really are, but she'll function as technical liaison with minimal access to the actual field operation.''

"What's my cover?"

"Mike Blanski, a physicist from the U.S. Department of Energy. Since Wezhardt has been around spooks before, she'll probably see right through you."

"Especially," Bolan added, "if I have to discuss solid-state physics with her. What am I expected to do over there?"

"Find out who's behind this and neutralize them. Find out if they've implanted any other military personnel and neutralize them, too."

"Any ideas on the 'who' I'm supposed to stop?"

"Not many. Wezhardt's firm, the Patton hospital and the U.S. Embassy are under discreet surveillance by relays of men and women. They drive plumbers' vans, utility trucks, that sort of thing. Two at a time and they're very good at it. They seem to know when *they're* being watched, and disappear. They haven't been identified as yet. A few years ago, I'd say they were working for the KGB or Stasi."

"That's the problem with the end of the cold war," Kurtzman commented with a smile. "It's not so easy to ID the player on the other side."

"True," Brognola said, "but whoever they are, they're ruthless enough to snuff Lesnick, and inventive enough to do it in a way that allowed them to tamper with a total of twenty-four thousand kilotons of destructive force at the same time. That doesn't sound like much, since Cheyenne Mountain can deliver missiles of hundreds of megatons, but keep this in mind—the bomb that wiped out Hiroshima was only twenty kilotons."

Bolan had been scanning the dossier on Lesnick. He was reading the hastily compiled list of the officer's known associates in Germany when he came across a certain name.

"Helmur Ganth," Bolan read aloud. "Stockbroker. That's the

second time in forty-eight hours I've come across the name of Ganth."

"What do you mean?" Brognola asked.

In simple, unadorned language, Bolan told him what had transpired in Brazil.

"Every piece of hardware was of German manufacture," Bolan said, a cold note entering his voice. "The perps spoke German. And, of course, Dr. Tohrbach, the man you sent me to rescue, turned out to be Karl Teudt, formerly of the Reich Main Security Office."

If Bolan expected Brognola to react with dismay or shame, he was disappointed. Brognola only nodded.

"I suspected as much. It's an axiom in the intelligence community that when Interpol makes a request for someone on our team to diddle around in South America on behalf of a German-born, naturalized American citizen of a certain age, you can bet an ex-Nazi is involved."

"Thanks for letting me in on your suspicion," Bolan said dryly.

Brognola sighed. "Striker, one way to keep Stony Man Farm functional is to perform occasional favors for government agencies. That way, I can call in the favors when I need to protect our people. I'm sorry about those Indians and what you went through down there, but I hope you understand that if I'd known the true nature of the request, I would've refused it."

"You might not want to tell the State Department that I smell ex-Nazis in this mess. Or maybe not so ex."

Kurtzman glanced at his computer monitor and said, "Your sense of smell is as sharp as ever, Mack. Let me put this on-screen and you can read it for yourself."

Kurtzman tapped a key on his console, and the overhead lights dimmed. Simultaneously light swelled from the four walls surrounding the table. The walls flickered, and large text pixeled across them.

"I've accessed the World War II historical database from the National Archives," Kurtzman said. "This is compiled from a couple of OSS reports, dated 1946. It was intended as a briefing document for the Nuremberg prosecutors."

Brognola squinted at the copy. "What's this about?"

"Read it and find out," Kurtzman retorted.

In its present form, the Thulegesellschaft, or Thule Society, dates back to 1910–1912. It was a proto-Nazi occult group with connections to Aleister Crowley's Golden Dawn cult. But the roots of the society stretch back at least to the sixth century, and perhaps further.

According to tradition, a secret society known as the Silent Tribunal originated after the conquest of Saxony in 772 by Charlemagne. The powers of the tribunal were wide. They exacted summary executions on any transgressor of Charlemagne's laws. The tribunal's symbol was a three-bladed knife known as a Dag, and replicas of this instrument were stuck into trees as a warning to others that they were searching for a miscreant, and no interference would be tolerated.

This organization existed in various forms and names until it surfaced fifty years ago as the Thule Society. The premise of the society is simple: the organization was named after the Thulians, a nation of Aryan superbeings, progenitors of the Germanic peoples. They enjoyed a utopian civilization until eighty-five thousand years ago, when it was wiped away by a cataclysm, much like the one that supposedly destroyed Atlantis. Therefore the Thulists believe they are representatives by descent of the true master race.

It is suspected that Hitler joined the Thule Society shortly after 1918, when he was assigned to a highly secret counterintelligence unit that engaged in acts of domestic terrorism, assassinating German leaders who had negotiated Germany's surrender.

The Thule group was supported by the German high command and it held secret courts and condemned people who they felt had betrayed the Aryan nation. Many prominent Germans were in favor of this violence and terrorism and were documented members of the Thule. For example, the police president of Munich, Franz Gurtner, was a member of the inner circle of the Thule, and he later was appointed minister of justice of the Third Reich. Rudolf Hess was also a high-ranking Thulist.

As time passed, the Thule became a magnet for wealthy international businessmen. Without funding from industry, German and international, the Thule could have never become so powerful. Almost every major industrial concern in Europe and Britain—oil companies, agricultural firms, banks and shipping companies—made sizable donations to the society. Many top military leaders of Japan belonged to their own version of the Thule Society, a group known as the Black Dragons, which was philosophically identical.

It is not an exaggeration to state that the Thule Society was the most important organization behind the rise of Nazism. Most, if not all, of the symbols used by the Nazis were ancient mystical symbols first used by the Silent Tribunal and then the Thule. The swastika, the death's-head, the rune-inscribed daggers and the SS lightning bolt were developed by the Thule.

After Hitler reformed the German Worker's Party into the Nazi Party, he made it mandatory that high-ranking members of the party, and later the SS, had to be inducted into the Thule.

However, the ranks of this society did not pledge loyalty to Hitler; on the contrary, Hitler pledged his loyalty to the society. He claimed his true guidance came from supernatural sources. The Thulists referred to their hidden masters as "supermen" who lived in a subterranean world and Hitler was supposedly in touch with them, as were other members of Thule leadership.

They believed the "supermen" would return to the surface of the earth to rule it as soon as the Nazis completed their racial-purification program and established the Thousand Year Reich. Indeed, in 1942, Hitler dispatched a naval expedition to a remote island in the North Atlantic in order to discover the hidden entrance to the land of Thule.

The preoccupation with mystical lore may explain Hitler's obsession with collecting artifacts and icons from the ancient past. A primary belief of the society was that in order to consolidate its position as the future masters of the world, it had to accumulate all the trappings of sacred kingship. There is no complete list of the artifacts supposedly in the Nazis' possession, but according to a report provided by a Lieutenant Teudt of the Reich Main Security Office, the relics are of immense spiritual importance to the inner circle of the society.

It is unfortunate that the Nazi defeat and reported death of Hitler has not ended the influence of the Thulists in the world. It was clearly more than a political movement; it was a religion, a holy order, and religions can only be suppressed, not destroyed.

Brognola removed the cigar stub from his mouth, looked at it and stuck it between his teeth again. "Why didn't any of this come out at Nuremberg?"

Kurtzman was busy with his keyboard again. "Just a wild guess, but I imagine the prosecutors were worried that the Nazis on trial could make a fairly convincing insanity plea."

"It's no crazier than Medellín drug lords practicing black magic or Santeria," Bolan said.

Kurtzman's computer was equipped to handle multiple functions. While Bolan and Brognola had been talking, he entered Helmur Ganth's name, cross-referencing it with files on high-ranking Nazi officials.

The text blurred from the wall screens and was replaced by a black-and-white photograph of a man in his midthirties wearing the black uniform and peaked cap of an SS officer. The man was standing beside a small boy, his gloved hand resting on his shoulder. The boy was wearing the shorts-and-neckerchief ensemble of the Hitler Youth.

"Oberführer Eric Ganth, commander of the Brandenberg Division. The kid is his only child, Helmur. The picture was taken in 1941."

Another black-and-white photo popped up beside the boy's head. This showed the smiling face of a middle-aged, gray-haired man wearing formal evening clothes. "Helmur Ganth as he appeared at a diplomatic function six years ago in Washington."

Kurtzman manipulated the mouse and superimposed the image of the man over that of the boy's. "A chip off the old block, looks like."

"If we suspected everybody in Europe who had a family member in the SS," Brognola growled, "then we'd have most of Western Europe under surveillance. Not to mention South America."

"You wouldn't have to go to those lengths," Bolan said. "Nazi garbage should have been flushed away fifty years ago. Instead, some people, maybe with good intentions, preserved aspects of it. And it's spread again. Nazi groups, like the skinheads and some of these paramilitary militias, have been revived in America, Germany and other countries."

"We don't know if this Thule Society or Nazis or Girl Scouts are behind this," Brognola countered. "It's all supposition, so far, no matter what Teudt told you."

"Until we have proof that satisfies you," Bolan said, "let me assume the opposition is the Thule Society. It makes sound tactical sense. So don't put shackles on me."

"I won't, Striker. But if it *is* the Thule, they know how to make themselves invisible through protective coloration. Don't you think the Justice Department has tried to apprehend some of these Nazis with intelligence ties?" Brognola squeezed the air with one fist. "It's like trying to prosecute smoke."

"Mack," Kurtzman said, "these guys have a lot of protection. You're going to piss off a bunch of powerful folks if you lift the rock off this situation and find a bunch of Nazi bugs crawling out from under it. The alliance between American intelligence and the Nazis at the end of the war isn't something they want publicized."

"Exactly," Brognola said. "If what you suspect is true, then the architects of the Nazi Party, the SS and the Third Reich are your targets. They've kept their secrets for a hell of a long time. This is the old guard you're going up against."

"The devil's guard, more like it," Bolan said. "But just to know where I'll stand with the intel net in Germany, we should send a jacket to the G-2 officer in charge about Thule. He'll either accept the possibility or he won't."

"And if he doesn't?" Brognola asked. "G-2 may not want to accept the likelihood or the responsibility that bastards they absorbed into their own spheres are working against them."

"I know that, Hal. I also know that half a century ago, the Nazis missed being the first nuclear power by a hair. I think they're now rectifying that. You said you can't apprehend these people?"

"Yeah," Brognola answered heavily.

Bolan's tone became low and cold. "These people—Thulists, Nazis, whatever they are—can't be prosecuted. But there's no reason they can't receive justice."

5

June 2, Berlin

Helmur Ganth raised his crystal snifter of Asbach Uralt brandy to the four men around the table. "Gentlemen, I salute you."

The oak-paneled conference room in the Wust and Wimmer office overlooking the Wilhelmstrasse gave an appropriately Old World setting to the function Ganth presided over.

The four men at the table responded to the toast with varying degrees of enthusiasm.

Ganth turned and raised his goblet to the oil portrait of Eric Ganth, which dominated the wall behind him. *"Prosit!"* he said loudly.

Eric Ganth had initiated his son, Helmur, into the Order of Thule upon his eighteenth birthday. He had told him that the Order, unlike the Odessa group, wasn't an organization devoted to fulfilling Hitler's dream of a thousand-year reich. Rather, Hitler had failed to fulfill the Order's dream.

On that long-ago birthday, Eric Ganth had said to his son, "Forget the Party, forget Hitler. He may have danced, but it is the Order that called the tune."

Helmur Ganth and every man in the elegant room knew the tune.

The portly and balding Professor Jorg Weisenburg was one of Europe's leading electronic specialists, or he had been until a heart condition had forced him to retire. His father had worked on Germany's secret electromagnetic research team, building on the discoveries of Marconi, Tesla and Hertz to construct offensive and defensive devices. Before the elder Weisenburg's work was completed, he died in the Allied bombing of Dresden.

Weisenburg had lost a father, but he gained his research papers and an undying hatred of Western democracy.

That hatred was shared by the elderly, spectacled psychiatrist who sat next him. Dr. Hito Asoka had developed a number of psychological weapons to use against Allied prisoners of war, especially in the fields of behavior modification and mind control. While still at university, Asoka had been enlisted into the Black Dragon Society, and after the surrender, he had asked to be inducted into the Order.

For the past thirty-five years, Asoka had chaired the substance-abuse program of the Nachsinnen Clinic, which specialized in the treatment of wealthy Berliners for acute alcoholism and drug addiction. His program was copied all over the continent, and more than one staffer at the U.S. consulate with a drinking problem had been referred to his clinic.

The man seated beside Asoka was a rail-thin, crew-cut seventy-eight-year-old retired colonel of South Africa's security police. Born in Pretoria, he had moved to Frankfurt when his nation's apartheid policy had ended and was hired as a NATO security consultant. His name was Arlen deMilteer, and though he had fought against Rommel in North Africa, he had always believed in his heart that the Allies were fighting on the wrong side.

Partly because of his German ancestry and the pride in his Aryan blood, he had been instrumental in helping hundreds of high-ranking German prisoners of war escape to South Africa. He had kept in contact with them, and they had put him in contact with the innermost circle of the Order. Through his numerous acquaintances in NATO, he kept the Order well-informed on military matters.

DeMilteer didn't consider himself a true fascist; he was merely a well-bred racist of the old school who was horrified by the revolts staged in his country's black townships. He had no desire to live in a nation where blacks were treated as equals.

The man next to him wasn't sipping brandy, but a goblet full of orange juice. He was a thick-bodied, heavyset man, with black, wavy hair. His complexion was swarthy, except for the paler hue of his upper lip where he had recently shaved off a bushy mustache. He was wearing a beautifully tailored Armani suit. He was more recognizable to newspaper readers and CNN watchers when he was mustached and dressed in a set of green military fatigues with a beret set at a jaunty angle on his head.

His colleagues referred to him only as "Abdul," even though that wasn't his name. As the ruler of one of the most hated countries in the Mideast, Abdul was consumed with paranoia every time he set foot out of his own sandy, oil-rich nation. Because his face was so well-known, even to the average citizen, he was afraid his presence could compromise the security of the Order, so he always took pains to disguise himself. Though he knew the conference room of Wust and Wimmer couldn't possibly be bugged, he insisted that he be called "Abdul" during his rare visits.

The Order tolerated this eccentricity, since Abdul's fears weren't without grounds. Any number of intelligence and counterterrorist agencies had a kill-on-sight contract on him. The Order made sure Abdul was always under its protection in Europe. Besides, the tyrant enjoyed a daily oil income of just under three million dollars, and he had already invested twenty million into the Order's coffers.

Abdul had joined the Order because he saw no reason to share his country's oil revenues with its dirt-poor citizenry, and he also saw the Order's project as the simplest, most practical way to end U.S. influence in his part of the world.

At the end of the table sat Heinrich Heine, clasping his snifter with trembling hands. His bald head wobbled on his scarf-sheathed neck. He didn't join the toast. Social fripperies only irritated him. The ancient rituals of the Order he participated in, but toasting the portrait of a dead man didn't interest him.

Heine had been involved with the Order since 1912. He had found and matriculated Hitler, transforming him into a shrewd orator and a frighteningly persuasive propagandist.

When the propagandist became führer, then madman, Heine had killed him, pulling the trigger himself. At Heine's orders, his stunned aides had carried his body into the garden of the Reich

Chancellery and burned it with gasoline. Heine had chosen April 30, Walpurgis Night, to sacrifice Hitler. It was all part of an ancient ritual.

The Order of Thule wasn't a large organization, nor did it need to be. It had a thousand-year legacy that was preserved from generation to generation, though Heine was concerned about passing on the torch to unworthy hands.

Though the Order financed such noisy, crude groups as the National Front, the German Alternative, the Christian Identity Movement in England and the White Aryan Resistance in America, Heine despised the young, drunken rabble. However, it was traditional to place several levels of attention-getting expendables between Order leadership and public-relations efforts like the Nazi Party.

As well as the skinheads and neo-Nazis, the Order maintained a well-armed troop of soldiers, consisting primarily of former East and West German border patrolmen. Most of them had nowhere to go after the Wall collapsed, and were happy to find a new place for their talents. The majority of them spent their time in a special wing of the Nachsinnen Clinic where Asoka had given them new identities and diagnosed them with a multitude of mental, emotional and substance-abuse ailments. Any government official glancing through the patient records would find that these men were chronics, dangerous to the community and themselves, and their treatment was ongoing.

Ganth drained off the brandy in his goblet and announced, "The news from Site 611 is excellent. The computers were rebooted with our disks. No one is the wiser."

"Did Lesnick's illness raise inquiries of an unusual nature?" Asoka asked.

Ganth nodded toward deMilteer. "Colonel?"

DeMilteer shook his head. In his guttural Afrikaans accent he said, "The transmitter was found, I'm afraid, and at last report, it was taken to Ostara Development for study. They may not know what it is. I think we can assume everything is under control."

"Let us assume nothing," Ganth responded stiffly. "We have

planned our campaign carefully and provided for all contingencies, but we must allow for an X factor.''

Weisenburg said, ''I'm familiar with the people at Ostara. One of the scientists there, a woman named Wezhardt, may realize the transmitter's purpose—''

''We have her under surveillance,'' Ganth interrupted. ''I doubt your excellent craftsmanship will be recognized. And if so, the end result is the same—we control the nuclear arsenal at Site 611. I also learned from my conduit in the U.S. Embassy that an expert in solid-state physics is due to arrive tomorrow.''

''Then we may have to reconsider the timetable,'' Asoka said. ''Move it up.''

''Good. When will we strike?'' Abdul asked.

Ganth smiled at the dictator patronizingly. ''His Excellency is premature. We do not intend to launch the missiles. The fear we will instill when the Americans and the government learn they do not have control over their toys will make them more than eager to deal with us.''

''Fear,'' Asoka added, ''is the best motivator.''

Abdul scowled. ''What is the point of owning a weapon we will not use?''

Ganth kept his smile in place. ''Our mission is what it has always been, Excellency—to seize control while Germany is in tumult, to force the NATO powers to recognize us as the true power behind the republic. It is unimportant whether the United Nations shares that recognition, or even learns about us. We are not in this for publicity.''

The last remark was a pointed comment about Abdul's apparent fondness for making threatening television speeches.

Abdul glanced around the table. ''That is all very well for you and for the rest of you. You promised that my nation would gain much from this undertaking. All I see coming out of this is a prolonged game of saber rattling.''

Heine spoke up in a sharp, whip-crack voice. ''The gain is that one of the conditions we set is the lifting of embargoes and sanctions against your country. You will supply us with oil, we will supply you with medicines, technologies and everything you need to rebuild your military.''

Heine turned from Abdul and lifted his eyes toward Ganth. "The news from Site 611 is excellent, you said. It is less so from Brazil, is it not?"

Ganth shifted uneasily. "Sir—"

"An entire village of Indians slaughtered," Heine spit. "One of our aircraft and its crew destroyed. And the Dag was not recovered."

For all his devotion to the Order, Ganth didn't share Heine's obsession with relics, no matter how important they were to the lore and legend of the society.

"Sir," Ganth said patiently, "Teudt's body was finally found. The traitor is dead, the Order avenged. What else do you want?"

By way of an answer, Heine hurled the contents of his snifter into Ganth's face. Ganth blinked as the liquor stung his eyes, but he didn't otherwise move.

Placing his hands flat on the tabletop, Heine levered his body erect. His arms trembled, but he forced himself to stand, his eyes blazing in his seamed face.

"After all these years," Heine said in a low, deadly voice, "you still do not understand. We are conquerors. As in ancient times, we took the relics of national and religious power as symbols of our victories. The powers of rulership in these objects were transferred to us. It is more than an empty, symbolic gesture. It has an actual, functional reason."

Taking a deep breath, Heine went on, "The Dag represents the roots of our Order. If it is in the possession of an enemy, those roots are cut. If we no longer control our past, then we will not command the present or the future. Do you understand me?"

DeMilteer snorted. "*I* don't. You've kept me out of this black-magic hocus-pocus so far, and I like it that way. Don't start dragging me into it now."

Heine focused his gaze on the South African. For a moment, his face was convulsed by homicidal rage. Then it relaxed. The furious flame in his eyes guttered out, and he smiled. Then he laughed.

"Leave it to our Afrikaner friend," Heine said, "to bring us back down to reality. Hocus-pocus, indeed."

The tension around the table broke, and everyone shared a laugh, including Abdul. Ganth wiped the brandy from his face with a silk handkerchief.

Then Heine's hand darted inside his coat. It came back out gripping the Walther. The pistol spit a flat crack of sound. The bullet took deMilteer in the forehead, punching a neat blue-edged hole barely half an inch above his right eyebrow. DeMilteer's head snapped back violently.

The high back and raised arms of his chair kept the man from falling, though his body sagged down toward the floor. Cordite stung the eyes and nostrils.

Heine met the stares of shocked faces with calm eyes. "Does anyone else care to speak of hocus-pocus?"

There was no answer, and Heine replaced the pistol beneath his coat. In a matter-of-fact voice he said, "I had already marked deMilteer for expulsion, so don't fear that his sudden vacancy creates either a problem or a vacuum. He served us well, but he showed signs of becoming an inconvenience."

Heine turned toward Ganth. "Helmur?"

"Sir!"

"You will use our contacts in Interpol, in the CIA, in the embassies or anyone else that is required to learn the identity of the man seen in Brazil. He will have the Dag if anyone does."

"I understand, sir."

Heine carefully eased himself back into his wheelchair. He waved a diffident hand. "Get someone up here to clean up this mess so we can continue with other business."

Ganth went to the telephone and picked up the old-fashioned French-style receiver. He dialed the mail room and spoke to the supervisor. "Please send Xauz up to the conference room with six memo pads. At once."

In less than a minute came the arranged double-knock signal at the heavy door. Ganth unbolted it and allowed Xauz to enter. He was a young man wearing the standard uniform of all Wust and Wimmer male employees—a single-breasted navy blue blazer bearing the firm's monogrammed insignia on the pocket, white shirt and narrow black necktie. Only his footwear didn't conform to the dress code; he wore pointy-toed American cowboy boots made of glistening rattlesnake skin.

Though Ganth was accustomed to Xauz's size, he nevertheless felt an instant's apprehension when the young man stalked past him into the room and insolently tossed the memo pads onto the table.

Xauz's arms and legs were like tree trunks, and great muscles rippled beneath the blazer with each motion. His closely shaved head, bearing only a bristly covering of hair, towered nearly seven feet above the floor. His forehead was high, and his gray eyes clear and alert.

Ganth gestured to deMilteer's body. "Get him out of here, Xauz. Then stand by."

Xauz nodded and bent over deMilteer, sliding his huge hands under the corpse's armpits. He hummed softly as he swung the dead South African astride the wide yoke of his shoulders, then carried deMilteer through a door built into a carved oak panel. A passage led to the basement of the building next door, then to a fenced-off alley.

After Xauz shut the door panel, the meeting resumed. Ganth would attend to cleaning up the blood and viscera personally, and he would also arrange for deMilteer to be found in his Frankfurt home, a recently fired Walther in his hand and a suicide note on the table. Numerous samples of deMilteer's handwriting were in his possession, and there was an excellent forger languishing at Asoka's clinic.

The next half hour was devoted to fairly routine details regarding finances and the acquisition of new ordnance to replace that lost in Brazil. The hit list of antifascist officials in the government who would oppose their terms was updated.

The meeting adjourned at six. Abdul left first, through the hidden wall panel that would bring him out to the alley, where his driver was waiting. Asoka and Weisenburg left by the main door on the first floor. Inasmuch as they could prove they had legitimate business with Wimmer and Wust, there was no reason for them to skulk through basements and alleys.

Ganth was left alone with Heine. The old man's outburst appeared to have drained him. His hairless head trembled.

"Are you feeling unwell, sir?" Ganth asked.

Without lifting his head, Heine said hoarsely, "I should've killed that swine of an Arab, as well as the Afrikaner. He will prove to be a problem."

Hesitantly Ganth said, "Sir, we need no more dissension."

"True," Heine replied bitterly. "We had enough of that in Brazil, didn't we?"

"We will find that man. We will find the Dag. You have my oath on it."

Heine uttered a low, derisive laugh. "I trust you will obey that oath with more dedication than shown by Teudt."

With effort, Heine raised his head. "Our Interpol contacts told us where to find Teudt. They also reported that someone leaked the Teudt's radio message to the American State Department, and they in turn contacted another agency. Find out what that agency might be. When you learn that, you will learn who that agency dispatched. And you will find the Dag."

Heine wasn't making a suggestion. There was no point in arguing with the old man, of trying to point out that six Pershing II missiles were worth a hundred—no, a thousand—ancient ceremonial daggers. Ganth toyed momentarily with the notion of crafting a replica and offering it as the genuine article. But Heine would see through the deception. And kill him.

"Helmur," Heine said quietly, "did you speak the truth to Abdul when you told him the missiles would only be launched as a last resort?"

"Of course, sir."

"He is right. There is no point in owning a weapon you do not intend to use. We are not seeking a balance of power."

Ganth's belly went cold. "Sir, is there a point in conquering a radioactive wasteland? The range of the missiles is limited. We would be destroying large pieces of the fatherland we wish to repossess."

"Do you not think the Americans will figure that out and guess we are only bluffing?"

"I think they may suspect that, but they won't take the chance."

Heine nodded. "Perhaps. Let me see the box."

Ganth hesitated.

Heine raised his head and snarled. "The box!"

Reluctantly Ganth went to the portrait of his father and grasped one of the mortised corners of the frame. It swung away from the wall on small, almost invisible hinges. Built into the wall was the military gray metallic surface of a safe door. It bore no locks or handles. There was a glassy rectangle midway between the top and bottom hinges. Ganth placed four fingers of his right hand on the rectangle. The safe door buzzed and opened.

He reached in and removed a black metal box about the size of a cigar box, but much heavier. He carried it carefully to the conference table and placed it before Heine.

With one forefinger, Ganth slid a wafer of metal open on the top of the box. Within it were coiled fiber-optic cables, coaxial input and output leads and an entire layer of microprocessors. The box was state-of-the-art in miniaturization.

Heine bent over it, one eyebrow lifted. "According to our friend Weisenburg, this little box can launch our missiles?"

"In conjunction with the rewritten programs," Ganth said. "The box is designed to be connected to a microwave transmitter that resembles a citizen's-band radio antenna. Theoretically we would drive the vehicle to within half a kilometer of the site, connect it with a keyboard and transmit the appropriate commands."

"Theoretically?"

"Obviously, sir, we have tested the device, but not on the actual missiles. To launch them would tend to invalidate our overall objective."

Heine chuckled. "Would it? What if I suggested we alter that overall objective in order to bridge the gap between the theoretical and the practical?"

Ganth swallowed. He didn't allow the fear, the hatred he felt toward the old man at that moment to show on his face.

"What is your answer, Helmur?"

Ganth stiffened and thrust out his right arm. "Honor Is Loyalty."

Heine smiled and caressed the black box. "Yes. Isn't it just."

6

June 3

The Learjet knifed through the night sky, following the air corridor designated for Western aircraft. Looking out the window at the lights of Berlin below, Bolan reflected that only a few years ago, MiGs from the Eastern side would have been buzzing them.

"We're on our final approach to Tempelhof airport," Charlie Mott said over the speaker.

Bolan slipped on the headset connecting him to the cockpit. "Everything still green?"

"Yeah," the pilot replied. "I received a message from Hal twenty minutes ago. Green as the fields of Ireland. He said to tell you not to waste time soaking up the local culture."

"I've been to strip joints before," Bolan said.

Mott laughed. He was one of the Farm's top pilots, second only to Jack Grimaldi in ability.

The jet descended in a steep glide toward the intersecting network of runways. Mott made a smooth landing and taxied the jet toward the terminal.

Bolan studied the airport. It was a huge, sprawling complex, sleek and ultramodern in design. He tried to imagine what it had looked like fifty years ago, after the Soviet armored infantry divisions had finished shelling the hell out of it.

The jet rolled to a stop. As attendants chocked the tires and wheeled a ramp to the door, Mott emerged from the cockpit.

"You can disembark now. Your luggage will be forwarded to the consulate, except your carryon."

Bolan shifted the position of the Beretta 93-R in its shoulder holster beneath his black leather jacket.

"Customs has already been dealt with," the pilot continued. "The chamber of commerce has sent a rep to meet you."

Mott employed the euphemism for the Verfassungschutz, the secret service. Bolan wasn't looking forward to meeting them. He knew the officers consisted primarily of former Gehlen Organization men.

Though most of the ex-Gestapo agents were probably retired or dead, Bolan couldn't shake the echo of Honor Is Loyalty from his mind.

The main promenade of the terminal was crowded with camera-laden people. Bolan caught at least a dozen different accents and dialects as soon as he entered. His eyes swept about, looking for his contact and simultaneously checking to see if anyone seemed unusually curious about him.

Not too very long before, the Tempelhof had been the jumping-off point for thousands of assorted spies, assassins and miscellaneous intelligence agents serving at least forty different organizations of a dozen different nations. Most of the anonymous cold warriors had moved their bases of operations to the Mideast and Africa, but Bolan spotted several men and women carrying the "spook" aura.

He also spotted a pack of tattooed and shaved-headed young men, swaggering about the promenade, elbowing aside tourists and talking in loud, aggressive voices. As they approached him, an outside member of the pack swung directly in his path. Bolan stopped and fixed a slit-eyed look on the young man's face. His right hand made a casual show of stealing inside his jacket.

The man's eyes caught Bolan's gaze. He blinked and, at the last second, veered to one side, avoiding him completely.

"Mr. Blanski?" said a low feminine voice behind him.

Bolan turned. The photograph of Ilona Wezhardt hadn't done her justice. She was a beauty all the way, with warm brown eyes only slightly darker than her complexion. She was full lipped, and even the casual attire of slacks and flannel shirt didn't conceal her trim but shapely figure. Her gaze was direct and intelligent behind the lenses of her glasses.

She extended a hand, and Bolan shook it formally. "I'm Blanski. You're Dr. Wezhardt."

"And you're a little late," she said. "Everyone is waiting, so we'll have to hustle."

Her English was perfect, touched only with a slight accent.

They started moving through the terminal. "I'm to conduct you to the consulate. They asked me to meet you because embassy officials might be recognized here."

"The old watchers never sleep," Bolan said.

"Something like that."

It was chilly outside the terminal, the temperature in the low forties. Bolan glanced around casually at the crowds streaming in and out of the many glass-and-chrome doors. He saw nothing that made him suspect they were under observation, but his sixth sense, his soldier's instinct that had helped him survive hundreds of killzones, was on the alert. All he saw that seemed the slightest bit out of place was a VW minivan parked at a service apron several hundred feet away.

The side panels were emblazoned with the words The Perfect Plug in German. Beneath the words was an illustration of a hand jamming a cork into the end of a leaky pipe.

Wezhardt led the way to a gray Opel sedan parked at the curb. A sandy-haired young man was leaning against the rear door.

"This is Pete," Wezhardt said, "our driver."

Bolan extended a hand. "Mike Blanski."

"Good to meet you." Pete opened the door, and Bolan and Wezhardt climbed in.

The Opel left the Tempelhof parking area and took the crosstown extension. Even at close to ten o' clock, the traffic was heavy.

"Why the consulate?" Bolan asked.

"My office is under surveillance," Wezhardt replied. "At least, that's what I'm told. The embassy has the least chance of being bugged."

"By whom?"

"That is what everyone is still trying to figure out." She looked at Bolan quizzically. "Do you have any ideas?"

He shrugged and changed the subject. "I understand you've been a great help on the technical side of this."

It was Wezhardt's turn to shrug. "Germany is the electronics capital of Europe. I've acted as a consultant to your government and my own on a number of occasions."

"Your government?"

Wezhardt faced him. "I realize I don't look like the standard German, Mr. Blanski. My hair, my eyes and my skin aren't the Aryan norm, but I am German nevertheless."

Bolan smiled. "You misunderstand me. I'm curious about why the republic needed your expertise, and if it was for a similar reason that sent me here."

Wezhardt laughed sheepishly. "I apologize. I can be a little sensitive. My grandfather was an American serviceman stationed here at the end of the war, and though having a black American as a family member is hardly unique, it's not commonplace. I was on the receiving end of a lot of harassment growing up. Even now. Especially now."

"What do you mean?"

"I'm sure you're aware of the nationalistic fervor sweeping my country since reunification. The slogan is *Deutschland Den Deutschen.*"

"Germany For The Germans," Bolan said.

Wezhardt nodded. "Anyone who doesn't have the prerequisite blond hair, blue eyes and pale skin is a target for harassment, even violence. Being born in this country doesn't make any difference, or make you safe."

"Sounds familiar," Bolan said.

"Yes," Wezhardt replied bitterly. "I'm afraid it does."

The Opel exited from the crosstown onto Luisen Street. It was a fairly broad, smoothly paved avenue, wide enough to accommodate four lanes of traffic. Pete kept the car in the right-hand lane.

As they were crossing a short bridge spanning the Spree River, Bolan suddenly straightened. His eyes had caught sight of something in the rearview mirror. He turned his head and looked behind them.

"We're being tailed."

"What?" Wezhardt turned, too, and for a handful of seconds she stared at the VW minibus several car lengths behind them. "You mean that plumber's van?"

"I saw it at the airport."

"So?"

"Intel states one of the vehicles suspected of spying on the Patton hospital and your office was a plumber's van."

Wezhardt's eyes widened. The van was rushing up behind them. Bolan could only see one figure in the cab, but in the cargo compartment, he glimpsed someone moving, and light glinted on something shiny and metallic.

The minibus hung on the Opel's back bumper for several seconds, then it accelerated, swerved and came abreast of the driver's-side door. The side door of the minibus slid open about three feet, and Bolan was looking into a goggled and masked face.

The face was sheathed in a silvery, metalliclike hood that draped down over the shoulders, and thick goggles had tinted lenses. In hands covered by heavy, silver gauntlets, Bolan saw a metal parabolic dish a little over two feet in diameter. A gleaming rod, topped by a crystalline cone, jutted from the center. A thick, insulated cable stretched from the back of the dish and into the cargo compartment of the van. Even though the sedan's windows were rolled up, he heard the steady whine of an electric motor.

Bolan didn't know what the dish was, but the crystal-topped rod looked like the muzzle of a weapon. Grabbing Wezhardt's head, he shoved her to the floorboards, at the same time drawing the Beretta with his free hand.

No noise, no light, no smoke came from the parabolic dish. But suddenly Bolan could feel intense heat, as if a giant acetylene torch had been turned on the car. The headlights of the minibus dimmed.

Pete, reacting to the sudden heat, looked back, glimpsed the dish and gave a cry of fear and anger. He accelerated, trying to outrun the van. The minibus kept pace, and its driver wrenched the wheel sharply.

Pete had no choice but to swerve onto the next side street to avoid a collision. It was a narrow, cobblestoned lane, with old buildings on either side. The minibus turned with the Opel, hugging it close.

The glass on the window beside Pete's head suddenly darkened and cracked. Heat blasted inward. Before Bolan's eyes, Pete shrieked in agony and clawed at his face. Then he wilted over the steering wheel. With a jarring thump, the Opel jumped the curb and plunged down the sidewalk.

Like a coiled spring, Bolan leaned forward and grasped the steering wheel. He cursed and gritted his teeth. It was scalding hot. He gave it a twist to the left, and the front tires left the sidewalk, slewing over the cobblestones. The rear end swung around in a semicircle.

The vehicle bounced over the facing curb and hit the brick facade of a building at an angle, its grillework almost inside a recessed doorway. Fortunately Pete's foot had slipped from the gas pedal, but the sedan's momentum was still sufficient to nearly hurl Bolan into the dashboard.

"What the hell's going on, Blanski?" Wezhardt cried.

As she heaved herself up, there was a squeal of brakes as the minibus sought to check its speed. It stopped, went into reverse and the metal dish swung around toward the Opel.

In one movement, Bolan thrust open the rear door on the side facing the building and shoved Wezhardt onto the sidewalk. Only a space of four feet separated the body of the sedan from the front of the building. Both of them hunkered down at the rear of the Opel.

Instantly the car beneath their hands became very hot. The back window nearest the van gave way in a spiderweb pattern of cracks, and glass showered onto the seat. The invisible torch was seeking out Bolan and the woman as they crouched between metal and brick.

Bolan felt his skin prickling, and the fine hairs in his nostrils seemed to vibrate. He felt rather than heard a feathery buzzing against his eardrums. His molars began to hurt, and his eyes stung, as if particles of sand were swimming in them. The gun in his hand heated up.

Though his vision was blurred, Bolan fired the Beretta through the open back door, the bullet whipping out the broken window and punching a hole in the van's half-open side door.

The dish turned toward him, and Wezhardt pulled him to one side. Bolan closed the door, and he and the woman crawled along the car's length to the front fender. Bolan could hear nothing but the van's engine, the muted whine of the electric generator and the persistent buzz in his ears. The small space between the front of the car and the recessed doorway grew stiflingly hot.

A high-pitched shriek like a dozen boiling teakettles split the night. The fuel tank of the sedan had ignited. The cap had been blown off by the pressure, and a foot-long jet of burning gasoline was whistling through the vent.

Bolan pulled Wezhardt toward the doorway. He didn't waste time trying the knob. He put two 9 mm slugs into the lock, rammed his shoulder into the door and he and Wezhardt fell into the foyer of the building.

They rolled to one side, against the wall, just as the Opel's fuel tank blew. The entire rear end of the car ripped open, spewing burning gasoline in all directions.

The detonation was like a thunderclap. Bolan felt the concussion against his back, despite the protection of the wall. A wave of fire crested and crashed through the open doorway.

Bolan raised his head to eye level with a window, pushing aside the heavy curtain. Through a part in the flames, he saw the dish withdrawn into the van. With a screech of rubber and a clashing of gears, the minibus leaped ahead and roared down the street.

"Are you all right?" Bolan asked Wezhardt, holstering the Beretta.

She nodded, hugging herself. She was scared, but still in control. She touched her face. "I lost my glasses somewhere. When the frames heated up and expanded, the lenses must've fallen out."

Bolan ripped down a curtain and used it to extinguish the burning gasoline in the foyer. Wezhardt helped him stamp out the flames, saying, "We've got to call the consulate and the fire brigade."

They heard windows on both sides of the street opening,

frightened people shouting. The flames from the burning car were threatening to burn the building they were in. Fortunately the building seemed deserted.

"Let's find the back door," Bolan suggested.

As they walked through the building, the first of the rising and falling wails of sirens echoed from the street. At the rear of the building they came to a heavy door marked as the fire exit.

They found themselves in a narrow alley. They strode quickly through it to a point up the block from the burning car. A crowd had gathered around the fire truck as the firemen used foam spray to smother the blaze. Police cruisers were speeding toward the scene.

Wezhardt stared at the dying inferno, the makeshift funeral pyre for Pete. "They almost got us, too," she murmured. "If not for you."

She glanced down at the nearly imperceptible bulge made by the Beretta inside Bolan's jacket. He knew the question she was going to ask, so he asked a preemptive one of his own. "What kind of weapon was that?"

Wezhardt frowned. "It wasn't a weapon...not exactly. It looked like a miniature version of a Gunn oscillator."

"A what?"

"A method of microwave generation, named for its discoverer, J. B. Gunn. Over twenty years ago, it was quite the advance in solid-state physics. The Gunn effect microwave devices replaced clumsy tubes used in radar and other applications. A lot of different types of solid-state devices were based on Gunn's findings."

"In other words," Bolan said, "a Gunn gun?"

Wezhardt laughed. "A pretty obvious joke, Mr. Blanski. During the attack, did you experience a prickling of the skin and feel a pressure against your eardrums?"

"And my back teeth started to hurt."

"Microwave radiation interacting with your metal fillings. We were lucky we caught only a fractional spillover of the microwaves, or we would've ended up like Pete."

"Seems like pretty advanced gear."

"Not really. The principles have been used since the thirties.

Marconi may've developed the first microwave 'death ray' back in 1935."

Still standing in the mouth of the alley, Wezhardt removed a cellular telephone from her handbag. She flipped it open, raised the antenna and swore in German. "I was afraid of this. Some of the circuits have been damaged."

There was a pay phone kiosk only a hundred yards up the block. Bolan walked with her to it. As she dialed the number, Bolan watched the activity down the street. Other fire engines and police cruisers were arriving. Uniformed officers kept the curious and morbid crowd back.

Even at this distance, Bolan could smell the sweetish odor of burned human flesh in the air. Anger rose in him, but he clamped it down. He had to be as cold and as calculating as the men in the van, or the men who gave them their orders.

He knew the attack hadn't been on impulse; there had been a leak, and his arrival in Berlin was expected. The attack served a twofold purpose. The first and most obvious was the intended elimination of himself and Ilona Wezhardt. Bomb experts could sift through the wreckage of the sedan for weeks and find no trace of an explosive device. Their deaths would be listed as due to a tragic accident, rather than assassination.

The second purpose was psychological—to show the American and German authorities that new and deadly technology was in the hands of people who had no compunction about using it.

Wezhardt hung up the phone. "A car from the embassy will be here any minute."

"Did you get a good look at the van?"

"You shoved me down to the floor. Did you?"

"It was a VW minibus, maybe ten years old. The front license-plate number was A838R. Not that it means much, since the plate was probably a phony."

"The van can't be traced?"

"Not that one." Bolan casually nodded up the block behind her. "*That* one may be a different story."

Wezhardt stiffened, but she didn't turn. Instead, she dug around in her purse and produced a small compact. Popping it open, she made a nonchalant show of applying lipstick while she eyed the mirror.

"Good thing I'm farsighted," she murmured. "Do you mean that florist's van?"

Bolan nodded. The van was a much newer model, and it was parked diagonally next to a storefront.

"What should we do?" Wezhardt asked.

"Nothing. They've already made us. If we start acting twitchy, they'll know we've made *them*, and I want them to hang around for a while."

"You know," Wezhardt said, snapping the compact shut, "it could be what it appears to be."

"Could be," Bolan replied. "But professionals work in teams, like relays, so if the target escapes the first team, the baton can be handed off to a second."

"Are we in danger?"

"I doubt it. Even if they have one of those oscillators, the hardmen in the plumber's van had to get right on top of us for it to be effective. These guys are probably spotters."

"Should we tell the police?"

"Absolutely not. Let's see what they do when our ride gets here."

The ride arrived within the next five minutes. A young redheaded man pulled up next to the phone kiosk in a Mercedes. Bolan slid in the front seat next to him.

"The name is Darryl," he said, flashing State Department credentials. Hooking a thumb over his shoulder at the activity behind them, he added, "Heard about that on the police scanner. Pete is dead?"

"Yeah," Bolan replied. "You knew him?"

Darryl's hands tightened on the wheel and his jaw muscles knotted. "I knew him."

"We may have a line on his killers. Interested?"

"My orders are to bring you to the embassy as quickly and as directly as I can. I'll be bucking for a reprimand."

"I'll take the responsibility."

Darryl sighed. "What have you got?"

"That florist's van. Cruise past it, see what it does."

Darryl hesitated. "You packing?"

"Yeah. You?"

"No, but screw it."

He engaged the clutch, and the Mercedes rolled forward.

7

Darryl steered the car carefully around the van, giving it no more than a casual glance. He drove up the block to a cross street, then hung a right. Expertly he spun the wheel, did a 180-degree turn and parallel-parked in a space between a Renault and a flatbed truck. He turned off the lights, but kept the engine running.

They sat in the car, waiting. The florist's van appeared at the intersection and turned left, away from them.

"They're not interested in following us," Wezhardt said, relieved.

"Why should they?" Darryl replied. "They saw us turn in the direction of the embassy."

Darryl was an experienced tail. He waited until a full block separated the Mercedes and the van before he pulled out, turning on the lights again. The van took a circuitous route for the next twenty minutes. It rolled past the Kaiser Wilhelm Memorial Church, took a right, then passed the Berlin Zoological Gardens.

The van turned off on Hardenburg Street, skirting the campus of Technische University. The traffic was still heavy, so Darryl wasn't as concerned about maintaining as much distance between the Mercedes and the van as before. He weaved in and out between cars, changing lanes every so often, hanging back, then accelerating.

The van's taillights suddenly shone bright as it braked for a left turn. Darryl eased up on the gas and shifted to the far right lane. The van had stopped at a gated driveway. Beyond the driveway was a four-story stone building, set back at least a hundred yards from the street. The lawn was ringed by a very tall wrought-iron fence.

As the Mercedes cruised past, the gate swung open to admit the van, which drove up to park in front of wide entrance steps. Darryl very quickly double-parked across the street.

Two men climbed out of the van. One opened the side door and removed a huge bouquet of flowers.

"A little late for a delivery," Bolan observed, leaning forward and staring past the bars of the gate. The two men were of approximately the same height and weight. He got a better look at them when they reached the lighted porch. Both were blond, the one carrying the bouquet a little taller and heavier than his companion. They both wore green coveralls with the name of the florist stenciled across the back. The tall man rang the bell, the door opened and they entered.

"What is this place?" Wezhardt asked.

Darryl reached for the car phone. "I can find out."

"No," Bolan said. "These people have access to sophisticated electronic gear. It's likely they have a monitoring setup to listen in to all radio and cellular phone transmissions. They might even have the consulate bugged."

Darryl frowned. "No way." But he didn't make the call.

"Move up the block a little," Bolan suggested. "If this is a legitimate delivery, they'll be coming out soon."

Darryl guided the Mercedes up the street, then U-turned so the nose of the car was aligned with the driveway. By leaning forward, they could see the van.

Within three minutes, the pair of deliverymen came out of the building and climbed back into their vehicle. As it rolled back onto the avenue, Bolan said, "They've pulled a switch on us."

"What?" Darryl asked as he put the Mercedes into gear. "It's the same van."

"The same van, but different guys in the same clothes. They look enough like the first two to pass a quick inspection."

Darryl seemed reluctant to accept Bolan's assessment. "What do you want me to do?"

"We know where the first pair are. Let's see where these guys take us."

The Mercedes followed the van for twenty-five blocks at a discreet distance back into metropolitan Berlin. Nightclubs, cabarets, bars and strip joints lined both sides of the street. Neon lights glared in a variety of colors; people clogged the sidewalks. Music thumped from inside the clubs, and raucous, drunken laughter seemed to come from every direction.

"Action city," Darryl commented with a sour smile. "Think maybe they're looking to celebrate?"

The van finally stopped at a storefront. The name and illustration on the plate-glass window was identical to that painted on the van. A garage door beside the storefront was rising, and the van moved beneath it before it was fully raised. The Mercedes rolled past without slowing.

"Now what?" Wezhardt asked.

"Let's get to the embassy," Bolan said. "That building on Hardenburg needs to be checked out. I think we've found our hardsite."

"You know," Wezhardt said, "you don't talk like any representative of the Department of Energy I've ever met."

"How many have you met, Dr. Wezhardt?"

"You'd be surprised, Mr. Blanski."

Darryl chuckled, and drove them through winding and twisting streets until they reached an alley off Clayalee leading to a chain-link gate. He braked in front of it, spoke briefly into the car phone and the gate swung open for them. He parked the Mercedes in an underground garage full of different makes of cars.

"Our secret fleet," Darryl explained. "The ones without diplomatic plates."

Darryl led Bolan and Wezhardt to a back entrance of a white-stone building, into a dimly lit hallway and then into a small, windowless room.

There were three men sitting at a round table. Darryl left the room. Wezhardt knew them and made quick introductions. Major Art Hyams was the representative of both G-2 and NATO intelligence, Lieutenant Roman Kinnard was the shift supervisor at Site 611 and a middle-aged man introduced only as Straub was a section chief of the Verfassungschutz.

Straub looked Bolan over with bleak eyes; the soldier knew

the long-nosed German had been in the business long enough to realize that he was a specialist, and that his name and credentials were fake. Then again, "Straub" probably wasn't his real name, either.

The discussion began slowly. Bolan briefed the three men on the most recent attack, and Wezhardt offered her opinion on the technology used against them. Hyams and Straub only grunted. They were cagey with each other, regardless of their common cause. It took Straub five minutes of monosyllabic answers before he admitted that the Russians had been informed of the current situation.

"Just what," Bolan asked, "*is* the current situation?"

Hyams nodded to Kinnard, who without preamble declared, "The Pershings at the site are no longer under our control."

By the lack of reaction, Bolan realized this was old news to both Hyams and Straub. "Bring me up-to-date, Lieutenant."

"After the system crash, we rebooted as quickly as we could. The database was downloaded from our mainframes, so the only software we actually needed to install were secondary analogs— access codes, targeting and trajectory programs, recognition signals and launch commands. Everything seemed to work fine, so I just relegated the cause of the crash to a glitch. When Lesnick collapsed, there was too much excitement to run a level-four diagnostic. Besides, we needed to relink with Cheyenne Mountain ASAP."

Kinnard took a very deep breath. "When the major informed me of the probable cause of Lesnick's death, I immediately suspected an electromagnetic pulse. I was ordered to conduct a level-four diagnostic. I did. Superficially the system is fully operable. But evidently the software we used to reboot had been tampered with."

"Tampered with?" Bolan repeated. "Explain."

"One of the diskettes had been replaced with one containing a program that infiltrated the primary and rewrote it. On the surface, everything is green. But the launch code has been rewritten and our attempts to delete it resulted in an immediate lock-out. I'm afraid that if we try to physically disarm or remove the warheads, the launch code will be transmitted."

"There's no way to interrupt the link between the computers and the missiles?" Bolan asked.

"We don't know yet," Hyams said. "This new program could have insinuated itself so completely in our systems that anything we do could trigger a launch. That includes moving them."

Bolan nodded. "Any idea who made the software switch, Lieutenant?"

Kinnard cleared his throat. "Aside from myself and other shift supervisors, you mean? There are only two keys to the disk locker. Each supervisor is handed one at the beginning of the watch. The second is kept in a combination-lock cabinet. Neither I nor the other three supervisors had the combination."

"But Lieutenant-Colonel Lesnick did," Hyams said. "Hard to believe that he would turn traitor, but all evidence points to it."

"Maybe not," Wezhardt said.

Straub looked at her levelly. "You think he may be innocent?"

"He may have done the software switch, but he might not have had full knowledge of what he was doing."

"We considered the possibility of brain-washing and hypnotic suggestion and drugs," Hyams said. "But his whereabouts and movements over the last three months are fully accounted for. That kind of conditioning, of thought-pattern reversal, requires a long time and a specialized environment, no matter what you see in the movies."

"I've been brought on board as a consultant because of my expertise in solid-state physics," Wezhardt said, an edge to her voice. "The effects of microwave radiation on the human body go far beyond simply cooking it from within. Exposure in the range of 0.5 kilohertz to 30 megahertz increases the gamma globulin and leukocyte count in the blood, enlarges the thyroid and causes deviations in brain patterns. Even at low intensity, microwaves can seriously alter the rhythm of brain waves, causing drastic perceptual distortions. Since our adversaries possess a variety of microwave devices, I believe Lesnick had his mind tampered with."

Straub allowed himself a small smile. "It was revealed fifteen years ago that the Soviet Union was bombarding the northwestern United States with low-frequency microwaves. As I recall, they were trying to influence behavior by electronic means. It wasn't very effective, since your country began a massive military buildup."

"You're not suggesting Russians are behind this?" Hyams demanded.

"Did you read the jacket that was modemed over?" Bolan asked.

Straub's jaw muscles tightened. "I read it. Ridiculous. If the Order of Thule ever existed, it died when Hitler did."

"I don't buy the Nazi theory, either," Hyams added. "There's no intel indicating any major movement either by the neo-Nazi groups or what's left of the Odessa."

"Let's stop sidestepping, gentlemen," Bolan said grimly. "Both of you know all about the Order. Hundreds, even thousands of SS men became part of Interpol and CIA operations after the war, not to mention the Gehlen Organization. It may be bad taste to mention it, but the vipers we thought we'd tamed fifty years ago have reared up and sunk their fangs into us again."

Straub's eyes narrowed. "I was never a Nazi."

"I'm not implying that you were or are," Bolan responded. "But what about this acquaintance of Lesnick's, this Helmur Ganth? You read the report on his father—"

"We know about Ganth's father," Straub broke in coldly. "It is hardly a revelation. Would you hold a son guilty for the sins of the father, Herr Blanski?"

"We checked out Ganth and his firm," Hyams said. "Impeccable credentials. Lesnick was only one of a dozen American officers who are clients of Wimmer and Wust. Ganth deals in stocks, bonds, hog futures, mutual bonds, that sort of thing. If he has any Nazi connections beyond his old man, we couldn't find them."

"That doesn't mean that he finds the philosophy uncongenial," Bolan stated. "The fact is, this embassy, Major, and your agency, Straub, probably have a few people lurking around who do appreciate that philosophy. The trap laid for me points to it."

"It's extremely likely," Wezhardt said. "Remember, Nazi scientists made the first breakthroughs in microwave researches. Not all of them are dead.''

"Assuming your suspicions are true," Hyams said, "what's their objective with the Pershings?''

Bolan shrugged. "Blackmail, maybe. To force NATO and the German government to deal with them, to accede to whatever demands they make. Or maybe they simply intend to blow up a large piece of real estate just to show they can. The missiles are only a means to an end.''

"If that is so," Straub said, "then they will make a demand of both our governments very soon.''

"They might want to keep their success a secret as long as they can," Bolan said. "They might not make a demand until they're certain we're on to them.''

Hyams sighed and dry-washed his face with his hands. "We're up against a tight timetable, but we don't know by whose schedule. Those missiles are virtually time-bombs, and we have no idea in hell how long or how short the fuses are.''

There was a knock at the door.

"Come!" Hyams ordered, and Darryl entered, holding a sheet of computer printout.

"We have the vitals on that building on Hardenburg. It's a privately owned substance-abuse clinic, run by a Dr. Hito Asoka. He's a very reputable psychiatrist, sometimes makes the rounds on talk shows. He's been chairman of the place since the sixties. He has no ties with any fascist or Marxist doctrines. The place is as clean and upstanding as it can be without having a halo around it. However, here's an interesting item—the place has a special wing in the rear for the care of chronic cases. You know, heavy-duty juicers and dopers. This wing is patrolled by armed guards and attack dogs.''

Straub fluttered a dismissive hand. "Many institutions have that kind of security.''

"State-run mental asylums, maybe," Bolan said. "This one has two of the black-hats holed up inside.''

He locked gazes with Straub. "We need the full treatment. Do you agree?''

Straub returned that unblinking stare for a few silent seconds, then shifted his eyes toward Hyams. "Very well. I authorize a wiretap and round-the-clock surveillance. My people will interact with yours, Major."

"These guys are pros," Bolan argue. "So don't send in agents dressed as vacuum-cleaner salesmen or put paving crews outside on the street."

Both Hyams and Straub glared at him. "We're not amateurs," the G-2 officer snapped.

"Neither are they. They've already scored three times against us."

"Your luggage arrived a little while ago, Mr. Blanski," Darryl said. "Do you want it brought in here?"

"Yeah, thanks."

Straub stood, military trim and ramrod erect. "I will see to the surveillance, Major, and contact you when my people are ready."

He nodded to Wezhardt and pointedly ignored Bolan as he left. Hyams looked at Wezhardt and Kinnard. "You two are dismissed. Thank you for your time, Doctor, and I apologize for the incident this evening. Quarters have been arranged for you here. Under the circumstances, I think it's best you remain here tonight."

Wezhardt opened her mouth to say something, then closed it. As she walked to the door, she murmured, "Good night, Mr. Blanski."

Darryl returned with two large vinyl-covered cases on a hand truck. He dumped them, took a quick look at Hyams's face, then left, shutting the door carefully behind him.

Bolan heaved the larger case onto the table and unlatched it. Inside was a Remington Autoloader USAS-12 shotgun and a pair of rotary drum, 20-round magazines. He checked out the mechanisms of the weapon, sighting down its length. Bolan laid it aside and lifted out his combat harness, and a foam-cushioned box containing a dozen Dutch V-40 minigrenades.

Hyams watched Bolan's inspection of the ordnance with a sour expression. He made a noisy show of removing the plastic wrap from a cigar and lighting it.

"Something on your mind, Major?" Bolan asked as he looked over his Desert Eagle.

"I don't know who the hell you really are, or who the hell you *think* you are," Hyams growled around the cigar, "but you're some kind of spook. But not from the Company. Otherwise you wouldn't have such a hard-on about Nazis and this Thule shit. At least not in Germany."

"Why not?"

"We don't give much of a damn about who played on whose team fifty years ago. WWII is becoming a very long time ago. They're on our side now."

"Alliances of convenience under extenuating circumstances are one thing, Major. But those circumstances are pretty inconvenient now, wouldn't you say?"

Hyams blew a wreath a smoke. "I read the jacket about this Order of yours. There's not one shred of proof or supporting evidence beyond that old OSS report."

"You sound pretty positive, Major."

"You know something I don't?"

By way of a reply, Bolan opened the second, smaller case. He removed the protective bubble wrap and tossed the Dag onto the table.

Hyams looked at it with a bored eye. "That supposed to mean something?"

"It's the supporting evidence. An ancient relic from the early days of the Order. It was in the possession of a former Gestapo intelligence officer who held on to it for fifty years as a way to balance out some of the evil he'd done during the war. The Order wants it back. They killed a village full of Brazilian Indians to get it just last week."

"Why do you have it?"

"Bait. Or flypaper. Take your pick."

Hyams sighed. "Listen, Blanski—if that's your real name, which I doubt—the surviving old Nazi guard are scattered all over the world, living new lives under new identities. They want nothing more than to spend the rest of their days in peace."

"You think the rise of neo-Nazism in Germany coinciding with the fall of communism is just happpenstance?" Bolan asked.

"What else?"

"Tactics. If the Order kept the driving spirit of Nazism alive, then it was to their benefit to help the Western democracies destroy communism in Europe. It's easier to fight one enemy than two."

Hyams snorted. "Bullshit. You're talking about some kind of long-range objective, planned over fifty years ago. If that were so, they'd have to take into account that a lot of their people would be dead by now."

"They recruited new people. While Allied intelligence was busy assimilating them into postwar intelligence networks, the Order was busy assimilating new people into *their* network."

"You're paranoid."

"Experienced. These guys couldn't operate without elements in the government giving them Get Out Of Jail Free cards. Same way the Mafia or the Colombian cartels get a grip on a country or a city. They don't have to conquer with guns and bombs. Not when somebody on the inside hands them the keys on a silver platter, simply by looking the other way."

"We're talking terrorism here, Blanski. Plain and simple, not a scheme to build a Fourth Reich."

"When's the last time you were briefed on international terrorism, Major?"

"I keep up with the latest intel."

"Then you've heard of the Third Position. The slogan is Hitler And Mao United In Struggle. Two extremes of the political spectrum coming together in dead center. An alliance of convenience, to spread death and terror around the world."

"We used the ex-SS guys to help us fight the Communists. They were beaten, the Reds weren't. It was expedient."

"That fight is over," Bolan said quietly. "The circumstances of the alliance no longer exist. It's past time to treat these people as what they really are."

Bolan slammed an ammo clip into the butt of the Desert Eagle and jacked a round into the chamber.

"I'm taking these guys out," he said calmly. "With or without your help."

8

June 4

Heine wheeled himself through the doorway, rubber wheels squealing on the bare concrete floor. The small room was packed with chassis after chassis, module upon module of electronic gear. A bank of monitor screens flickered with gray-and-white images. Pilot lights of a powerful radio glowed red and green. Two complex recording units with vertically mounted spools and an eighteen-channel console ran the length of one wall. A locked file cabinet stood in a corner.

Sven was standing before one of the monitor screens and he turned as he heard the squeak of rubber. "I've cued the tape for you, sir."

Heine didn't reply. He wheeled his chair to the screen and watched the video record of the minibus assault on the Opel. The tape had been recorded by the team of observers in the florist's van. Hidden inside a bouquet of flowers, it had been delivered late the previous night to the clinic. Heine, who had quarters in the Nachsinnen, had been called by Sven to look at the tape. Sven was wearing the neat white coat of a hospital attendant. Beneath it, in a hip holster, was a small .25-caliber FIE Titan pistol.

Heine watched the explosion of the Opel, rewound the tape and watched it again. "Nicely done."

Sven cleared his throat. "Fast-forward it, sir."

"Why? The black woman and the American went up in smoke. That's what is important."

"Not exactly, sir." Sven steeled himself for Heine's outraged reaction. His hand stole beneath his coat, and his fingers touched the butt of the Titan. He kept his eyes on Heine's right hand, making sure it didn't dart inside his coat to grab the Walther holstered there. Sven had heard of deMilteer's "expulsion," and he had no intention of having his employment terminated in the same manner.

Heine didn't show any anger, but Sven wasn't relieved. Heine's long fingers pressed a button on the console, and images on the monitor screen sped up. Flames licked crazily, and people raced to and fro and official vehicles careened around corners and disgorged passengers, all to an inhuman tempo, like an old Keystone Kops comedy.

Sven leaned forward and pointed. "*There*, sir."

The pace of the tape returned to normal. The quality of the image was poor, dim and backlit by flames dancing from the burning automobile. A man and a woman emerged from the mouth of an alley, paused and approached a telephone kiosk. They were facing the hidden camera.

"How did they escape?" Heine asked.

"I'm not certain, sir. According to Otto, the oscillator operator, the American was armed. We hadn't counted on that."

"Why would a representative of the Department of Energy be armed?"

"I don't think that is who he really works for, sir. And I believe he is the same man we saw on the riverbank in Brazil."

"The same man who destroyed our aircraft and shot down two of your comrades?"

"Yes, sir. Though I only caught a glimpse of him when I put the searchlight on him, I'm sure he is the one. The swine was carrying a strongbox."

"That man is no swine," Heine muttered.

"We retraced his path on the riverbank and found Teudt dead in an underground passage. Obviously this man found Teudt alive."

"And," Heine said, "Teudt gave him the Dag."

"Our latest intel indicates this man's name is Michael Blanski. We checked, and though there is a computer personnel record of a Michael Blanski employed by the Department of Energy, his credentials seem incomplete."

"A cover," Heine snapped. "The U.S. has dispatched a specialist, and I doubt, even with our contacts, we will learn his real identity. But that is meaningless. I know who he is."

Sven was startled. "You recognize him?"

Heine didn't answer. "Contact Helmur. We must neutralize this man, and Helmur can take care of it in a less spectacular fashion than the last attempt."

Sven didn't move. "With all due respect, sir, I request the contract. The men he killed in South America were friends of mine and—"

"Contact Helmur!" Heine barked. "Immediately!"

Sven hurried away, making sure Heine didn't turn with the Walther in his hand. Heine ignored him. He pushed his wheelchair back and thought about the face on the screen.

His lips drew back in a smile. For the first time in decades, Heine was filled with fear, and he took a secret delight in the emotion.

It was somehow fitting, even inevitable, that this American warrior would have the Dag. Though the man's face was unmarked, Heine could see the scars on his soul. This was a warrior of many battlefields, a man who had always emerged victorious, stained with the blood of his enemies. The man had been wounded, true enough, but each wound was a badge of honor, each scar representing a triumph.

This man was no mere soldier, performing his duty for God and country. Heine had told Sven that he knew who the man was, and he did, without knowing anything about him at all.

He knew, with a terrible certainty, that the dark man was Vengeance, Justice and Death.

ILONA WEZHARDT'S OFFICE at Ostara Development offered few clues to her interests. The walls held mostly works of art—black-and-white Japanese block prints, swirling abstracts and colorful Expressionist scenes from turn-of-the-century Europe. A framed diploma from MIT hung on the wall behind her desk.

The desk was very large and very old, with many pigeonholes.

A framed, hand-tinted photograph of a black man wearing the uniform of the U.S. Army Air Corps was the only personal item on it.

Bolan guessed the man in the photo was Wezhardt's grandfather, but he didn't question her. He was more interested in the device she was fiddling with on the desktop.

It was a metal, oblong gadget studded with dials and buttons, about two and half feet long by two wide. A glass-covered digital readout dominated the face, and a telescoping antenna extended from the top.

"This can detect and register microwave radiation at up to five hundred yards," she said.

"What if it picks up emissions from microwave ovens?" Bolan asked.

Wezhardt carefully pointed out dials and controls. "It can be adjusted to register wavelengths of certain frequencies. Ovens usually operate on a different band than the Gunn oscillator."

The sun was setting. Bolan had accompanied Wezhardt to her office to pick up the device so it could be turned over to the surveillance team posted around the Nachsinnen Clinic. At last report, approximately eight hours of constant observation had turned up nothing unusual or suspicious. The wiretaps hadn't been hooked in, and Wezhardt had cautioned against using long-range listening devices, since their energy transmissions could be detected.

Wezhardt stowed the device inside of a large, leather carrying case. Bolan went with her to the Volvo the embassy had provided. Hyams hadn't been happy about them driving across Berlin without an armed escort, but Bolan had pointed out that it was extremely unlikely another hit had been scheduled so soon, and even if it was, the radiation detector would let them know if the Gunn oscillator was being deployed again.

Wezhardt put the device in the back seat, turned it on and raised the antenna. She drove so Bolan could have his hands free; the Beretta was snug in its shoulder rig, and the Desert Eagle rode in a cross-draw belly holster under his partially zipped jacket.

As they passed the company's sign, with its graphic of a

woman with stars floating from her hair, Bolan asked, "Ostara. Does that mean anything special?"

Wezhardt smiled. "Ostara is the Teutonic moon goddess. Her festival is celebrated each spring, like Easter."

She glanced over at him. "Do you have a deity, Mr. Blanski, besides the god of the gun?"

Bolan didn't look at her. He was scanning the area ahead of them and checking their backtrack in the side mirror. "I don't worship guns, Doctor, any more than a stonecutter worships a chisel."

"So they're just the tools of your trade, is that it?"

"More or less."

"And what is your trade, besides masquerading unsuccessfully as a physicist?"

"On-call garbageman and sanitation expert." He didn't smile when he said it.

Wezhardt glanced again at the harsh profile. She'd worked with intelligence agents before, but this man was different.

"Don't you ever find it tiring?" she asked. "Going to wherever you're ordered to go to clean up somebody else's mess?"

"I'm not ordered," Bolan replied. "I pick and choose. I can only do so much, so I go where the need is the greatest."

"The need for what?"

"Scale balancing, loose-end tying. Justice."

Bolan turned his head toward her, and for a moment their eyes met. A horn blaring from behind them commanded Wezhardt's attention; Bolan's hand made an instinctive streak to the butt of the Desert Eagle. Both of them eyed the mirrors. A young man in denim astride a motor scooter was signaling for a left turn behind them. He was wearing a bright, shiny white helmet.

Wezhardt let out an uneasy laugh. "Just a kid."

Bolan kept his eyes on the mirror until he was positive the woman's assessment was correct. The rider turned off left and disappeared into the mouth of an alley. Bolan released the butt of the pistol, but he didn't relax.

"Do you think you could find that florist's shop we went by last night?" he asked.

After a second of silent surprise, Wezhardt said, "Sure. I guess so. Why?"

"The primary hardsite is already covered. I want to double-check we haven't overlooked a secondary target."

"What about that plumber's van?"

"Hyams said there was no company called the Perfect Plug. It's likely that van is inside the florist's garage, or hidden on the grounds of the clinic."

By the time their Volvo reached the area of the florist's shop, the sun had fully set. They drove past the storefront. The window was dark, the garage door down. There was no signal from the detector in the back seat. Wezhardt had to drive slowly and tap the brakes several times to avoid running over drunken bar patrons who kept stumbling into the cobblestoned street.

Loud music blasted from the neon-lit nightclubs and strip joints. Packs of young people, arms entwined in crapulous affection, clogged the sidewalks.

Wezhardt managed to find a parking space a hundred yards or so down the street. Checking the detector, she announced, "Still nothing."

Bolan opened the door and got out. "Stay here."

Wezhardt didn't say anything, but she got out of the Volvo and joined him on the sidewalk. She stared at him with amused, defiant eyes. Bolan sighed once, and they walked up the sidewalk to the florist's. They were forced to step aside once to make way for a weaving collection of drunken, laughing young women.

At the shop, Bolan peered through the window and saw only what he expected to see: flowers, and a large rack holding an assortment of cards. The door was locked, and the garage door was secured from the inside.

"Think there's a back entrance?" Bolan asked.

The sound of glass shattering against stone cut off Wezhardt's response. Bolan spun. Three men were reeling across the street toward them. One had dropped a beer bottle on the cobblestones. All of them appeared drunk, but they were walking faster than drunks would have been expected to.

They were young, shaved-headed, wearing metal-studded denim jackets, fingerless leather gloves and provocative smiles.

One was of medium height and build, the second rather small and acne spotted.

The third was one of the biggest men Bolan had ever seen. Rather than the heavy laced boots his companions wore, his feet were shod in pointy-toed cowboy boots.

"Hey," the big man said in reasonably good English. "They're closed. Find another place to buy your black bitch flowers."

Bolan sized him up quickly. He was huge, nearly seven feet tall and probably tipped the scales at close to three hundred pounds, none of it fat. He was also doing a very poor job of pretending to be drunk.

His two companions laughed at the giant's wit. Bolan recognized the smaller man's jawline; he'd seen him only a short time before astride a motor scooter.

Bolan stepped in front of Wezhardt. She breathed, "Don't. It's a trap."

He knew it was a trap. If it was sprung successfully, he and Wezhardt would be written off as just two more victims of random neo-Nazi violence. He also knew the trap was prepared on impulse, a surveillance team forced to act as assassins. The three weren't professionals, and that made the situation a little less formidable.

Staring into the hulking giant's face, Bolan asked mildly, "What's your name, son?"

The young man blinked. After a second's hesitation, he said with a smirk, "They call me Xauz. What's it to you, foreigner?"

"I always want to know the name of every idiot I kill. Makes record keeping easier."

Xauz gaped at him in outraged surprise. "You know-it-all American—I'll tear your head off!"

As Xauz crossed the intervening few feet of sidewalk, Bolan saw that the smallest skinhead had pulled a sawed-off bat from beneath his jacket. Bolan stepped back, his hand closing around the butt of the Desert Eagle.

Metal glinted from the knuckles of Xauz's right fist. Bolan sprang to the left, away from the brass-reinforced punch. As

Xauz's fist brushed the collar of his jacket, Bolan slashed the barrel of the Desert Eagle across the bridge of the giant's nose.

Blood gushed forth, splashing into Xauz's eyes. He stumbled forward, pawing at his face. He slammed into the garage door with a loud bang, uttering a scream of rage and pain.

Bolan whirled on his companions. The little guy with the ball bat stared too long at Xauz. The Executioner slashed the barrel of the pistol across the side of his head, splitting the scalp. Blood pouring down his face, he staggered against his companion.

The remaining skinhead pushed his senseless partner out of the way and rushed forward, head down, hands balled into fists. Bolan didn't use the Desert Eagle on him. He pivoted on one foot and drove a roundhouse kick into the man's lower belly. The skinhead folded over Bolan's leg, then flopped down on the sidewalk, making gagging sounds.

Xauz turned, breathing heavily through his mouth. He glared at Bolan and the Desert Eagle in his hand. He didn't move.

Deliberately Bolan handed the pistol to the wide-eyed Wezhardt. He faced Xauz and smiled. The youth charged at him, hands outstretched.

Bolan quickly stepped inside his adversary's outflung arms and kicked his right kneecap. The pop of the patella being forcefully removed from the femur was clearly audible, even over the throbbing beat of music.

Xauz went down on the sidewalk, plucking at his maimed leg and yelling in agony. He gaped up at Bolan with astonished horror. His right hand was splayed out on the sidewalk, and Bolan put the heel of his right boot on it, twisted sharply and heard the bones crack. Xauz screamed as Bolan maintained the pressure. He bent and pulled the brass knuckles from his hand.

Bolan slipped the knucks over the fingers of his right hand and waited until the skinhead he'd belly-kicked shambled erect. He was breathing in great, bubbling gasps, hands over his stomach.

Without putting much of his weight behind it, Bolan snapped a jab to the skinhead's jaw. Metal met flesh and bone with an ugly crack. The skinhead staggered a few feet, then fell in a loose-limbed heap to the sidewalk.

Bolan turned back to Xauz. He was still smiling that small, cold smile. At the sight of it, Xauz managed to control his pain and tried to force himself to his feet.

The soldier waited until Xauz had achieved a half-crouching posture, then he delivered the toe of his right boot full into Xauz's mouth. The youth went over on his back, spitting blood and bone splinters.

Bolan strode over to him and Xauz cringed, scooting on the seat of his pants until his back was pressed against the garage door.

"The master race," Bolan said, his voice heavy with contempt. He gestured to Wezhardt, who slipped the .44 into his hand. He went to one knee beside Xauz and planted the bore of the pistol against his forehead.

"I'm going to ask you a few questions," Bolan said. "If you don't answer them, if I think you're lying or if I simply don't like your attitude, I'll blow your head off. Do we understand each other?"

Squeezing his eyes shut, Xauz nodded several times. "*Ja, ja.*"

"Who do you work for?"

"Wust and Wimmer."

"What do you do?"

"Mail-room clerk."

"Who ordered you to kill us?"

Xauz hesitated, and Bolan dug the bore into his forehead.

"No one. My orders were to watch the store. See who showed up. I didn't have orders to kill you."

"So you did this on your own initiative. A skinhead with ambition. Who gave you the orders?"

"Herr Ganth."

Bolan stood and holstered the Desert Eagle. "Do you know what a Dag is?"

"No."

"It doesn't matter. Tell him I have it."

Bolan took Wezhardt by the arm and led her back to the Volvo. She was trembling. "Want me to drive, Doctor?"

Wezhardt gave him an angry look and quickly slid behind the

wheel. When they were mobile again, she snapped, "Why did you brutalize that kid?"

"He intended to do more than brutalize you," Bolan replied. "You might very well have crippled him."

"I might very well have educated him. Size, strength and arrogance counts for only so much. He'll have time to think about that over the next few months while he's taking his meals through a straw and walking around on crutches."

9

When Bolan and Wezhardt entered the small office in the consulate, Major Hyams was waiting for them. He ignored the radiation detector Wezhardt placed on the table and snarled, "Just what the hell did you hope to accomplish, Blanski?"

"To draw the enemy into the open."

"And to draw a lot of unwanted attention!"

Wezhardt looked from Hyams to Bolan and demanded, "What're you talking about?"

"The major had us tailed," Bolan said.

"What?" Wezhardt said raggedly. "Then why didn't you help us with those skinheads?"

Hyams didn't answer. He kept glaring at Bolan. "We had the florist's shop covered, Blanski. There was no need for you to go there."

"Good of you to share that with me."

"Now, because of that little street theater performance of yours, the enemy won't go near it."

"They don't have to," Bolan replied. "I have a name and a place. Helmur Ganth of Wust and Wimmer."

Hyams sighed in exasperation. "Didn't we go over that already? Ganth is clean—"

"And one of the skinheads, maybe all three, works at his firm," Bolan interrupted. "Straub can arrange formal charges against them. They're low-level thugs, not pros. One of them will spill and we can go after Ganth all nice and neat and legal."

Hyams thought that over for a handful of seconds. He opened his mouth to speak, but the telephone on the table rang. Hyams picked up the receiver and spoke into it. Then he fell silent, just listening. After a minute, he hung up. His face had paled by several shades. He sank into a chair and rubbed his forehead.

"What is it?" Bolan asked.

Hyams cleared his throat and began speaking in a monotone.

An ambulance had picked up the three young men Bolan had left on the sidewalk. They had been ferried to the nearest hospital. Less than ten minutes after they had been admitted to the emergency room, two men—one with a raincoat slung over his right arm—entered the emergency room and announced they were relatives of the three young men.

The admissions nurse informed them that the men were being treated and their injuries were such that it was unlikely they would be released that night.

Whereupon one of the men shot the nurse through the head with a .25-caliber automatic.

Then the two men walked quickly into the examination room where the three skinheads were being attended to by a pair of physicians. The man with the raincoat flung it aside to reveal the muzzle of an Uzi. He shot down the two doctors.

The largest of the three skinheads screamed something before several bullets perforated his cranium. The other two were dispatched by a prolonged burst of autofire.

The pair of raiders calmly left the emergency room. On their way out, the man armed with the .25-caliber pistol shot a security guard who tried to block their way. The nurse was dead and so were the three skinheads and one of the doctors. The other was on the critical list with multiple gunshot wounds. The security guard was expected to die before dawn.

The entire sequence of events had happened in the past forty-five minutes.

"Oh, my God," Wezhardt gasped when Hyams finished his account.

She looked at Bolan with horror-stricken eyes. Then, with one hand covering her mouth she ran out of the room. Bolan didn't go after her. There was nothing he could say.

A frustrated and angry Hyams stared at him. "So much for nice, neat and legal, Blanski. Your leads just evaporated."

"No," Bolan said. "I forced their hand. They killed three of their own to keep their secrets, but they know they'll have to make a move very soon. We have to get busy to checkmate it.''

"How do you figure to do that?"

"By hitting their hardsite when they least expect it."

"When?"

"Tonight."

"Goddammit, we don't have any evidence that the clinic is anything than what it appears to be."

"That's why we need to hit it. Get Straub over here with maps of the sewer lines in the Hardenburg district."

Hyams chewed his lower lip for a moment. The friction between two military veterans, each accustomed to playing out a mission his own way, heated up the small room.

Bolan said calmly, "Major, I have the authority I need to make this come to pass. You know I do. Let's knock off the game of push-me-shove-you. We don't have the time for it."

Hyams snorted and picked up the phone. He muttered into it for a few seconds, then dropped the receiver back into its cradle. "Straub's on his way."

"Good. I'll order us some coffee."

The pot of black coffee arrived before the Verfassungschutz officer. Bolan had just finished his first cup when Straub walked in, carrying a briefcase.

"Here is what you requested," he said to Hyams.

Straub spread out a large chart on the table and Bolan went over his plan, point by point. Straub mentioned certain problems and even made a few useful suggestions.

"You've used these sewers before?" Bolan asked.

Straub nodded. "Before the Wall came down, we occasionally infiltrated agents into East Berlin through them."

"A pretty clandestine border crossing," Bolan replied. "And smelly, too."

Straub ignored the comment. "I have little doubt that you can penetrate the clinic. Whether you can get out is a different matter altogether. After last night and tonight's event, those inside will be on full alert."

"I've taken that into account. The risk factor is high, but acceptable."

"I suggest a reserve standby force, waiting to execute a diversionary tactic if you need assistance."

Bolan considered the proposal. "Agreed, as long as it's a strike force of no more than twenty men. And keep the unit incommunicado from all outside contact from the moment you brief them."

Straub angled an eyebrow. "What are you implying, Herr Blanski?"

"Nothing. I'm making a straight-from-the-hip statement. There's a leak somewhere between the consulate, G-2 and your secret service. I don't know who, and at the moment, I don't care. I just want to make sure I won't waltz into another trap."

Straub didn't become angry or huffy. "I understand. My department will provide you with the newest and best equipment."

"Thank you."

A rendezvous and timetable were set. Bolan shook Straub's outstretched hand, and the secret service officer left the room.

"You must be slipping," Hyams drawled. "You didn't offend him this time."

Bolan didn't reply. He poured himself another cup of coffee.

Hyams watched him sourly and asked, "What if you get in there and find absolutely nothing of value? It'll be a pretty embarrassing diplomatic incident."

He seemed pleased by the possibility.

"I don't embarrass easily, Major. If that's the case, you can watch me eat crow with a side order of humble pie."

"What if you get in there and find a hell of a lot more than you expect? You're just one man."

Bolan shrugged, sipping at his coffee. "I'm one man who makes a point of paying my bills. If the second scenario is the case, then I'll pay off what I owe and add in a lot of interest."

THE REPORT of the massacre at the hospital reached Ganth at a little after nine o'clock. He was working late when the secured line between his private office and the Nachsinnen Clinic rang.

Asoka provided the details. Ganth was shaken, appalled and greatly disturbed by the vision of the next day's headlines. He demanded to know who had ordered the raid.

"Heinrich, who else?" Asoka said. "When the report of the accident came in from one of our informants on the police department, Heinrich dispatched Otto and Sven to the hospital."

"I thought as much," Ganth said bitterly. "What Heinrich has done is intolerable. Our men have acted like cheap thugs."

"There's more," Asoka said. He hesitated, then added, "According to Otto, Xauz said he had a message for you, something the American told him."

A chill crept up the buttons of Ganth's spine. "A message for me? The American knows my name?"

"Evidently. Xauz probably told him that he worked for Wust and Wimmer."

"What was the message?"

"The American told Xauz to say to you that he has the Dag."

Ganth swore into the mouthpiece, and swore again when he noticed that his hands were shaking. "Did Otto tell Heinrich about this?"

"Of course," Asoka answered. "And Heinrich flew into a rage. He demands that the American be apprehended at any cost, and forced to reveal the Dag's whereabouts. He even said something about storming the U.S. Embassy, or kidnapping the Wezhardt woman and holding her for ransom."

"Good God," Ganth muttered.

"It is my opinion that Heinrich is suffering from a severe dissociative disorder," the Japanese psychiatrist said. "Partly due to age and partly due to a long-term psychosis. We can no longer trust his judgment."

"Of course not," Ganth snapped. "This sort of violence will only anger the very people in the government we wish to influence. If they come to believe we are common terrorists, or a leftover scrap of storm troopers, they will not even consider our proposal."

"I agree," Asoka said. "Heinrich must be isolated from the circle."

"Easier said than done," Ganth replied. "Many of the soldiers in the special wing are undisciplined hoodlums, loyal to Heinrich, not to our objective."

"They are expert survivors, Helmur. They might not be loyal

to our cause, but they will not wish to leave the sanctuary I've provided for them.''

"We'll have to move up our timetable,'' Ganth said. "I'll draft the communiqué tonight. In the interim, remove Heinrich from the general population. If anyone in the wing asks, just say that he needs special medical treatment.''

Asoka agreed and hung up. Ganth sat at his desk, swiftly calculating the odds of how soon he could expect the Berlin police or the Verfassungschutz to ask him questions about Xauz. He knew the young giant should have been eliminated, since the Order's security couldn't be compromised, but the public manner in which it was done raised far more questions than answers.

Heinrich, unfortunately, was becoming a security risk, as well. If the old man continued to be intractable, he would notify Asoka to kill him, preferably by injection, introducing an embolism into his bloodstream. Because of his advanced age, the few soldiers loyal to him wouldn't become unduly suspicious.

It would be a very difficult decision to make. Ganth admired Heinrich Heine as he admired no other man, with the exception of his father. But it was Heinrich who had told him to plan for all foreseeable contingencies, as a good strategist should. In contemplating Heinrich's death, he was simply following the old man's advice.

Certainly he would regret killing the man; Heinrich had almost single-handedly kept the Order of Thule from being consumed in the same inferno that consumed the Third Reich.

Through the SS, Heinrich had seen that the Order had maintained its own research centers and factories, many of which even Hitler and Himmler didn't know about.

Ganth couldn't help but chuckle at the memory of how the Allies had raced hither and thither all over Germany to recover the Third Reich's legendary "secret weapons.''

When the Allies did discover a few research centers, all they found were frustratingly incomplete documents, isolated parts of obviously complex components and a treasure trove of electronic odds and ends that could have belonged to just about anything.

Heinrich, Eric Ganth and Jorg Weisenburg had overseen the completion of many of the so-called secret weapons, including the miniaturized microwave transmitters. The Order had access to technology as much as five years or more ahead of the most advanced industries.

But Heinrich looked on the technologies developed by Nazi scientists as mere toys. As much as he disparaged Hitler as a madman, Heinrich himself was just as obsessive and perhaps just as insane. He believed in reincarnation, Atlantis and a world of Aryan gods lying just beneath his feet.

Though Ganth believed in the basic philosophy of the Order, he was a pragmatic man. He didn't entertain for one second that any of the myths and legends about the land of Ultima Thule were anything other than parables.

Heinrich had told him that the concentration camps were never designed to simply imprison the racially inferior; he claimed they were imitations of the social order of Thule, and were useful in performing mass human sacrificial rites.

Helmur Ganth and Heinrich Heine were in complete agreement in one area, at least—human freedom led only to unchecked lunacy. Freedom and democracy never worked. They led only to self-indulgence, conflict and waste, and perpetuated the stagnancy of the human mind.

The nuclear missiles were, like humanity in general, only tools to be used to build a better, cleaner world. Ganth had no intention of launching them, because he knew that many people in the German, Russian, British and American governments believed in the tenets of the Order.

The world was out of control, freedom and democracy led to revolution and chaos, and the Order would transform Germany into the prototypical nation of the future, a standard by which other countries would measure themselves.

The Order of Thule wouldn't accomplish this through armies or death camps or brutal repression. Ganth knew that nuclear blackmail would accomplish only so much. The Pershings were only fulcrums to move the government and NATO to the proper position to agree to their terms. After all, the agreement would be covert, and every European nation would benefit.

In the final analysis, the world of politics was only a chess game, the pieces were property and the game was only played by an elite who hid behind closed doors.

With nuclear missiles as keys, those doors would be unlocked and the Order of Thule would be invited to join in the game.

10

June 5

It was nearly 2:30 a.m. when Bolan entered the pump house some eight blocks from the Nachsinnen Clinic. Straub and a pair of Verfassungschutz men were waiting for him. Bolan pulled on the rubberized black wet suit while Straub explained the operation of the ear transceiver and throat mike to him. The flesh-colored transceiver fitted snugly into Bolan's right ear, and a thin but tough filament stretched down to a small microphone that adhered to a spot near his larynx. The battery pack was equally small, and fitted into a back pocket of the wet suit.

Wezhardt and Hyams were stationed in a truck half a block away from the clinic with the radiation detector. If it picked up microwave emissions, Wezhardt would let him know over the radio.

Straub handed him the diving mask. It was a self-contained unit, equipped with a very small oxygen tank that provided enough air for at least fifteen minutes. There was no need for bulky back tanks that would interfere with his movements or speed.

One of the men handed Bolan a waterproof knapsack. Inside it was his Desert Eagle, his combat harness, the broken-down Remington Autoloader with one ammo drum and a night-vision headset. There were also a few odds and ends that Bolan thought might come in handy.

Straub was uneasy with all the weaponry. "I thought this was primarily a recon mission, Herr Blanski, not a commando raid."

"A recon mission can turn into a raid at a moment's notice,"

Bolan replied, shrugging into the knapsack. "If that happens, I want to be prepared for it. I hope to get in and out without any contact with the people inside."

Straub glanced at his watch and gestured to his two men. They lifted away the heavy manhole cover, revealing the entrance to municipal sewer hole 501.

"My people are all in position," Straub said. "On rooftops, in parked automobiles and we have a Hotspur Hussar Land Rover standing by, as well."

"Let's hope I don't need it."

Bolan adjusted the oxygen flow into his face mask, gave the thumbs-up signal and clambered down metal rungs into the dark concrete cylinder. He clung to the last rung, then dropped down into the sewer. It was about ten feet in diameter and filled almost to the top with a steady rushing stream that carried Berlin's garbage. The current wasn't overpowering, but Bolan allowed himself to be carried along with it.

The soldier detached the waterproof flashlight at his waist and shone it ahead of him, looking for the intersection where he would have to turn off to the right. It came up very quickly, and Bolan kicked his flipper-encased feet against the current until he made the turn. He rolled and flowed down the sewer, aiming the flashlight up at the concrete tunnel's roof.

He saw the iron circle marked 83 and seized the bottom rung of the short, rust-eaten ladder that stretched down from it. He pulled himself up from the main current and hung there for a moment, steadying his breathing. He pushed the face mask up on his forehead and touched the throat mike.

"I'm here," he whispered.

Wezhardt's crisp tones sounded in his ear. "No signals from the detector."

"Acknowledged."

Bolan began to push up against the manhole cover, trying not to shove too hard, because he couldn't guess what lay on the other side. Rust showered down from the rim. Finally the heavy metal disk shifted, and he managed to shoulder it up and to one side without making too much noise beyond a grinding sound.

Bolan struggled up, panting from the exertion. He was in complete darkness and rather than turn on the flashlight, he opened the pouch and removed his combat harness and an infrared night-vision headset. Slipping the goggles over his eyes and turning on the infrared beams, he saw he was standing in a low-ceilinged chamber, a maintenance tunnel of some sort with walls made of blocks of rough-hewn stone. The blocks looked very old.

It probably led to the basement or subcellar of Dr. Asoka's clinic. Bolan activated the microphone and whispered, "I'm in."

"Acknowledged," Wezhardt said. "All clear."

Bolan kicked out of his flippers, strapped on the Desert Eagle and snapped together the Remington. Cradling the shotgun in the crook of his left arm, he walked slowly down the dark shaft. Despite the headset, the room was still too dimly lit to be seen clearly. He walked carefully some fifty feet before the passage curved to the left. Just around the curve was a heavy metal door. It was locked.

From a pouch on the harness, he took a small squeeze tube and spread the thermite paste around the edges of the hinges, then stepped back quickly. As the paste was exposed to oxygen, it flared into a clinging white fire that burned through the hinges until the door was held upright only by half-liquid threads of metal.

The flames died, and Bolan gingerly pulled against the door. It grated, hung for a moment, then fell toward him. He caught the heavy door and carefully eased it to the floor.

He peered into a wide, high-ceilinged room. Stacks of wooden crates were arranged neatly across the floor in a rectangular pattern. An old coal-burning furnace squatted against the far wall.

Bolan inspected one of the boxes, which was extremely heavy. Using his combat knife, he pried up the wooden lid. The crate contained a dozen handguns, Glock 17s. He checked another crate, this one longer and narrower. It held six Heckler & Koch 94 autocarbines, the same ones the men on the Madeira River had carried.

The soldier opened several other crates at random, finding incendiary grenades, blocks of C-4 plastic explosive, clips of ammunition and Kevlar bulletproof vests. There was enough hardware to supply a small army. He found no electronic paraphernalia, nothing that seemed to relate to microwave emitters inside people's mouths.

Tapping the throat mike, he said quietly, "I've found something. This place is definitely dirty. There's enough ordnance in here to take a city."

Hyams's voice filtered into his ear. "Then get the hell out Blanski. Straub can arrange for a warrant and have the place busted by noon."

"Negative," Bolan whispered. "The rest of the stuff, the microwave gear, must be upstairs in the clinic. That's the real evidence."

Wezhardt's voice, touched with concern, said, "Blanski. Mike. You've done enough. Let the authorities handle it from here on out."

"It's easier to go up than retreat the way I came in. That is, if I can find a way out of here. Stand by. Don't call me, I'll call you."

Bolan looked around the room. By the eerie, wavering infrared light, he saw no way out of the chamber. No door or stairway. He paced around the supply depot, looking for a concealed panel or a trapdoor or even a dumbwaiter shaft. He didn't look long before overhead lights blazed into life with such suddenness he was momentarily dazzled.

The soldier pushed the goggles onto his forehead and squatted near a crate. He heard the sounds of footfalls, then metallic clinkings as if a key were being inserted into a lock. He risked a quick glance around the corner of the crate.

A man was stepping out from inside the furnace. He swung the door to one side and bent low to enter the arsenal. He had long blond hair, tied back in a flowing ponytail, and wore the white coat of a medic. Whistling tunelessly, he walked over to a crate less than ten feet from Bolan's position and lifted the lid.

Drawing an FIE Titan pistol from beneath the coat, he ejected the clip, took a fresh one from the crate and slid it into the butt. As he was holstering the weapon, he turned and saw the metal door lying flat just outside the room.

He bellowed in surprised rage and pulled the pistol, looking wildly around the room, questing for a target. Bolan wasn't certain if the room was soundproofed, so he didn't use either of his guns. Instead, he leaned out and flipped his combat knife across the room.

The man was turned away from Bolan, and the blade entered the back of his right knee, the razor-keen point slicing through the front, splitting the cap. The man screamed and staggered to one side, slamming against a stack of crates. He struggled to turn and face Bolan. He raised his pistol.

The soldier buttstroked his jaw with the stock of the shotgun. The man went down on his left side, eyes glassy, and pointed the pistol at Bolan's midsection. The Executioner kicked the pistol aside and struck twice more with the stock of the shotgun. The man slumped down unconscious.

Moving quickly, he bound the man with his own belt and improvised a gag with strips torn from the white coat. He yanked the knife free and resheathed it. Though the blood flow was heavy, it wasn't critical. Bolan fashioned a pressure bandage from the coat and dragged the man to a far corner and arranged a number of crates around him.

Bolan entered the furnace and saw a light switch on the wall, as well as a flight of narrow stairs that stretched up at least fifty feet. He turned the light out, fitted the night-vision goggles over his eyes again and climbed the stairs quietly.

When he reached the door at the top of the steps, Bolan carefully edged it open and found himself in another room. He smelled it before he could see it. Garbage cans were arrayed in rows along the wall. He moved to a door at the far end of the room, pushed it open slightly and found himself in a large kitchen appointed with all the modern appliances.

Stepping to the nearest window, he peered out beyond the wire mesh. At first he saw nothing but neatly trimmed shrubbery, then a man wearing a white coat appeared around a corner. A lean Doberman pinscher strained against the leash the man had wrapped around his left hand. In his right, he casually carried an H&K autocarbine.

Bolan's underground route had taken him directly into the special wing of the institution, where the arsenal and the men who used it were sequestered. The wing was probably connected to the main building by a single corridor.

He glided silently through the kitchen, the rubberized soles of his combat boots making almost no noise. He went through a huge dining hall and found himself in a corridor that was dimly lit from overhead bulbs encased in wire cages. The corridor was lined with numbered doors.

A small circle of glass was set in each door. Bolan peered through one and saw a tiny room, almost a cubicle, with a snoring man sprawled on a narrow cot.

Bolan moved on, senses alert, finger on the trigger of the shotgun. He heard the murmur of voices somewhere ahead of him, so he slowed his pace. The voices were coming from inside one of the rooms, so he carefully looked through the window in the door.

A heavyset Japanese man was engaged in a heated discussion with a very old, bald man in a wheelchair. The room was far more spacious than the other he had seen. Both men were speaking in German, so Bolan had difficulty in understanding the entire exchange, but at one point the old man addressed the Japanese as "Asoka."

It seemed odd that the director of the institute would make personal visits with his patients, especially at four o' clock in the morning.

The old man was trembling, with rage it seemed. He rattled off a rapid-fire stream of German, which Bolan guessed were insults.

Asoka turned toward the door, and Bolan slid away from it, his back pressing against the wall. He recalled that Teudt had said Heinrich was well past ninety.

He didn't know who Heinrich was, or had been, but there was something in Asoka's voice that made it certain he was afraid of the old man.

The corridor opened up into a room filled with armchairs, book-laden shelves and tables scattered with newspapers and magazines. A large-screen TV dominated one wall. Bolan kept on going, entered another corridor, then came to a sudden stop.

Two men stood in the corridor. They were clad in the white coats of clinic attendants, but the way they held their Titan pistols showed plainly they were combat veterans.

One of the men spoke into a compact walkie-talkie. The other snarled something in German and gestured with his gun. Bolan understood enough of what he said to get the gist: it had something to do with putting down his weapons and raising his hands or having his brains blown out.

"No habla," Bolan said.

In excellent English, the heavier of the two snarled, "You *habla* as well as I do. Drop the shotgun, or I'll put my initials in your forehead."

Bolan eased the gun, barrel first, to the floor. Then, with a flick of the wrist, the barrel came up and he squeezed the trigger. The sound of 20-gauge buckshot exploding from the bore of the Remington was deafening. The heavy man took the shot in his lower belly. As though he had been slapped off his feet by a giant invisible hand, he catapulted backward down the corridor.

Diving headfirst, Bolan went into a somersault and the bullet fired at him by the second man seared the air well above him. Coming out of the roll, Bolan triggered the shotgun again. The shot pounded the man's chest, picking him up and knocking him down like a disjointed puppet.

Bolan regained his feet and ran, leaping over the shattered bodies of the two Germans, keeping his finger on the Remington's trigger. He had chosen it as his close-assault weapon because it was fairly lightweight, could be manipulated with one hand and the recoil was manageable because of the gun's gas system operation.

"Situation critical," he said into the throat mike. "I've been discovered."

An alarm began to warble the second after he uttered the words.

There was no response from the transceiver, only a crash of static.

Doors began to open, and voices began to shout questions and curses. A man in boxer shorts popped out of a room just as Bolan passed. The guy made a grab for him, and Bolan slammed the barrel of the Remington alongside his head, and he staggered back into his room.

The soldier veered toward a pair of double doors and shouldered them open. He was standing in a tiled shower room. At least a dozen shower heads projected from the wall, and each shower stall was separated from the other by a waist-high tiled wall.

Bolan started turning water faucets, adjusting the temperature to scalding hot. He went from handle to handle, letting jet streams of water burst forth and produce billowing clouds of steam. The steam would mask his movements, and the noise of the spray would cover any sounds he might make. Using the barrel of the shotgun, he smashed the fluorescent tubes of the overhead light fixtures, then squatted in a corner, between a bench and a row of lockers. He had a clear view of the doors.

The steamy air became stifling. The night-vision goggles gave all surfaces a strange, unshadowed appearance. The heat radiating from the shower stalls was like a glowing, molten bath.

The doors burst open, and three men armed with autocarbines rushed in. One tried the light switch and cursed when it didn't work. The infrared light of the headset made the men stand out as dark blobs, the only cool things in the room.

Standing shoulder to shoulder, they opened up with the carbines, raking the dark shower room with hammering autofire. The racket was deafening as streams of slugs shattered tiles, ricocheted from the chrome shower heads and stitched holes in the walls.

None of the bullets came near Bolan's position. Resting the shotgun across his left forearm, he squeezed the trigger.

The man closest to the Remington was blasted off his feet and hurled against his companion, who in turn staggered against the man next to him. Bullets went wild, chewing up the ceiling panels. Plaster dust and chunks of drywall rained to the floor.

The Remington boomed repeatedly.

Two of the men were swept back through the double doors, carbines falling from nerveless hands. The third was smashed violently against the wall, blood exploding from a plate-sized cavity in his torso.

From the other side of the doors, a frenzied voice shrieked orders in rapid-fire German. Bolan recognized the voice of Asoka. The pudgy psychiatrist was screaming about the noise, fearing it would be heard out on the street.

Bolan doubted that, but at least he wouldn't be subjected to grenades being lobbed at him.

Standing up, he made a quick circuit of the muggy room,

making sure there wasn't another way in or out. There wasn't. Tilting his head back, he studied the ceiling panels, wondering if there might be decent-sized crawl spaces.

Bolan tried the throat mike again. The static still hissed in his ear, but this time he heard Wezhardt's voice, faint and faraway. She sounded frantic, calling his name over and over again.

"I'm reading you, Doctor," Bolan said.

"Thank God. Some sort of jamming umbrella went into effect a few minutes ago. It took us a while to boost the signal."

"When the alarm went off, the jamming frequency was probably activated automatically."

"Where are you?" she asked. "We've had reports of gunfire."

"I'm inside the clinic proper, probably on the first floor. I'm bottled up in a shower room."

There was a sudden crash of static, drowning out most of Wezhardt's response. "—out of there?"

"Repeat," Bolan said.

Beyond the double doors, Bolan heard noises of activity— hurried footfalls, whispering voices and the steady squeak-creak of wheels.

Wezhardt's voice came again, overriding the static. It was urgent, holding a note of terror. "—read me? Dammit, Mike, do you read? Respond!"

"I'm here."

"You've got to get out of there fast! Now! The radiation detector has just registered a strong signal. They've powered up one of their microwave emitters, probably the Gunn oscillator."

Bolan glanced toward the doors.

"Mike! Acknowledge! Mike!"

"Acknowledged."

The squeaking outside the doors stopped.

A low hum sounded and Wezhardt's response, if she had one, dissolved in a blur of static.

11

Bolan instantly grasped the strategy. The enemy would maneuver the Gunn gun to the closed doors and flood the shower room with microwave radiation. Then, at their leisure, they would recover his corpse, fried from the oscillator and parboiled from the steam.

The whole room was beginning to heat up. Not the muggy heat from the steam, but a dry, baking heat that made his skin prickle. He felt a thudding pressure against his eardrums.

Fiery pain suddenly seared the calf of his right leg. The blade of his sheathed combat knife was melting the rubberized wet suit beneath. Bolan snatched it out and flung it away, scorching his fingers in the process.

Going to the wall farther from the doors, Bolan tapped the tiles with the stock of the shotgun. After several tries, he was rewarded with a hollow echo. Bracing his legs wide, and shielding his lower face with his left hand, Bolan began to fire the Remington at the wall. Round after round blew the tile, plaster and wood to bits.

He kept pumping the trigger, hoping the heat from the Gunn gun wouldn't ignite the cartridges in the Desert Eagle or the shells inside the Remington's ammo drum.

Finally he stopped firing, and, using the stock of the shotgun as a bludgeon, he battered his way out of the shower room.

Men were waiting for him in the weight room beyond, and they drove him back with a steady fusillade of small-arms fire. Bolan didn't return it; to find a target meant exposing himself to the hail of bullets.

The gunfire tapered off and ceased. A laughing voice called, "Hey, American—hot enough for you?"

In fact, it was. The heat in the shower room was unbearable. The steam drew sweat out of him, and the microwave emissions dried it out instantly. Fortunately he wasn't in the center of the room, or he would have succumbed by now. Still, the invisible fan of radiation was touching him.

He risked a quick peek through the hole into the room beyond. It was filled with exercise equipment, lead weights and benches. He didn't get a good look because the gunfire resumed.

Bolan hugged the wall, hearing slugs snapping through the hole to smash more tiles.

A new voice cut through the gunfire in German, as sharp as a whip crack. "Halt, you idiots!"

The firing stopped again. The voice called out, in English, "American, can you hear me?"

Bolan didn't respond. He was gulping air in great gasps.

"You will not be harmed if you come out. I want only one thing from you."

Throat dry as dirt, tongue like a piece of shoe leather, Bolan managed to husk out, "The Dag?"

"Where is it? Is it safe?" The sharp voice hummed with tension, with want. "Name your price. What do you say, American?"

Bolan knew he couldn't stay much longer in the superheated shower room. Pretending to go along would at least buy him time.

"I'm coming out," he called.

He rose slowly and peered around the edges of the hole. He saw no one and started to step through.

Then the lights went out.

Nobody in the weight room moved or spoke for a second or two. They were stunned and uncertain in the sudden darkness. Bolan didn't hesitate. He charged forward, his night-vision headset illuminating six figures near the doorway.

The Remington roared, and the figures scattered in all directions. Bolan dropped into a crouch just in time to avoid a bullet that whistled over his head. He fired again, and saw one of the shadow-shapes fall heavily against the wall. Three more explosive shots cleared the room entirely. When he squeezed the trigger again, there was nothing but a dry click.

Dropping the Remington, Bolan drew the Desert Eagle and rushed for the door. A man standing just outside it reacted to the rustle of his wet suit and slashed out with the barrel of his carbine.

The night-vision headset caught most of the impact, and the blow cracked the lenses of the goggles and smashed the infrared light projector. Bolan was immediately in the dark, but he rolled away and fired the automatic in the direction of the blow.

The .44-caliber round took the man in the right shoulder. The wounded man lurched down the corridor, wild with pain, dazed from the shock of impact.

"Schissen! Schissen!" he screamed.

The answering burst of carbine fire from his comrades was quick and deadly. A dozen .30-caliber slugs at close range chopped his head to pieces and nearly cut him in two.

Pulling off the ruined headset, Bolan sprinted down the corridor in the opposite direction, unhooking the flashlight from his belt. A carbine cracked from behind him, and he turned a corner. He pressed the throat mike.

"Ilona, are you there?"

Her voice, static free, said, "Yes. We managed to short out the power to the clinic. Hope it was in time."

"It was, thanks. The jamming umbrella is down, as well as the Gunn gun."

"Good. Straub's people are moving in. Try to stay alive until they reach you."

Bolan stopped beside a small window and knocked the glass out of the pane with the Desert Eagle. The window was barred on the outside, but he had an unobstructed view of the front of the clinic.

From across the street, two members of Straub's unit fired a missile from a Grail Blowpipe launcher. The missile impacted on the wrought-iron gate and blew it askew on its hinges.

The Hotspur Hussar Armored Land Rover roared to the gate, the barricade remover smashing into the gate and knocking it aside. A machine gun began chattering from a window above Bolan, the bullets striking sparks from the vehicle's body.

A small port opened on the roof of the Land Rover, and a two-foot-long projectile sprang from it. Bolan heard it smash a window on the floor above, then the slamming concussion of a flash bomb. The machine-gun fire ceased.

A dozen helmeted men in body armor, armed with the stubby West German G-11 rifles, raced through the open gate and across the lawn. More autofire sounded from inside the clinic, and two of the men went down.

The rear door of the Land Rover opened, disgorging six men who rushed the front door and vanished from Bolan's field of vision. He heard steady gunfire, some from handguns, much more from automatic weapons. People were shouting, swearing and running.

Then he heard a new noise—screams of women, hoarse shouts of terror from men. The legitimate patients of the clinic were awake and terrified as the noise of battle mounted.

The mercenaries were fighting back stubbornly and skillfully, for they had nothing to lose, and therefore everything to fight for. It was crucial that they be kept too busy to dip into the collection of weaponry in the subcellar.

Bolan left the window, intending to be as great a threat to the mercenaries inside as the specialists were outside.

ASOKA HAD WHEELED Heine into the monitor room in the basement. Picking up the phone, he tried calling Ganth, but the phone was dead. Sven was nearby, holding a flashlight in one hand and a Gewehr 3-A3 assault rifle in the other.

The chubby psychiatrist was perspiring freely, his shirt already soaked through. Heine sat in the wheelchair, watching his frantic activities with a derisive smirk.

Sliding open the drawers of the file cabinet, Asoka tossed matches into each one. The documents were flash paper, and they ignited instantly. Though the documents were encrypted, there was always a chance that a clever cryptographer could decipher them.

"You seem worried, Hito," Heine said with a smile.

Asoka ignored him, though he was far more than worried. He was terrified. He had no idea how many men were besieging the clinic, and the possibility they outnumbered the mercenaries was bone chilling. Not counting the soldiers the American had killed, there were only forty-three defenders. He had to concentrate on the problem of escape.

"We cannot stay here," Sven said worriedly.

Heine wheeled himself to a switch-studded metal panel on the wall. "True. So let us even the odds a bit."

He flicked the switch that started the emergency generator, suddenly illuminating the entire interior of the building. The monitor screens flashed to life. They showed nothing but snow. Sven got busy resetting them.

"Now that power is restored," Heine said cheerfully, "our men can contend on equal terms with the visiting team."

His gnarled fingers touched another switch on the panel. "And we can also compound our visitors' handicap."

Asoka rushed toward him. "*Don't!* Heinrich, for the love of God—!"

Heine yanked the Walther from inside his coat and waved off the Japanese psychiatrist. "Back off."

"Heinrich," Asoka pleaded. "That is monstrous. Please, don't do it."

"Shut up, you fat son of a bitch!" Heine snarled. "It's fifty years too late to retreat into your Hippocratic oath!"

Heine threw the switch, closing the circuit that controlled all the doors of the legitimate patients' rooms.

From the monitor console, Sven announced, "I've got cameras two, four and eight reset."

On the screens, panicky patients stumbled out of their rooms in wild confusion. Some wandered dazedly in the corridors, and others headed toward the front door.

Asoka, Heine and Sven watched as a quartet of armored and helmeted raiders smashed down the front door with a battering ram. A group of mercenaries waited for them in the foyer. They had made a barricade from heaped furniture. The Verfassungsschutz specialists exchanged fire with the mercenaries. Stray patients wandered into the cross fire. They seemed indifferent to the bullets.

The raiders stopped firing, but the mercenaries shot through the patients. The invaders were forced to retreat back out the door.

Heine laughed and looked up at Asoka's sweat-filmed face. He smiled sweetly. "I wish to leave now."

Asoka turned away from Heine, covering his face with shaking hands. Heine raised the Walther and squeezed the trigger. The bullet hit the psychiatrist near the base of the skull, shoving him forward face-first against the wall. He slid down it lifelessly.

To Sven, Heine said, "Let's go, my boy. Our work here is done."

WHEN THE POWER came back on, Bolan's first thought was of the Gunn oscillator trained on the shower room. Reversing direction, he sprinted back down the corridor. When he reached the double doors, he saw two of his kills still lying on the floor, but the microwave emitter was gone.

He heard gunfire down the hallway, and distant masculine screams. He headed in that direction.

Rounding a corner, he saw a row of barred windows with the glass knocked out of them. Three white-coated mercenaries fired handguns out the window. One of them wore the silver protective garb and was positioned behind the parabolic dish of the oscillator, which was much larger than the one Bolan had seen the night before. It was mounted on a wheeled tripod type of contrivance. A heavy cord ran from the electric motor on the base of the dish to a wall outlet.

The oscillator operator was swinging the dish back and forth out the center window. The wave of invisible radiation fanned out and washed over Straub's men on the lawn. Five of them were writhing in horrible agony on the ground, screaming, convulsed with the awful pain of their bodies cooking from within.

Even as Bolan raced forward, he glimpsed the rifle in the hands of one Verfassungschutz specialist explode with enough force to shred his face and hands and send pieces of the weapon flying like shrapnel.

Bolan increased his pace. Because of the heavy fire, the mercenaries didn't hear his rushing approach. But they certainly felt it.

The first shot from the .44 drilled into a man's head, lifting the top of his dark blond scalp and flinging it toward the ceiling.

The second 240-grain blockbuster punched a mercenary in the side of the neck, sending him cartwheeling down the corridor, leaving a red spray in his wake, like a liquid banner.

The hooded oscillator operator frantically tried to swivel the dish toward Bolan. The soldier launched himself over it. He collided with the man and both of them went down, but Bolan's knee was in his adversary's gut.

The oscillator fell over, the funnel of radiation splashing against the ceiling.

The man beneath Bolan was strong, but his movements were hampered by the heavy gloves. He closed one hand around the long barrel of the Desert Eagle and struggled to yank it away.

Bolan couldn't get to the man's eyes because of the goggles, and the mercenary couldn't claw for Bolan's because of his padded hands, so they wrestled and wrenched at the pistol.

For a very long moment, they were motionless, locked in straining combat, sweat breaking out on Bolan's forehead, breath coming in harsh gasps from beneath the mercenary's hood.

The mercenary jacked a knee into Bolan's left kidney, but the Executioner ignored the pain and grabbed a fistful of the silver hood. He pulled on it at the same time the man arched his back and bucked Bolan off.

Bolan threw himself backward, using the man's strength against him. The hood came off, but the mercenary didn't release his grip on the gun barrel. Planting a foot against the man's sternum, Bolan levered him up and over.

The man's bare head landed in the parabolic dish of the oscillator. He had time for one high-pitched cry and a convulsive shudder before there was a sound like a paper bag bursting.

A nauseating stench filled the corridor. Bile rose in Bolan's throat as he carefully walked around the silver dish. The mercenary's head was out of shape. His brain had cooked and exploded within the skull. Only the scalp kept his cranium intact. Viscera oozed from the eyes, ears and nostrils.

Bolan yanked the cord from the wall outlet, and the electric hum ceased. It seemed strange that such a ghastly, deadly weapon worked off house current, like any other appliance.

He fired a round into the electric motor of the oscillator, just to make sure it couldn't be used again.

12

Bolan continued down the corridor, following the sound of heavy, continuous gunfire. He went through a door and realized he was in the main building of the institution. Sidling up to a corner, he hazarded a quick look around it.

In the front foyer, three mercenaries were directing carbine and pistol fire out the battered-down front door from behind an overturned table.

The bullet-riddled bodies of at least four patients, three men and a woman, were wallowing in their own blood on the floor. They had been caught in the cross fire between the table and the open front door.

Bolan announced his participation in the firefight with three rapidly fired rounds from the Desert Eagle.

The first bullet hit a mercenary broadside, punching a deep, ugly cavity in his right rib cage. Bullets two and three spun the second mercenary like a top, blood spurting from mortal wounds in his head and upper back.

The third mercenary swung his body and pistol toward Bolan, rising from behind the overturned the table, snarling in rage.

A rifle burst from one of the specialists outside the door opened his skull in a spray of crimson.

In a crouch, Bolan crept across the floor to where a carbine lay in the outflung hand of a dead mercenary. Grabbing it by the barrel, he retreated, knowing that he was just as likely to be cut down by friendly fire as he was by the enemy's.

He went through a side door and up a short flight of carpeted stairs leading to a long hallway. The windows faced the front lawn.

At least ten men were blazing away with carbines out of a bay window. A crate of ammo clips was pushed against the wall.

The mercenaries had arranged themselves in two rows, so while one line reloaded, the other line could keep the invaders at bay. The fire from Straub's unit had accounted for three of them already.

Bolan had no intention of making a kamikaze charge down the corridor. There was little doubt he could decimate the mercenaries, but there was also little doubt he would stop at least a dozen .30-caliber slugs in the process.

He inspected the ceiling. This stretch of corridor had interlocking acoustical panels in the ceiling. He holstered the .44 and slid the Heckler & Koch carbine through his combat harness.

Springing into the air, Bolan grasped the top edge of the door frame, a ledge about two inches wide, and chinned himself up until he was able to push one panel aside.

He clambered up into a crawl space. There were small crosspieces of two-by-fours joining heavy rafters, and he crawled along them, putting his weight on the wood. When the sound of gunfire was very loud, he stretched out on a rafter and carefully tugged aside a corner of a pane.

The mercenaries were almost directly below his position, their backs to him. Bolan unslung the autocarbine and inserted the barrel into the small space between the tiles. Gripping it in his left hand, he made sure his body was shielded by the rafter before he squeezed the trigger.

Over the rattling roar and the clink of ejected cartridges, Bolan heard cries of shock, pain and anger. Return fire raked the ceiling, showering him with panel chips and splinters.

He withdrew the carbine and shifted position, feeling the rafter beneath him shudder as a couple of rounds nicked it. He dropped the empty weapon and slid back, weathering the storm of bullets that chewed up the panels only a foot below him.

The autofire ceased, to be replaced by the rapid scuff and scutter of running feet. Clinging to the rafter with one arm, Bolan drew the Desert Eagle and swung down, kicking out several bullet-blasted panels and dropping lightly to the floor.

Six of the mercenaries were running down the corridor, one

supporting another. They left four of their number, either wounded or dead, on the floorboards.

Bolan went after them, pausing only long enough to pick up a carbine and slam a loaded magazine into it. He crouch-walked beneath the bay window. A fusillade of shots still zipped between the bars, pockmarking the opposite wall.

He ran full out down the corridor. One of the mercenaries turned and sent a strafing burst of .30-caliber slugs toward him. Bolan managed to press himself against the wall, avoiding the swarm of lead. He brought his carbine into target acquisition, finger tensed on the trigger.

Then he saw the naked woman.

She pirouetted from a room, dancing, twirling on her toes like a ballerina. She was young, blond and very graceful, and she crooned a song in a lovely, melodic voice. She blocked Bolan's line of fire, but he knew the mercenaries couldn't have cared less if she put herself in front of theirs.

Bolan bounded forward, catching her and falling with her to the floor just as a stream of autofire burned the air where she had been posing. Lifting his head, he saw the men turn left through an arch.

The woman beneath him stared unfocusedly at Bolan. She smiled and caressed his face. *"Liebchen,"* she murmured.

Bolan pushed himself up and away from her. She seemed content to remain on the floor, singing softly to herself, so he started running again.

The entire building suddenly shuddered, shaken by a tremendous concussion. The floor heaved beneath Bolan's feet, sending him stumbling sideways against the wall. Plaster fell from the ceiling, and he heard windowpanes shattering all over the building.

From the sound and feel of the explosion, Bolan guessed that a grenade had detonated; whether it was due to the actions of the mercenaries or the specialists, he wasn't certain.

The Executioner turned left, beneath the arch, into a long, carpeted hallway. Almost at once, a door opened at the far end of the hall, and a man was framed there, with a Gewehr rifle at his shoulder.

Bolan dropped to the floor and fired once. The rifle was already stuttering, a stream of lead pouring into the hall. The slugs swept high, and by the time the gunner got his aim adjusted, blood was squirting from his chest where Bolan's shot had hit him. The man hurtled backward, his arms flailing, the rifle clattering to the floor.

The soldier stayed low and ejected the spent clip from the Desert Eagle, ramming in a fresh one detached from his combat harness. He chambered a round and got carefully to his feet, moving to a window. The glass was broken out of it, and he peered out past the bars.

The grounds of the clinic were filled with running, falling and leaping figures. Smoke poured from a corner of the building, and flames lanced out of a ground-floor window.

He saw a specialist, apparently blinded by the smoke, take half a dozen shots in his Kevlar-protected chest and fall down. Immediately a pack of mercenaries surrounded him, their Titan pistols snapping viciously. The bullets ripped the secret service man's face to pieces.

Bolan poked his carbine out the window and fired three times in quick succession, a mercenary falling to each round.

Some of the hardmen looked up at the window and raised their autocarbines. Bolan ducked back as a storm of shots ripped through the window and peeled long splinters from the opposite wall.

The howling sirens of fire engines and police cars sounded in the distance.

Turning from the window, the Executioner crept to the room at the end of the hall, out of which the mercenary had popped. He didn't waste time checking out the room. He simply threw himself at the door with a flying kick, knocking it off its hinges. He had both the Desert Eagle and the carbine spitting flame and thunder.

No one was in the room. It was a janitor's closet, loaded with mops, buckets, a water heater and a deep, rusted laundry sink. Bolan searched the walls and the floor with his eyes. Near the sink, he felt the floor give just a bit. He put a round from the

.44 into the floor. The bullet punched a hole, and a gout of powder mushroomed up. Not linoleum or cement, but mortar.

It was a false floor, mortar over wood.

He began a methodical search for the concealed switch and found it in the sink. The hot water handle lifted up and out. Hidden pivots creaked. The wall the sink was attached to swiveled open, revealing the dark throat of a small elevator shaft.

Snatching up a handful of rags, Bolan wrapped them around the greasy cable and slid down. He leathered the Desert Eagle and managed to navigate the cable while still holding the Heckler & Koch 94.

The shaft wasn't very deep, perhaps only twenty feet. He alighted noiselessly atop the lift car and used the barrel of the carbine to flip open the square emergency roof hatch. He leaned back against the wall of the shaft, anticipating a storm of gunfire blasting up from below.

When the gunfire wasn't forthcoming, he dropped into the car. The cage door was open and beyond it was a short corridor forming a T, with hallways branching to the left and the right.

There was also a gut-shot mercenary, lying facedown in a thickening pool of the blood. He was the one Bolan had wounded upstairs. When he died, his comrades had simply dropped him and gone on their way.

Bolan wasn't sure which way his quarry had taken, so he paused at the crossbar of the T and tested air currents with a moistened forefinger. He felt air moving from both directions, so on impulse he turned down the left-hand path.

The corridor led to a room filled with video monitors, electronic gear and file cabinets with open, smoking drawers. A pudgy man sat on the floor with his face jammed against the wall. Blood and brain matter were clotted on his collar.

Bolan toed him away from the wall and onto his back. The contorted face and glazed eyes of Asoka looked up at him. Judging by his expression, his last sensation hadn't been pain, but sorrow.

The solider glanced at the images on the monitor screens. There were scenes of white-coated mercenaries surrendering to the Verfassungschutz specialists, and a few who still were trying to dig in and shoot it out. A handful of walking wounded frantically stumbled toward cover.

On one screen was the image of a blond mercenary pushing a man in a wheelchair down a concrete hallway toward a metal-paneled door. Several armed men were clustered at the door, and Bolan recognized them as the same Germans he'd been pursuing.

Bolan whirled and sprinted from the room, down the corridor, past the intersection and through the right-hand hallway. The door at the end of the passage was closing, pushed from the outside. It shut with a heavy thud before he reached it, but he still slammed into it. The impact hurt his shoulder and sent jarring pain through his entire side.

He bounced back from it, the wind all but driven from his lungs. Stepping back, he examined the door. It had a combination lock, but no handle or knob.

He backed up halfway down the corridor and unlimbered the carbine. Holding down the trigger, he emptied the clip at the lock. He stood fast as ricochets whined and screamed around him, striking sparks from the sheet-metal and digging long gouges in the walls and ceiling.

When the firing pin clicked against the chamber, he dropped the carbine and drew the Desert Eagle. Holding it in a two-handed grip, he blasted the same small area of the door with .44-caliber rounds.

The circular lock was smashed, shattered and finally fell out to clatter on the floor.

Bolan ejected the clip, took a spare from the harness and slid it into the pistol's butt. He ran forward, launching a kick at the door, which crashed open.

He found himself in a long, low tunnel, evidently part of the old sewer system he had used to enter the clinic. Stagnant water lay ankle deep, and rats scuttled on the curving stones.

He heard an engine start down the passageway. Chambering a round into the pistol, Bolan sloshed through the water, following the sound. The stone floor slanted upward at a gradual angle, out of the sewage. He saw damp footprints and the tracks of wheelchair tires on the dry stones.

He reached the top of the ramp just as a minibus bearing the

Perfect Plug logo rounded a bend in the tunnel and was lost from view.

Bolan pressed the throat mike. Static crackled and hissed in his ear. When the power had been restored to the clinic, the jamming umbrella opened up again. He could only hope that one of the Verfassungschutz agents would spot the vehicle, but he was pretty sure that the minibus would emerge blocks away from the hellzone.

The soldier walked back down the passageway. He returned to the elevator and took it back up to the janitor's closet. The sound of battle had nearly faded, except for distant and sporadic gunfire. He walked down the hallway toward the front door of the clinic.

Straub was there, speaking into a walkie-talkie. Blood streaked his face from a minor laceration on his forehead.

"How did your recon mission go, Herr Blanski?" he inquired sarcastically.

13

The mop-up went slowly.

Little pockets of resistance still had to be dealt with, patients had to be rounded up, the dead tagged and bagged. The place was honeycombed with hidden rooms and secret passages.

When a specialist brought up the mercenary Bolan had wounded in the subterranean arsenal, Hyams suggested it might be fruitful if Bolan had a long, quiet talk with him. The G-2 officer said it was likely that the mercenary could cast some light on where all the concealed rooms and cubbyholes might be located.

The mercenary was more than willing to cooperate, on the condition he be given a painkiller for his leg. One of Straub's specialists found some medical supplies and gave him an injection of morphine. The man was so grateful, he even drew a crude map indicating all the secret bolt-holes he knew about.

By the time all that was accomplished, it was nearly eight o'clock.

Bolan went through every room, accompanied by Wezhardt and Hyams. They found bodies, wreckage and spent cartridges, but no sign of any advanced microwave gear.

In a antechamber off the kitchen, Wezhardt found a metal-paneled, padlocked door marked Danger! High Voltage! in German. To be on the safe side, Straub ordered one of his men in the underground room to turn off the emergency generator. Bolan shot out the lock and opened the door.

By the glow of flashlights, they found strange machines, some with parabolic dishes five feet in diameter, and tiny little devices small enough to fit inside someone's mouth.

Wezhardt examined the gadgets with complete concentration, occasionally murmuring to herself.

Straub ordered the power be restored, and when the lights came up, he took Bolan aside. Early-morning sunlight was streaming in through the windows.

Four medics came by, struggling with a body bag. It was unzipped over the head, and Asoka's face stared up at them.

"That was the man who kept the secrets," Straub said. "Until someone put a bullet in his brain."

"That someone used a .38," Bolan replied. He touched the butt of his holstered Desert Eagle. "I use a .44."

"So I've noticed by the number of corpses."

"If you have something to say, say it."

"Very well." Straub's face was inscrutable. "What right did you have to continue marauding through this institution after Major Hyams ordered you out?"

"If I had done what he said, by the time a warrant was processed, every bit of evidence would have disappeared. You know there's a leak."

"I also know that we don't know a damn thing more about who controls the missiles than we did two days ago."

"At least we've blown the cover off one of their safehouses."

"And staged a minor war," Straub said. "Eleven of my people are dead, six are seriously injured. I don't find that much of a trade-off."

"To be honest," Bolan said, turning away, "neither do I."

Straub grabbed his arm and spun him. "I'm not done with you, Blanski."

Bolan glanced down at Straub's hand, then fixed his eyes on the man's face. "I'm damn sorry about your people, but if you had tried to play this out legally, your people would have walked into an ambush and the casualties would have been far greater. Your problem is that you haven't been taking these guys seriously. I hope that's changed."

Straub's cellular phone suddenly buzzed. He released Bolan and took the phone from an inside pocket of his coat.

Bolan stalked away from him. He didn't blame Straub for being angry, but deaths were the luck of the draw. It was part and parcel of walking the hellfire trail, and Bolan knew the odds were he would fall on that trail, as well, sooner rather than later.

He found Wezhardt sitting on the floor with the gadgets spread out around her. She reminded Bolan of a kid on Christmas morning, busy opening all her gifts. Hyams was squatting near her. She looked up at his approach.

"Mike, this isn't like any sort of solid-state hardware I've ever seen."

"You don't know what it is?"

"I can venture a fairly good guess."

"Don't keep me in suspense."

Wezhardt gestured to the parabolic dishes. "These emitters, the oscillators are the clue. They transmit a very strong, very focused beam of radiation. They're all set for an exceptionally high frequency, not like the Gunn guns."

"And?"

"And any one of these oscillators could transmit a signal to penetrate a missile silo and trigger a launch."

"From here?" Bolan asked.

Wezhardt shook her head. "No, but the range doesn't have to be close, either. Theoretically, you could mount one of these oscillators on a vehicle and drive to within a kilometer or two of the silo and send out the appropriate frequency. It would have to be linked with a portable computer terminal or telemetry box to get the transmission code pulses just right."

"Who could do this?" Hyams demanded.

Wezhardt shrugged. "You. Me. Anyone with the most superficial knowledge of microwaves...and an electrical generator inside the vehicle."

"Any names occur to you that might fit the designs of these gadgets?" Bolan asked.

"Too many," Wezhardt replied. "Keep in mind that as early as 1935 there was talk coming out of Germany about death-ray projects, among other things. The Nazi military establishment had encouraged every kind of research in the field of lasers, radar and microwaves. Any number of scientists could have worked on these kind of emitters."

"Name one," Bolan suggested.

"Jorg Weisenburg," Wezhardt responded. "He used to be on the consulting staff of Ostara. He retired about a year ago. I remember him talking about some remarkable solid-state research and experiments his father was involved with for the SS during the war. It's possible that this gear is the product of those experiments."

"Would the personnel files of Ostara have his last known address?"

"Maybe. I'll check it out."

Straub was suddenly there, folding up his cellular phone. "I've just finished talking to my director," he said. "The enemy has made contact. Terms and conditions. I'm instructed to go to your embassy where we'll receive the full update."

"Christ," Hyams said tonelessly. "This is like something out of a bad movie...or a nightmare."

"Yeah," Bolan agreed, "and the bad movie and the nightmare are just now starting the second acts."

GANTH HAD GONE to bed rather late. Though he had been comforted by Asoka's assurances that he would deal with Heinrich, his nerves continued to be on edge.

He had devoted several hours to making a videotaped communiqué to the federal republic, making sure it ended up in the hands of the director of the secret service.

Once completed, it had been dispatched to the offices by a courier. Then Ganth was chauffeured to his palatial home in the Prenzlauer Berg district.

He took two sleeping pills and set the alarm clock for eight. He finally dozed off shortly before three o'clock.

He was awakened at quarter to six. It wasn't the clock, the telephone or one of his five-person serving staff, but a cold, round object pressing against his forehead.

Ganth's eyes snapped open, blinked and focused on the black barrel of the Walther P-38. His body jerked, but a terrifyingly familiar voice spoke from only two feet away.

"Don't move," the voice said. "Not one millimeter or I'll spread your brain all over the pillowcase."

Ganth lay rigid, frozen, barely breathing. "Heinrich."

"Very good, Helmur. You *can* obey simple commands. Not bad for an incompetent imbecile."

Ganth's eyes adjusted to the gloom. The faint light of dawn peeking in between the curtains showed him two men. One was Heine, gripping his Walther. The other was a tall blond man standing behind the wheelchair, holding a Glock 17. A long Sionics noise suppressor was threaded onto the muzzle.

Ganth tried to speak, but Heine pressed the bore of the pistol harder into his forehead.

"Shut up. I am very angry with you, understand? This morning's disaster was the final straw. You leave me no choice."

"Disaster?" Ganth murmured, his voice pitched low to disguise the tremble. "What are you talking about?"

"The clinic was overrun. I was forced to flee. They are on to us, Helmur."

"Overrun? By whom?"

"By the secret service and the American."

"How could this have happened? We had no warning!"

"I tried to explain it to you, Helmur. I tried to warn you. The American warrior has the Dag. As long as it serves his energy, his vision, he will be brought into conflict with the Order. We cannot destroy the Dag, so we must destroy the warrior."

Ganth had regained some of his composure. "It wasn't the Dag that brought him into conflict," he said as scornfully as he dared. "It was our conduit within the consulate. The idiot followed the man's orders to follow our observation team to the clinic."

"He had no choice, did he, without raising the American's suspicions? No, Helmur, you cannot transfer the blame for this morning's botch. You will take full responsibility."

"What about Hito?"

"Dead. I killed him myself."

Sheer terror flooded Ganth. He felt his bowels loosen, and he tried to jackknife up out of the bed, but Sven leaned over and slammed him back down, a hand jammed cruelly over his mouth. Ganth breathed in panicky whistles through his nostrils.

"Forget about your servants, Helmur. We have eliminated them from the game."

Sven removed his hand, and Ganth began to babble. He

claimed his rights as a high-ranking member of the Order; he told Heine that he didn't have the authority to do this.

"This entire operation was organized and planned under my direction," he said. "Lesnick was my contact, as is our conduit inside the American consulate. I've already sent a communiqué to the director of internal security. Only I have access to the black box. So you don't dare kill me."

Heine leaned back in his wheelchair and moved the gun muzzle back from Ganth's forehead.

"Much of what you say is true," he said meditatively. "The Order owes you much, despite the fact that Eric, your own father, told me to kill you if you put personal interests ahead of the Order's."

Ganth's eyes bulged. He was too shocked to speak.

Heine chuckled maliciously. "Oh, yes. He told me shortly before he died that egotism was your fatal flaw, and that I must make sure you were expendable."

Ganth became angry. "I am *not* expendable. The Order needs me. *You* need me!"

"Actually," Heine said calmly, "I need only the black box. And to get that, I need only a small part of you."

Heine glanced up at Sven and nodded. Ganth began a screaming rush from the bed, but the Glock in Sven's hand made a sound like a rubber mallet hitting concrete.

Blood bloomed in the center of Ganth's forehead, and the back of his skull broke open. He fell back limply onto the bed, his eyes gazing sightlessly at the ceiling.

Heine looked at the red-and-gray mess spattered on the pillow under Ganth's head and made a noise of disgust.

"I prefer the .38," he said. "A cleaner kill."

Heine lifted Ganth's slack right hand by the wrist. With a forefinger, he traced a line just below the wrist bone. "About *here,* I should say."

Sven nodded and stuck the Glock into his waistband. From a coat pocket, he withdrew a heavy clasp knife. He opened the five-inch blade and thumbed the cutting edge.

It was exceptionally sharp.

THERE WAS a portable television and VCR on the table of the small room when Bolan, Hyams and Straub entered.

Darryl was making adjustments and greeted everyone with a nervous smile. A large padded envelope sat on the table. Nodding to it, he said, "That arrived from your office a few minutes ago, Mr. Straub."

Hyams dismissed Darryl, and he and Bolan sat down. Straub removed a videocassette from the envelope and inserted it into the player.

An image flashed onto the screen, showing the shadowy head and shoulders of a man sitting in some shadowy place. The videographer had taken great pains to show nothing but a dark human outline.

The image spoke in a harsh, electronically distorted voice.

"Inasmuch as you will play this communication for the Americans, I will speak in English and save you the time and trouble of interpreting.

"My name, the organization I represent, are not important. What is important is that we control six thermonuclear missiles at an American missile site. That control cannot be wrested from us without incurring the most terrifying consequences. I should not have to add that what we accomplished at one site, we can accomplish at another."

"You son of a bitch," Hyams muttered.

"We have no intention of launching the missiles—at least, not yet. That is entirely up to you. We want Germany returned to the Germans. We have had enough of wasted time and opportunities, self-indulgence and corruption and decadence. We must reclaim our land, our superiority in the global community. We cannot do that while a weak and pallid democracy persists in allowing freedom to destroy us."

Straub snorted.

"Germany is finally one nation again," the image droned on, "but the freedom prevents us from sharing a united purpose. We must be disciplined and driven. Our people cry out for such a discipline. Our young people are desperate for a sane and safe Germany. We can save ourselves. Such a goal can be accomplished in a relatively short time, without bloodshed, without incident."

The man on the screen paused, as if for effect, and continued, "All we require is a covert cooperation between the government of Germany and the organization I represent. We will ask for certain legislation to be passed, certain laws to be created or repealed, certain trade agreements to be made. We realize the wheels of government turn slowly, and we can afford to be patient.

"However, you cannot afford to ignore us. Within two weeks, a motion to amend the constitution regarding the immigration laws will be presented to the parliament. The motion will be carried as a show of good faith. If it is not, then we will be forced to take extreme measures. If the motion is carried, then we will communicate with you again. If it is not, further communication is unnecessary. You know our position. Let us know yours."

The image faded and was replaced by hissing snow.

Straub reached over and turned off the television. "On the basis of this tape, my superiors in Bonn are convinced of a substantial plot against the security of the republic."

"No shit," Hyams said. "Has a course of action been discussed?"

"A show of thinking it over, at least for the moment," Straub replied.

"Two weeks is a long time to pretend to go along with these people," Bolan said. "The longer they have the missiles in their hands, the greater the temptation to play their trump card."

Straub rubbed the back of his neck. "Herr Blanski, not every member of my government may be pretending. There are a number of officials who were elected to their positions by subscribing to the tenets of Germany for the Germans. Their sympathies lie with what the man in the tape described as his own."

"Even so, I can't believe they'd allow a shadow government to pull their strings," Bolan said.

"And why not?" Straub demanded, some heat entering his voice. "Hasn't my country been the puppet of the U.S., NATO, the United Nations and the Soviet Union for over fifty years?"

"We're talking a large and well-financed fascist conspiracy here," Bolan said. "Do you want your country's strings pulled by a conspiracy?"

"Don't be so naive," Straub replied, his voice rising. "The entire world is part of a conspiracy! You think your country is any different? A select few decide all the issues."

"A neat, self-serving philosophy," Bolan said. "Justifies allowing totalitarianism to take over. The problem is, you'd have too many secrets to keep."

"So?" Straub's tone was challenging. "We Germans have always lived by the credo that the good of the many outweighs the good of the few."

"Fifty years ago, maybe. But that won't wash in today's political climate. If your own citizens won't censure you for knuckling under to blackmail, the rest of the world will."

Straub's eyes slitted. "And how would you deal with it, Herr Blanski?"

"There are only two ways to deal with a blackmailer. Expose him or kill him."

Hyams cleared his throat noisily. "Blanski, Straub, we're being a little premature. Let's find out which way the parliament jumps, then make plans."

Straub didn't take his eyes off Bolan. "Whatever plans are made will not include American intelligence. This is now a matter of internal security. We will proceed from this moment on with utter stealth and complete secrecy. Do you understand me?"

"I understand that stealth and secrecy are effective against an enemy," Bolan replied. "But when a democratic government practices them against its own citizens, you divorce everyone in that democracy from any understanding of the circumstances affecting their own lives. If that's your standard, then you don't have a government. All you have is a conspiracy."

Neither Straub nor Hyams replied.

"We have to grab Helmur Ganth and this man Weisenburg," Bolan went on, "and lean on them. Find out who the old man in the wheelchair is, why he was willing to trade my life for the Dag—"

Straub stood up so quickly his chair fell over backward.

"Enough!" he shouted. "I am the authority in this matter. It is not open for debate, for suggestions, for plans or counterplans! If I were not in your country's embassy, I would have you arrested, Blanski, as an enemy of the state. I still might, if you set foot on German soil again."

Motions sharp and violent, Straub ejected the videocassette, shoved it back in its envelope and stalked from the room.

After he had slammed the door behind him, Hyams said dryly, "I think you struck a nerve."

14

Bolan's first move after he went to his quarters was to get out of the wetsuit, then he rang Wezhardt at her office. She sounded clear-headed and alert, while he was beginning to feel the effects of too little sleep and too much exertion.

"I found Professor Weisenburg's address in the personnel records," she told him. "It's over a year old, but since he's lived in the same place for nearly thirty years, I doubt he's moved. Would you like me to call him?"

"No," Bolan replied. "If he's involved at all, once he learns of what happened at the clinic, he'll probably make himself scarce. No point in forewarning him."

"He lives at 88 Lindenalle. It's a residential section not too far from the Berliner Ring."

"Thanks. What are your plans for the day?"

"After I turn these gadgets we found over to the research unit, I'm going home, taking a bath, then a long nap. Care to join me?"

"That may not be wise, Doctor."

"If you want me to call you Mike, I insist you call me Ilona."

"That may not be wise, Ilona."

"I'm too tired to care, Mike."

She hung up.

Holstering the Beretta in the shoulder rig, Bolan slipped on his jacket, stowed two extra clips in the pockets and went down to the garage in the embassy basement, making sure to avoid Hyams. No one was there.

Bolan glanced over the board from which keys hung from

numbered hooks and started to take a set belonging to an Opel, when he heard the sound of metal on metal.

Following the sound through the parked cars, he saw a pair of coveralled legs sticking out from beneath a canary yellow Mercedes.

"Hello," he said quietly.

The legs twitched in surprise. Darryl slid out from beneath the car's engine block, tools in hand, eyes wide with surprise.

"Mr. Blanski. Shit, you scared me."

"Not only do you drive them, you work on them, too?"

"Sometimes. If it's minor stuff like changing out the oil filter. What can I do for you?"

"I need wheels and directions to Lindenalle."

Darryl stood and thumped the hood of the Mercedes. "I've just serviced this one and she carries some light armor in the bodywork. As for directions, I'll drive you."

"Not necessary."

Darryl smiled sheepishly. "I'm afraid it is, sir. Orders. I'm supposed to escort you and chauffeur you whenever you leave the embassy grounds. If the secret service wants to lean on you, they'll be less apt to do it with a consulate staff member as a witness."

Bolan considered it for a second, then nodded. "Let's do it."

Darryl hurried to a booth at the far end of the garage, unzipping the coverall. "Give me a minute to wash up and ring upstairs."

"I'd just as soon you didn't do that."

Darryl looked at him earnestly. "It's my job, sir. If I don't let my relief know I'm off the grounds, I'm in deep shit. The garage has to be manned by someone."

Bolan's eyes narrowed. "As long as he's the only person you talk to."

"It will be, sir. You have my word."

JORG WEISENBURG HAD BEEN an early riser for most of his life. But after the death of his wife of two years earlier, and the diagnosis of his heart condition, he tended to sleep until ten or so every morning.

When Inga, his wife of thirty-seven years, had died, Weisenburg had found fewer reasons to get out of bed at all, much less at the crack of dawn. Though the Order had given him something of a new purpose, he still felt hollow.

Ganth's scheme had been an interesting diversion, a tactical problem to solve. He had involved himself with it primarily to interrupt the tedium of his daily life. He consciously didn't dwell on the repercussions if it was successful or unsuccessful.

When he awoke at a little before ten, he heaved himself out of bed and turned on his favorite midmorning news program while his breakfast tea was steeping. He was unprepared for what he saw and heard, and his own reaction to it.

The usual banal banter between the program's hosts was absent. Instead, on the screen of the small color TV on the kitchen counter were scenes of carnage; tongues of fire licking from the ground-floor window of a building that was horrifyingly familiar, the sound of gunfire, running figures outlined by flames and the flashing lights of official vehicles and an on-the-spot correspondent speaking excitedly about the unbelievable events occurring at the Nachsinnen Clinic. A superimposed caption told him that the video had been made several hours before, in the predawn hours.

Weisenburg's weak heart gave several painful spasms. He gasped and sank into a kitchen chair, his face suddenly filmed by cold sweat. Blood pounded so loudly in his ears that he almost missed a report about a massacre at a local hospital late the previous night.

With trembling hands, he reached for his medicine box and gulped the pills that would restore his heartbeat to its normal rhythm.

His thoughts raced wildly, out of control. He thought about all the microwave emitters he had constructed and stored at the clinic; he thought about Hito, whom he was very fond of; he thought about poor deranged Heinrich, whom he admired but feared, who lived there.

Then he wondered why he hadn't been apprised of the raid on the clinic. He didn't dare call Hito, so he phoned Ganth on his secured office line. There was no answer, which was disturbing since the man was punctual about being at his office at 9:00 a.m. sharp, every morning.

He called the general switchboard of Wust and Wimmer and was connected to Ganth's secretary, who told him that he hadn't yet arrived. She seemed a little puzzled, but not concerned.

Weisenburg was more than concerned—he was frantic. He dialed Ganth's home; there was no answer, even though any one of five servants should have picked it up.

Weisenburg stared at the TV. On the screen, a young man, face covered with blood, was being rushed past the cameras toward a waiting ambulance. He looked very young. Memories of Dresden, of the Russian assault on Berlin, filled his mind.

He was suddenly so repulsed by the images and memories of violence that he nearly vomited. It was no longer a game or an intellectual or engineering challenge. It was terrifyingly, sickeningly real.

There was only one reason why he couldn't reach Ganth; he was either in custody or in flight, leaving Weisenburg, Hito and Heinrich to fend off the authorities who would shortly be pounding at their doors.

Moving faster than he had in years, Weisenburg rushed into his bedroom and began to toss clothes into an overnight bag. He made sure he had his passport and sufficient cash. He didn't want to use credit cards, since that would leave a paper trail. He dressed quickly and carelessly and half trotted to the front door. Fragments of a plan began to take shape in his mind—he would take a taxi to the airport and book passage on a flight to Brazil. No, Canada—no, he wouldn't take a flight at all; he would pay the cabbie to drive him to Poland.

All this ran through Weisenburg's brain as he locked the front door and turned to leave the stoop.

"Professor Jorg Weisenburg?" a cold voice asked behind him.

His heart gave a great lurch. The world seemed to tilt to one side, then the other. When it steadied, he felt strangely calm and he turned around slowly, attempting an air of dignity.

"I am he." Since the voice addressed him in English, he would respond in kind.

A tall man stood at the bottom of the stoop. He was dark

haired, with eyes that were like chunks of blue ice. The face, though dispassionate and cold with resolve, wasn't cruel or brutal. This man was a professional, and Weisenburg decided to extend him professional courtesy.

"Who are you, sir?" he asked.

"I represent American military interests in Europe," the man said. "I need to ask you a few questions about solid-state hardware. Microwave emitters, specifically."

"I am not under arrest?"

"I don't have that authority, sir, though I'm sure it can be arranged."

"I understand." Weisenburg saw a yellow Mercedes parked behind the man at the curb. "Shall I accompany you?"

"Yes, to the American consulate."

"All right."

Weisenburg stepped down to the sidewalk. The man glanced down at the bag in his hand.

"Going someplace, Professor?"

Weisenburg laughed. His relief was such that he felt almost giddy. "Yes, I am. With you, remember?"

Bolan was a little surprised by the man's attitude and behavior. He had half expected not to find him home, and if he did, to encounter stiff-lipped German resistance. Weisenburg had the air of a man who had been harboring a secret for a long time, and now welcomed the opportunity to disclose it to someone, anyone.

A closed delivery truck, painted a drab olive green, suddenly rolled forward. Bolan had noticed it parked a hundred yards down the block when he had arrived, and had pointed it out to Darryl.

Taking Weisenburg's arm, Bolan quickly pulled him to the side of the stoop behind a four-foot-high brick wall that doubled as a planter. Weisenburg allowed himself to be led without question or protest.

The truck accelerated and roared past them. As it came abreast, two ports in the cargo compartment suddenly slid open. Bolan pushed Weisenburg down behind the wall just as machine-gun barrels were thrust out of each port. Darryl threw the Mercedes into reverse and backed up, shouting something at Bolan that he couldn't catch.

The whole street filled with the staccato hammering of auto-fire. Lead swept across the front of the ornamental wall, punching craters into it, shredding flowers and smashing the front windows of Weisenburg's home.

Even before the machine guns began to chatter, Bolan had thrown himself over Weisenburg, behind the shelter of the wall. The Beretta was in his hand. The truck raced past and jolted to a stop fifty feet up the street with a whine of brakes. The guns stopped stuttering. Its driver maneuvered the truck around in a U-turn, intending to come back for another broadside.

Bolan got to his knees and fired a round at the truck. The bullet glanced off the side. It was armored. The truck had half-way completed the turn.

Taking a breath and holding it, he steadied his gun hand on the top of the wall. The sound of the truck faded into nothing; he closed his ears to it. He brought one of the gun ports on the truck's opposite side into target acquisition. The small, rivet-rimmed oval was clear and sharp. In the center was the slender black barrel of the machine gun.

He shifted the blades of the front and rear sights a fraction to the right, then squeezed the trigger three times, all in the space of half a second.

All three bullets tore through the right-hand gun port, an area that could have been covered by the palm of a child's hand.

The gun barrel withdrew in a jerky, convulsive fashion. The second barrel was pulled back smoothly.

The truck completed its turn, seemed to hesitate, then roared past. Bolan stood, pulling the white-faced Weisenburg to his feet. Darryl leaped from the Mercedes, a .45-caliber Browning auto-matic held in both hands, and fired several rounds at the retreat-ing truck. He only stopped shooting when Bolan shouted at him.

"Forget it, it's like a tank," he said. "And we've attracted enough attention for the morning."

People were streaming from their homes, opening windows, shouting questions and yelling for someone to call the police.

Bolan manhandled Weisenburg into the rear of the Mercedes

and got in beside him. "Put your hands where I can see them, Professor."

Weisenburg obediently placed his shaking hands on his knees. Darryl climbed back behind the wheel. He was enraged.

"Let's get after those bastards!"

"Just what I had in mind," Bolan said.

As Darryl threw the Mercedes into pursuit down Lindenalle, Weisenburg kept his gaze on the floorboards.

"They were after you," Bolan stated.

"*Ja.* I suspected as much. But who are 'they'?"

"You don't know?"

"Not Hito," Weisenburg said softly.

"No, not Hito Asoka. He's dead."

The Mercedes took a curve with a squealing of rubber. Weisenburg grabbed blindly at an armrest. His eyes filled with tears.

"Dead. How?"

"Shot through the back of the head with a .38."

Weisenburg took a deep gulp of air. "Who?"

"I don't know. In his last moments, he was in the company of a few hardmen and an old man in a wheelchair."

Weisenburg sat frozen for a moment, then whispered, "Heinrich."

"Heinrich?"

"Heinrich Heine. The spiritual leader of the Order. A brilliant strategist."

"How does Helmur Ganth fit into this?"

Before Weisenburg could answer, Darryl wrenched the wheel and the Mercedes swung west at a corner. They were rapidly gaining on the truck. The area they raced through was an industrial district, containing large, ugly redbrick chemical works and vacant lots. Overgrown walls, many bearing fifty-year-old bullet scars, reared from the weed-choked ground.

The truck turned to the left around the corner of a soot-stained factory wall. Beyond it, Bolan saw docks and the waters of the Landwehrkanal.

Darryl eased off on the gas, and the Mercedes slowed to a crawl. It slowly nosed around the corner of the building. There, facing the Mercedes, not more than two hundred feet away, was the armored truck.

Bolan was so intent on it, he didn't notice Darryl reaching down and fiddling with a knob on the dash. A sheet of partition glass lunged up between the seats. With a pneumatic hiss and a thump, its top edge slid into the narrow metal channel running the width of the roof.

It was a standard feature of government vehicles that might have to transport prisoners.

Face taut, Bolan tried the door. It wouldn't open. He reached across Weisenburg and grasped the left-hand door latch. It was locked from the dash controls.

Bringing out the Beretta, he reversed it and struck the partition with the butt. Not surprisingly, the glass didn't even crack, much less break. He knew every window in the Mercedes was bulletproof.

Darryl looked over his shoulder, his face expressionless. He brought the car to a full stop and climbed out. He left the engine running.

"What is going on?" Weisenburg asked. "I don't understand."

"I'm afraid I do," Bolan said.

Without looking back, Darryl casually approached the truck. He paused to light a cigarette, shielding the lighter from the breeze with a hand, then continued on toward it. He waved at the cab.

One of the gun ports in the cargo compartment opened, a burst of autofire chewed up the asphalt, tracked Darryl, caught him and sent him reeling backward, arms windmilling, clothes flapping as though he were facing a stiff wind. He fell onto his back, arms outflung, the cigarette still burning between the fingers of his right hand.

"Dear God," Weisenburg croaked.

The telephone hooked on the back of the front seat suddenly rang. Weisenburg jumped at the sound of it; Bolan picked it up. Without preamble, a voice spoke. It was the same sharp tones he had heard outside of the shower room.

"We've never been formally introduced, but I had to speak with you nonetheless."

"Didn't we exchange a few words earlier this morning?"

"Wonderful, you recognize me. I wasn't sure if you would, with all the other distractions."

"Is this Heine?"

There was a moment of silence, then, "You adduced my identity with Jorg's help, I imagine."

"Do you want to talk to him?"

"No need. I had him marked for expulsion. It is my good fortune that I snared both of you in the same net."

"I take it you're in the truck?"

"Yes. I was forced to fire the gun that killed your driver, since you seriously wounded Otto. You are a magnificent marksman."

"Darryl was a member of your Order?"

There was a burst of genuinely amused laughter from the receiver. "By no means. He was simply one of a network of contacts we maintain in embassies of many countries all over the world. Normally they are not asked to compromise their positions so blatantly, but he was such a greedy young man, I knew tempting him with the promise of a fortune and a new identity would be sufficient for him to completely betray his country."

"Honor Is Loyalty," Bolan intoned.

"For very few, I'm afraid. Today, most men are loyal only to themselves."

"What you're loyal to is obvious, Heine. Like the Dag."

There was pain in Heine's reply. "Yes. I realize that by killing you, I may forfeit an opportunity to have it again in the Order's power, but I cannot risk leaving it in your possession. If I cannot have it, I must have your life. You are a warrior, and its energy cleaves to you, it inspires you, it alters probabilities. You should have died in Brazil, you should have died many times in the clinic, but the power of the Dag was with you. I cannot have that power turned against me. The energy circuit you share with the Dag must be broken, and regretfully that means you must die."

"You're afraid of me, is that it?"

"Do not seek to draw me into a—what is the word?—macho

debate. Yes, I am afraid of you, nor am I ashamed to admit it. Without the Dag, you are a nuisance. With it, you are a true threat to my plans, to the very existence of the Order.''

"What *are* your plans, Heine?"

"Don't be a fool!" Heine's voice was angry, insulted. "You think I'm the villain of the type of cheap cinematic melodramas you Americans love so much? You think I'll reveal anything to you before you die?"

"How are you going to arrange our deaths? Another Gunn oscillator?"

"No, none of Jorg's toys today. This is a simple explosive device, nothing too fancy. Half a kilo of trinitrotoluene attached to the oil pan of your car. The device is hooked to the battery, which, obviously, you cannot reach. When I hang up, the timing apparatus of the bomb, which is connected to the fan of the motor, will be set in motion. Thirty seconds after I break the connection, the bomb will explode.''

"You're a good one to talk about melodrama, Heine. Why go to all this trouble?"

There was a sigh. "It is not every man whose mind, whose heart is pure and fierce enough to tap into the energies of the Dag. Such a man is owed explanations. Goodbye, warrior. I salute you.''

The voice ceased speaking. A dial tone buzzed out of the receiver. Bolan replaced it on the hook and glanced at his wristwatch.

"Are we just going to sit here?" Weisenburg asked.

"Only for another twenty-eight seconds, Professor."

15

Twenty-eight seconds wasn't much time to formulate a plan. It wasn't even worth using the cellular telephone to call anyone, since all Bolan would have time for was a very brief overview of how and why he and Weisenburg came to be blown to bits.

He raised the Beretta and smashed out the plastic covering of the dome light in the roof of the Mercedes. With steady fingers, he unscrewed the small bulb and dropped it to the floor.

He jacked a round out of the Beretta. It was copper jacketed. He spit on it, making sure it was wet all the way around. Then he thrust the bullet into the empty bulb socket, jamming it against the two terminals.

There was a tiny flash of blue sparks as the current passed through the wet copper and short-circuited the electrical system. Heine's words about breaking power circuits had given him the idea.

The engine jerked and ceased to throb.

Bolan sat and waited. Less than fifteen seconds remained. If the fan belt continued a full revolution after the engine stopped, it would still actuate the timing mechanism and detonate the bomb. Another three seconds passed.

And nothing happened.

The voltage from the battery to the timing mechanism had been cut off, so the bomb wouldn't explode.

"Why did you do that?" Weisenburg asked, frowning.

Bolan didn't answer. He looked over at the truck. When Heine realized the car's engine was no longer running, more than likely he would order a more direct assault. A bullet striking the bomb

beneath the Mercedes chassis would detonate it, since trinitrotoluene was notoriously unstable.

The soldier didn't wait for the notion to occur to the men in
the truck. Telling Weisenburg to crouch down and protect his
face, he raised the Beretta and emptied it at the partition. The
gun thundered in the confines of the Mercedes in a deafening
rhythm. The smell of cordite became choking.

The bulletproof glass resisted the bullets, catching them in its
polymer coating. Cracks spread in a network of interconnecting
lines, but it didn't break.

But Bolan had blasted a crude X pattern across the face of the
partition, putting several rounds into the center, where the lines
intersected.

Leaning back, bracing himself against the seat, he launched a
straight leg kick at the center of the X. From the corner of his
eye, he saw the truck lurch into motion.

Bolan kicked again, ignoring the needles of pain shooting up
from his ankle to his knee. The partition gave a bit. He kicked
again, and the pane of glass folded inward, the top edge popping
out of the slot on the ceiling.

Leaning forward, he grasped the top and threw all his adren-
aline-charged strength into wrenching and yanking the partition
down and from side to side. He managed to open a space large
enough for him to fight and elbow his way through from the
back to the front seat.

To Bolan's surprise and relief, the truck gave the Mercedes a
wide berth, rolling past it and toward the street between the factory buildings. In retrospect, it wasn't so surprising; the Mercedes
was armored, and shooting at it would be a waste of time. Ramming it with the truck would cause the bomb to go off, and
damage their own vehicle. Until the bomb was disarmed, Bolan
couldn't start the car and pursue them.

With the dash control, he unlocked the back door, allowing
Weisenburg to get out. Bolan quickly crawled beneath the chassis
of the Mercedes to get a look at the device.

"What was all that about?" Weisenburg inquired.

While Bolan examined the package, he briefly explained to
the old man about the bomb. Like Heine had said, the explosive

device wasn't fancy. Two receiver leads ran from the battery to a timed detonator. The smaller of the wires belonged to the telephone-recharging pack.

To be on the safe side, Bolan crawled back out, raised the hood and disconnected the clamp from the positive terminal before he pulled the receiver from the detonator. He simply yanked the telephone lead from it. The package itself was wrapped in woven fiberglass and attached to the undercarriage by a pair of thin tin straps bolted to the frame. Judging by the crooked bolts, Darryl hadn't completely affixed it to the chassis when Bolan came upon him in the garage.

With the blade of his pocketknife, Bolan easily sawed through the straps and carefully slid the package from beneath the car. Though he was impatient to get started after Heine, he couldn't leave the bomb lying around for someone to stumble over.

Gingerly, as though he were walking on eggshells, Bolan carried the package over to the bank of the canal, both hands gripping the edges. When he reached the lip of the waterway, Bolan gently heaved the bomb up and away from him. Then he dropped flat, covering his head with both arms.

The package struck the water with a splash, floated for a second, then tipped onto one end. It started to sink.

A geyser of water thirty feet high suddenly appeared where the package had been, and the slamming concussion nearly rolled Bolan over. Echoes of the explosion rolled back from the factory buildings like the thunder of distant artillery. Water, muck and a few fish rained to the ground.

Bolan sprang to his feet and rushed back to the Mercedes. He quickly reconnected the battery, slammed down the hood and jumped in behind the wheel, ordering Weisenburg to get in beside him.

The Mercedes roared through the industrial district, Bolan paying no heed to speed-limit signs.

"Where would Heine be going, Professor?" he asked.

Weisenburg shook his head miserably. "I don't know."

"To Ganth's home or office?"

"Perhaps. I doubt it." Weisenburg massaged his temples. "Heinrich must have gone mad. Or senile."

"Why do you doubt it?"

Weisenburg started to say something, then clamped his mouth shut.

Bolan turned to face him. "Answer me. I just saved your life and I'm calling in the marker."

"The only thing at Ganth's office is the telemetry box," Weisenburg said, speaking so rapidly his words tumbled over one another. "But only Helmur can get to it."

"Why?"

"It's in a safe, electronically keyed to open by his fingertips."

"The telemetry box would trigger the launch of the missiles?"

"*Ja,* but that wasn't our plan. That would have been foolish, because of the limited range."

"You were running a bluff, is that it?"

"A bluff? I don't understand—oh, *ja.* We never intended to launch the things."

"Even though you could."

"*Ja,* but it was simply a fulcrum, a way to impose a balance of terror—"

The cellular phone on the dashboard rang. Bolan snatched it off the hook, wondering if it might be Heine again.

"Who is this?" It was Hyams's voice.

"Blanski."

"Where's Darryl?"

Bolan didn't respond to the question. He said instead, "I'm with Jorg Weisenburg."

"I know. I've already received the report about the shoot-out in front of his home. You'd better get your ass back here, Blanski. Straub is ready to have your balls removed, bronzed and used as a paperweight."

"Find Helmur Ganth. Weisenburg tells me that the telemetry box controlling the birds is at Wust and Wimmer."

"Ganth has been found," Hyams replied. "At his home. Shot through the brain and mutilated."

"Mutilated? How?"

"Some sick son-of-a-bitch cut off his right hand."

Pressing the receiver to his chest, Bolan asked Weisenburg, "The fingertips of which of Ganth's hands open the safe?"

Weisenburg's brow furrowed. "I believe it is his right hand."

Bolan put the receiver to his ear again. "Major, I don't have time to explain, but if you can reach Straub, tell him to get a unit to Wust and Wimmer and be on the lookout for an olive green delivery truck."

"Why?"

"And while you're at it, see if Straub knows anything about a Heinrich Heine."

"Goddammit, Blanski—"

Bolan hung up.

Under his steady questioning, Weisenburg told Bolan the most direct route to Wust and Wimmer, and admitted there was a secret entrance from an alley through a basement, though he had never used it. He seemed confused, disoriented and would occasionally mutter the name Inga.

Bolan sent the Mercedes flashing through the traffic, running as many red lights as he dared. After about twenty minutes, they reached Wilhelmstrasse.

"There it is," Weisenburg said, pointing to an old, three-story building with a gabled roof.

It was something of an oddity on the street, surrounded as it was by trendy boutiques and eight-story apartment buildings. There was no sign of the armored truck.

Bolan circled the block and slowly passed the mouths of several alleys, most of which were service entrances to the shops and stores. Then he saw the truck, parked facing away from the street, but butted up against a wrought-iron fence between the side of the Wust and Wimmer building and an apartment complex.

Bolan cruised down the street and parked. He inserted a full clip into the 93-R and chambered a round. Weisenburg gave him vague directions to the secret basement entrance, apologizing that he didn't know more.

"I do not understand," he said. "Why is Heinrich here? Helmur wouldn't give him the telemetry box, and even Heinrich isn't foolish enough to start something in full view of the employees and clients."

Grimly Bolan said, "Helmur is dead. Heinrich or one of his

Hitler Youth cut off his right hand. If what you've told me is true, he's sneaking in the back way, into the conference room, using Ganth's hand to open the safe, take the box and sneak out again. No one would be the wiser. Until some of your countrymen are vaporized by a thermonuclear blast.''

Weisenburg's mouth gaped open, and he stared at Bolan uncomprehendingly.

''I suggest you use the phone and call your secret service and give yourself up. Otherwise, Heinrich will only try to have you killed again. And the next time, I might not be around.''

Bolan got out of the car and walked quickly to the alley. The truck's engine was idling, so someone had been left behind. Making sure he was positioned in such a way that a man in the cab couldn't spot him in the rear- or side-view mirror, Bolan reached the rear bumper and crawled beneath it. It was a tight fit, and the diesel fumes nearly made him cough, but he navigated the length of the vehicle until he was directly beneath the cab.

Turning over onto his back, he listened for a moment, straining to catch any sound. He heard a muffled cough.

Bolan inched out from beneath the truck. The driver's-side door was directly above him. With his left hand, he reached up and rapped very loudly on the door, in the ''shave and a haircut'' rhythm.

Scuffling and a voice cursing in surprise sounded above him. The shocks creaked and the door was flung open. A hard-faced man with bushy eyebrows looked around, a Glock 17 in his hand.

Bolan shot him through the underside of the jaw. The 9 mm slug snapped the man's head back with such force, Bolan heard the vertebrae crack. He fell down across the seats. He wasn't worried about the gunshot being heard, since the traffic noise was so heavy, the sound would probably be attributed to a backfire.

Getting to his feet, Bolan reached in and turned the ignition key. The engine stopped, and he removed the keys, putting them in his pocket.

Stepping into the cab, he thrust open the small hatch separating it from the cargo compartment, hoping that Heine would be there.

He wasn't; no one was. There were bloodstains on the walls

and metal flooring, but then Heine had told him he had wounded a man named Otto. The soldier padded to the fence, found an unlocked gate and pushed it open. Set flush with the facade of the Wust and Wimmer building was a short set of stone steps leading down to a cellar door.

Bolan had no idea how many men he was facing. Not counting Heine, he had seen four mercenaries leaving the clinic. He had already neutralized Otto and had just now accounted for another, so that left only two to contend with—assuming that no more mercenaries had escaped the raid and joined up with them.

There was only one way to find out. Bolan went down the steps on the balls of his feet and tried the knob. It was unlocked.

He inched the door open, and his eyes roved over the maze of rusting pipes running at all angles about the room. A large, cracked porcelain sink was attached to a wall. The flagstones on the floor all seemed undisturbed.

Bolan walked in warily, senses alert. He heard nothing but the sounds from the street outside. Weisenburg didn't know where the concealed door to the passage leading to the conference room was located, but Bolan made an educated guess.

He reached the sink, tugged and twisted at the faucet handles and a section of wall behind the sink swiveled open with a crunch of hidden pivots.

Bolan wasn't surprised. It stood to reason that the designers of the hidden doors at the clinic were the same people and would lean toward standardized specs.

Peering around the edge of the panel, he saw only a narrow flight of wooden steps leading up into musty darkness. He put one foot into the passageway and onto the second step, which creaked slightly.

Over his head came a faint whoosh, a glint of some dark metal, and a stinging force ripped the Beretta from his hand.

16

Bolan flung himself backward, trying to shake some feeling back into his numbed hand. He heard his pistol skidding across the rough floor somewhere behind him.

A large red-haired man sprang from the narrow stairwell, whirling a kind metal flail or whip around in his right hand. It was a series of iron rods, linked together by metal rings. The handle was wrapped around with leather, and at the end was a heavy iron weight with beveled edges. It was about five feet long.

Bolan recognized the contraption as a *kau sin ke,* a Chinese hand weapon that could deliver a lethal, bone-crushing blow. He recognized the man using it as one of the mercenaries who had fled into the subterranean room of the clinic.

The man was smiling with genuine enjoyment. "I've been waiting for you. The men you shot down were my friends."

Bolan backed away, keeping his eyes on the man's feet. The whirling pieces of metal hummed through the air in a blurry circle. He knew better than to stare at it, because the spinning motion induced a mild hypnotic effect.

"What's your name?" he asked.

"What difference does that make, American?"

"I always want to know the names of every idiot I kill."

This man's reaction was different than that of Xauz. He was a professional. He merely grinned in appreciation.

"The name I go by is Ernst. It's not my real name, but it'll do until I come up with a better one."

Bolan feinted to the left, then leaped to the right, pivoted and swung his left leg up and around in a perfect crescent kick.

Ernst surged forward in the opposite direction. Bolan's boot grazed his head, but the weighted end of the *kau sin ke* slapped into Bolan's ribs, smashing all the wind out of him and knocking him backward.

Trying to ignore the needles of intense pain lancing up his rib cage, fighting for breath, Bolan recovered his balance. His eyes searched the cellar floor for the Beretta.

Ernst snapped the jointed lengths of iron at him like a bull-whip. Bolan ducked, and the weighted end crashed into the wall, knocking a fist-sized chunk of stone out of it.

While Ernst reeled in the *kau sin ke,* Bolan launched himself forward. Doubling the metal rods, the German met the Executioner's attack by whacking him across the midsection. Dazed and nauseated, Bolan managed to shift the weight of his body, and he caromed against Ernst, grabbing a handful of shirt as he went down. Both men fell heavily, Ernst striking his head against the flagstones.

Bolan struggled and heaved, and achieved a kneeling position atop the German. He pinioned Ernst's right wrist under his knee. With his free hand, Ernst gouged savagely at Bolan's eyes. Batting aside the hand, the Executioner rammed a straight right into the snarling face under him.

With a twist and sidewise wrench of his whole body, Ernst managed to shove Bolan to one side and club at him with the doubled *kau sin ke.* The blow glanced off Bolan's raised forearm. He rolled and got swiftly to his feet and planted a boot on the side of Ernst's neck as he tried to rise.

The man went over on his back, but he unleashed the full length of the *kau sin ke* in a snakelike strike directly at Bolan's head. The soldier leaned backward, and the weighted end only brushed the collar of his jacket. Arcing past him, it crashed to the floor, fracturing a flagstone.

Thrown off balance, Ernst tried to lift the heavy rods for a backhand blow, but Bolan took a quick step forward and kicked hard at his hand. There was a sharp snap as a wrist bone broke.

Ernst yelled with pain, and his fingers slackened around the leather-bound handle. Bolan kicked the *kau sin ke* out of the way.

Ernst hugged his broken wrist, and his left hand groped for something on his right hip. As he yelled a warning in German,

Bolan slashed down with a stiffened palm, his right arm like a pile driver. The edge of his hand chopped into the base of Ernst's neck. With a liquid gurgle, the man sagged to the floor and lay there unconscious.

Patting him down, Bolan found a Glock holstered behind his right hip. He removed it, made sure there was a round in the chamber, looked around the basement and found the Beretta in a dim corner.

Checking to make sure it hadn't picked up any dirt or grit, Bolan squeezed into the passage behind the sink and climbed the stairs as quickly but as quietly as he could.

It was very dark, but ahead and above he saw a thread-thin, rectangular outline of light. Reaching the panel at the top of the stairs, Bolan put his ear against the wood and heard a distant murmur of voices. He pushed against the panel gently, and it gave beneath his hand. He swung it open just enough so he could see where he was.

He saw three mercenaries, standing on one side of a long conference table. Two were armed, one with a sawed-off shotgun under his arm, the other shouldering one of the H&K 94 auto-carbines. Both had their attention riveted to a broad-shouldered man with long blond hair who was facing a square steel safe door set into the wall. There was no sign or sound of Heine. Apparently the Germans had just recently arrived at Wust and Wimmer, even though they had at least a fifteen-minute head start on him. Dropping Heine off somewhere had delayed them.

As Bolan watched, the blonde removed an object from beneath his coat. It was wrapped in cloth, and it was soaked through with rust red stains. The man undid the wrappings and revealed a human hand, severed at the wrist. Blood still dripped sluggishly from the ragged stump of the wrist.

The mercenary pressed four fingers of the amputated hand against a dark strip of glass running the width of door, and the safe swung open smoothly. The men exchanged grins and words in German.

The blonde dropped the hand carelessly on the floor, reached in and removed a black box. He held it carefully, almost reverently.

Bolan kicked open the panel.

All hell broke loose, which he had expected.

What he didn't expect was a fourth man in position against the opposite wall, armed with an autocarbine. He fired first, a steel-jacketed spray that ruined the old and artfully carved oak paneling.

Bolan went to his knees behind a chair at the end of the table, and his two pistols began to roar in a beautifully synchronized rhythm.

A pair of 9 mm slugs hit the man with the shotgun with a one-two punch, knocking him backward and forcing the barrels into the air as they blasted thunderously.

As plaster drifted from the ceiling like a heavy snowfall, a burst of autofire splintered the panel behind Bolan. He went flat to the floor, lunging beneath the table. His injured rib cage twinged, but he crawled forward, pistols blazing, pushing himself along with his knees and the sides of his feet.

A line of bullets spewed from an H&K 94, thudding into the table, but not penetrating the thick slab of mahogany. Bolan kept advancing, firing, the thunder of the gunfire deafening.

He saw one of the men jerk and quiver, then double over, bleeding from three wounds in his belly. He fell facedown barely four feet from Bolan, taken out of play permanently.

He watched as two pairs of feet and legs rushed through the big carved door at the end of the room. Bolan fired the Glock, and the bullet dug into the wall by the door frame, missing one leg by a fraction.

Bolan rolled out from beneath the table and got to his feet in the same lithe motion. He rushed through the door and found himself in a huge office. Roughly fifty desks, some enclosed by partitions, were occupied by computer terminals. Word-processing clerks and telephone salespeople were gaping at the men racing through the room, as were the executives who sat in a glassed-in row of offices.

A uniformed guard wearing a Sam Browne belt with a holstered revolver walked through the far door. When he saw the three running men, two nearly atop him and one wielding an automatic rifle, he went for his side arm. The autocarbine chattered, punching several holes in the man's shirtfront.

Immediately, screaming pandemonium exploded in the busy office. Women began to shriek, men shouted and took shelter beneath their desks, computer terminals toppled. More than a few ran in heedless, panicked flight between Bolan and the mercenaries.

He wasn't about to witness a repetition of innocent people being caught in a cross fire as had happened at the clinic, so Bolan held his fire and allowed the men to run through the office. He lost precious seconds dodging people, guns held in both hands.

When he reached the main corridor, he suddenly leaped to the left and forward on his stomach, sliding on the slick marble floor like a ballplayer approaching home plate. The impulsive move saved his life.

Before he had quite hit the floor, there was the stuttering report of the autocarbine, and the clanging impact of the bullets striking the bronze frame of the door behind him.

The man with the H&K 94 had been lying in ambush for him, covering his companion with the black box.

The slide took Bolan fifteen feet down the smooth surface of the floor. As he slid, he fired, working the triggers of both pistols. Ejected shells clattered on the marble in his wake.

Every bullet Bolan fired pierced the body of the mercenary. The shock of four bullets pounding simultaneously into his torso slammed him backward into a decorative pillar. Bouncing from it, he staggered forward, right into a final shot that hammered him between the eyes and emptied the Glock.

Bolan didn't wait to see the mercenary fall. Dropping the Glock, he was up and sprinting down the wide corridor toward a rear window, high up from the floor. He could see that the window was open and could also see the blond man scrambling frantically to get through it and out, encumbered as he was with the black box tucked under one arm. It seemed heavier than it looked.

Bolan got there just in time to catch the tail of the man's coat as it slid outside onto a fire escape. That would have been enough if the coat had held, but it didn't.

There was a ripping of fabric, an angry cry in German, and Bolan staggered backward from the force of his pull. There was almost an entire coat in his hands, but nothing in the window or the fire escape beyond. He heard running footfalls on the metal steps.

Bolan jumped the five feet up to the windowsill and swung his body over and out onto the fire escape. He heard police sirens and the squeal of tires from the front of the building, and he hoped it was Straub's people.

He descended the fire escape three steps at a time, pausing at each landing to see if he could get a clean shot at the mercenary. The crisscrossing steel beams and walkways blocked him. He knew the man was probably armed, and he also suspected that he had an escape route already plotted, one that didn't include the truck. That vehicle was too easy to spot and too cumbersome to maneuver.

Weisenburg had described Heine as a brilliant strategist, and that seemed true. The man had anticipated almost every other contingency, so Bolan assumed such a crucial mission as recovering the telemetry box wouldn't be left to chance, even if it was an eleventh-hour plan.

Between the metal slats, Bolan glimpsed the German dropping the last few feet from the fire escape to an enclosed courtyard below. He saw him run a few feet and whirl, the Glock in his right hand.

Just as the blonde fired, Bolan vaulted over the rail of the landing and dropped beneath the shot.

He took a hard fall onto the concrete, one that brought a sharp pain to his ribs. Climbing to his feet, he raced after the mercenary, who continued to fire at him without aiming. No bullets came anywhere near him, but when an amplified voice bellowed from behind him through a bullhorn, Bolan realized the shots served as an alarm to the police converging around the Wust and Wimmer building.

A shot sounded from behind him, and the bullet slashed a long white scar on the concrete a few feet in front of him. He cast a quick glance over his shoulder and saw men in black uniforms climbing over the wall of the courtyard. One was drawing a bead on him with his service pistol.

As far as the Berlin police officers knew, Bolan was one of the men who had shot and killed the security guard upstairs. And if Straub had enlisted their aid, he had told them that the intruders would be armed and dangerous. The events at the clinic were only a few hours old, and no one could really blame the police for subscribing, even temporarily, to the ''shoot first and get a statement later'' school.

Deliberately or by happenstance, matters had been arranged to put Bolan at odds with the local law, odds that very well could prove fatal.

He saw the mercenary reach the low wall encircling the courtyard, bound to the top and roll over it, automatic in one hand, the black box in the other. Bolan put on speed, but another shot from behind him struck the wall and sprayed stinging grains of stone into his face.

Whirling, Bolan fired three rounds, shooting over the heads of the police. The shots were close, for he wanted them to duck or seek cover—which they did. He was able to get over the wall without another shot being fired at him.

Bolan found himself in a narrow alley; buildings reared around him for an unbroken block. The blond man was racing down the alley as if he knew exactly where he was going. The Executioner shot off in pursuit, ejecting the spent clip from the Beretta and sliding in a full load on the run.

He saw his quarry turn right upon leaving the alley. Bolan followed him, then was forced to throw himself backward into a sheltering doorway.

The blond mercenary had the passenger's door of a late-model, gray Volvo open, and was pointing his pistol at the mouth of the alley. He pumped the trigger four times, random shots that served no purpose other than to keep Bolan pinned down.

With a high-pitched engine roar, the Volvo leaped away from the curb. Bolan didn't shoot at it. He realized he was on the street at the rear of Wust and Wimmer, and the Mercedes was still parked at the curb only a few hundred feet away.

Running toward it, he hoped the men in the Volvo wouldn't spray the tires with gunfire as they passed. Fortunately the car turned left down another side street before they came abreast of it.

To Bolan's surprise, Weisenburg was still in the car. As he started it and threw it into reverse, he asked, "Still here, Professor?"

"I did what you said. I called the secret service. They're sending a representative to meet me here."

"The meeting may have to be postponed."

It didn't occur to Bolan that the old physicist may have experienced enough violence and fast action for one day. He was far too valuable as a source of information to let him out of his sight. Bolan simply told him to make sure his seat belt was secure and wheeled the Mercedes down the side street after the Volvo.

Bolan took the turn just as a group of police officers raced around the corner of the Wust and Wimmer building, blaring their whistles and waving at him.

His foot jammed the accelerator pedal, and the Mercedes whipped away from the angry cluster of police and took the next corner just as guns began to blast.

The Volvo was several car lengths ahead on a broad avenue. The noontime traffic was heavy, but not particularly slow. Official vehicles were appearing at almost every intersection. A quick glance in the mirror showed another in the rear.

The Volvo turned right, back in the direction of Wilhelmstrasse. Bolan followed, knowing that the men he was pursuing were intimately familiar with the maze of back alleys and side streets. They could afford to engage in a cat-and-mouse chase with Bolan, but he knew it was one he would lose with the police added to the mix.

Trying to imitate every move of the Volvo took Bolan in a zigzag, pretzel course, circling the same blocks over and over.

As the Volvo turned at another corner, a police car rolled into sight, spotting Bolan just as he made the swing.

Sirens screamed from the next block and were answered from a side street.

The men in the Volvo had led Bolan into the opposite end of

the cordon, which the police had been forming around the blocks and streets bordering Wilhelmstrasse and the Wust and Wimmer building.

A police car lunged from the curb, and Bolan was forced to slam on the brakes. Police leaped from it, brandishing pistols, shouting orders. Bolan's hands gripped the wheel, knowing that he might succeed in running the blockade, but not without people dying.

He put the car in neutral, placed the Beretta on the dashboard and locked his hands behind his head. Weapons were thrust in through the windows, voices growled orders. The doors were jerked open; Weisenburg was hauled out by the collar, Bolan by the arms.

He was slapped against the side of the car, frisked roughly, then spun back around. Straub stood there, staring at him with bleak gray eyes.

"Cuff him," he said quietly. He spoke in English so Bolan would be sure to understand him.

17

Bolan wasn't in the cuffs for very long, maybe twenty minutes. That was as long as it took for a pair of neatly dressed men to drive him to a nondescript building not far from the Europa Centre.

He was ushered in through a back entrance, and the cuffs were removed just before he was shoved into a small holding cell.

Bolan didn't resist the treatment. Nothing was to be gained by arguing or struggling. Even though he knew Straub intended to do nothing more than flex his authority as the Verfassungschutz section chief, Bolan wasn't intimidated. He was only concerned about the delay in getting back to the battle.

There was a narrow metal bunk attached to the wall. Using his jacket as a pillow, Bolan lay down and waited. He had a pretty good idea of what would happen during the rest of the afternoon.

When Hyams found out about his detention, he would notify his superior, who would notify someone in Washington, who in turn would notify Brognola. After a couple of hours of international telephone calls, some high official in the German government would notify Straub to stop playing power games and release the American specialist and let him get back to business.

Though not particularly comforted by this scenario, Bolan was able to relax enough to fall asleep.

The sound of the door bolt being thrown back awoke him. He didn't know what time it was, but he was sure several hours had passed. One of the neatly dressed men gestured for him to come out and follow him down a corridor to a frosted-glass door.

He opened it, gestured for Bolan to enter, then closed it behind him. Bolan was in a busy and crowded room.

Phones were ringing, fax machines were spewing paper, cigarette smoke filled the air. Men and women were talking, studying maps, jogging back and forth with sheaves of paper in their hands.

Bolan had been in enough war rooms to recognize one when he saw it. Obviously this division of the secret service was trying to coordinate their activities with other local law-enforcement and intelligence agencies.

Seeing an open office door, Bolan jostled through the crowd toward it. Inside were Straub, Wezhardt, Hyams and Weisenburg. They were seated at a table and glanced up when he entered. All of them looked tense, worried and, in Weisenburg's case, half-exhausted.

On a desktop against the far wall, Bolan saw his equipment cases and his Beretta, snug inside its shoulder holster. He took a chair at the table, asking, "Have you been waiting for me?"

Hyams cleared his throat. "Yes. There were a few diplomatic feathers that needed to be smoothed first. It's under control."

Straub pursed his lips, as though he were tasting something extremely sour. "Do not expect an apology from me, Herr Blanski."

"I don't. And don't expect one from me."

"Your cowboy tactics could not be tolerated," Straub said, ignoring Bolan's response. "As it is, the news media is harassing the police and my agency unmercifully. They demand answers."

"That's why I made contact with Professor Weisenburg. He may be able to supply some."

All eyes turned toward the old man. His hands were flat on the table, and he was staring at them unblinkingly.

"What do you want to know?" Weisenburg's voice was barely above a whisper.

"Some background first," Straub said. "How long have you been a member of the Order of Thule?"

"Since the end of the war. Eric Ganth, who had been my father's SS superior at the Reinickendorf West research station, contacted me. I was very angry, very upset by my father's death, by the destruction of Germany. I met Heinrich, Helmur, Teudt, Hito and a few others who have since passed away. I was initiated in January 1946.

"The Order was explained to me as a society that would isolate the true Aryan race from the rest of substandard humanity. It was a dream that would live on beyond the death of Hitler, that superseded the Third Reich. We would become the true rulers of the earth."

"How was this to come to pass?" Bolan asked. He was trying very hard not to be sarcastic.

Weisenburg shrugged. "Through the slow infiltration of decadent political systems, through the use of higher technologies, through cleverness, through simple Aryan superiority."

"What about the higher technologies?" Wezhardt asked.

"The German scientific establishment worked exclusively for the military," Weisenburg replied. "Almost all of that work was concerned with producing advanced weaponry, the so-called Nazi secret weapons that so obsessed the Allies toward the end of the war. One of the major breakthroughs was in the field of electromagnetism, specifically microwaves, building on the work of Tesla and Marconi. My father designed and built an emitter that short-circuited the ignition systems of aircraft engines at a hundred meters. Another emitter was built to ignite flammable materials from a distance.

"My father's intention, aborted by his death in Dresden, was to expand the effective radius of the emitters and at the same time reduce their size. His successors did not have access to his notes, so when the Reinickendorf facility was evacuated and transferred to an underground complex in the Alpine redoubt, most of his research, his prototypes were lost. Eric Ganth retrieved them and gave them to me."

"And you were so grateful to receive your father's legacy," Straub said, "you agreed to build on his work for the greater glory of the Thule society."

Weisenburg was silent for a moment, then nodded. "That is essentially it."

"That was over fifty years ago," Bolan stated. "Other industries must have made your father's achievements in solid-state physics obsolete."

Anger flickered in Weisenburg's eyes. "Many of his discoveries were duplicated. Some were realized, but never acted upon. Most were employed in a very pedestrian fashion, such as in radar, communications and ovens. Other of my father's discoveries were stumbled across by accident and classified as top secret. Your own Navy has experimented with Maser weapons, which are nothing more than microwave emitters."

"How many of these things did you build?" Hyams asked.

"Ten, twenty, maybe thirty."

"There weren't that many found at the clinic," Wezhardt said.

"I wasn't responsible for the storage of the devices," Weisenburg replied. "It would have been unforgivably foolish to keep them all in the same place."

"They weren't all of the same type," she countered.

"Quite a few were modifications of my father's prototypes. Others were built using the principles discovered by others."

"Like the Gunn oscillator," said Wezhardt.

"*Ja.*"

"Tell us about Heinrich Heine," Bolan ordered.

A visible shudder shook Weisenburg. "He held the rank of Standartenführer, but he really served as a high priest. As a young man, I idolized him. Later, I feared him. As should you."

"Explain."

"The common assumption is that the true power of the Third Reich was held by Hitler, Himmler, Göring, Bormann and a handful of others. In many ways, the true guiding force behind Germany's war was Heinrich Heine. I was truly astonished by the extent of the power and influence he wielded.

"Heinrich was regarded as a demigod by both Hitler and Himmler. He was cold, brilliant, relentless and nearly inhuman. He designed a new world order based on ancient occult principles. He saw the war as not just a struggle for territory or even power, but an opportunity to restore the planet to its true superhuman rulers."

"What kind of bullshit is this?" Hyams demanded.

Weisenburg smirked. "The truth was hidden by German technology, German science and German organization. The great innovation of the Third Reich was to mix occultism with technology. Your own government wanted that mix. Why else were so many Nazi scientists imported into America after the war?''

"What did Heine do after Hitler died?" Bolan asked.

"After he executed Hitler, you mean?"

Weisenburg seemed to enjoy the expressions of shock and disbelief on the faces of the people around the table.

"According to Heinrich, he killed him, sacrificed him on April 30, Walpurgis Night, one of the major mystical dates in the old Teutonic religions. He chose that date to restore some balance to the powers Hitler had misused.

"In any event, Heinrich lived in many places around the world. He acted as a liaison between SS officers seeking asylum and U.S. and British intelligence organizations, advised the Odessa and, as far as I know, helped Josef Mengele stay hidden when all of Israeli intelligence was scouring South America for him.''

"Was he the mastermind of this scheme?" Straub asked.

"No, that was Helmur. It has been in the planning stages for nearly three years.''

"Why so long?"

"Heinrich insisted on waiting until the most favorable time before implementing the project.''

"Why was this the most favorable time?" Bolan asked.

"Fifty years ago last month, Heinrich, Eric Ganth and Gustav Teudt buried a casket containing the holiest relics of the Order in a glacier on Hochfeiler peak. The casket was exhumed, but one of the relics was missing, and Heinrich believed our project might not succeed unless it was recovered.''

"The Dag," said Bolan.

"*Ja.*" Weisenburg stared at him steadily. "He fears its power, fears you because you now wield it.''

"Was Aubrey Lesnick a member of this Order of yours?" Hyams demanded.

Weisenburg snorted. "Don't be ridiculous. He was simply a pawn. An important one, but a pawn nonetheless.''

"Did he cooperate with you willingly?" Straub asked.

"After a fashion. He was a business and occasional social associate of Helmur's, you see. During his visits to Helmur's office and home, Lesnick was subjected to low-level microwave fields, which made him extremely susceptible not only to suggestion, but to behavior modification.

"It required several months of treatment in order to be undetectable, and was not a permanent alteration. That is why Helmur more or less overruled Heinrich's objections to implementing the project before the Dag was recovered."

"Who else is involved in this?" Bolan asked.

"Aside from myself, only Hito and Helmur, and a man named deMilteer, who Heinrich killed three days ago. And another man we called Abdul."

"Abdul?" Hyams echoed.

With a smile, Weisenburg told them Abdul's true name.

"Bullshit!" Hyams snarled, thumping his fist on the tabletop. "Bullshit!"

"He was very enthusiastic about the project," Weisenburg said. "He contributed many millions of dollars to it. However, he may be dead already, since Heinrich is obviously liquidating everyone he considers a security risk."

"Which seems to be everyone but himself," Bolan noted. "What about the soldiers and the skinheads? How many of them are there?"

Weisenburg shrugged. "The soldiers were Heinrich's province—Helmur recruited the young toughs. I don't know the actual numbers."

"Does Heine understand the workings of the telemetry box?" Wezhardt asked.

"There is no reason why he shouldn't. He knows the missiles' rewritten transmission code, and the box is keyed to it."

"How do you think he will employ it?"

Weisenburg shook his head. "I have no idea. The simplest method would be a wheeled vehicle equipped with a microwave emitter that could be driven to the general area of the missile site. However, the emitter could just as easily be mounted on an aircraft."

"Do you have any idea where Heine might be?" Straub inquired.

"No. He could be anywhere in or outside of Berlin. Though I am unaware of its actual location, I was led to believe the Order maintains a place where aircraft and vehicles are stored."

"I see." Straub sighed heavily. "Unless you have something to add, Professor, you will be returned to detention."

"Good. I am very tired. And hungry."

"I will make sure you are fed."

As he stood, Wezhardt reached out and grabbed his hand. "You're not the slightest bit sorry about any of this, are you?" She sounded more puzzled than angry.

Weisenburg gently pulled away from her. "Ilona, I am too old, too dead inside to be sorry about much of anything."

Straub walked Weisenburg to the door and turned him over to one of the neatly dressed men.

Hyams pinched the bridge of his nose, then massaged his temples. "This is crazy. How the hell do we deal with something like this? This isn't terrorism. This isn't the action of a hostile government. This is insanity."

"At least we have some solid information to go on," Bolan said. "And we know the target is Site 611."

Hyams pulled an attaché case from beneath the table and took a large aerial map from it.

"This is a view of the Site 611 grounds," he said, tapping it. "It's in a pretty inaccessible place. Only one road in and out to the silo itself."

"Where's the main highway?" Bolan asked.

"There isn't one. Just a lot of country lanes, cow paths, things like that. The nearest people, dairy farmers, are about three miles away."

"Should be an easy area to stake out," said Bolan, studying the map. "With such little traffic, strange vehicles will be easy to stop. Assuming Heine doesn't come by air."

"The airspace is restricted."

"I doubt he'll let a little thing like that stop him," Bolan replied wryly.

"Won't they want to wait for a response to their demands before they take action?" Hyams asked.

"Nuclear blackmail isn't the plan any longer," Bolan said. "It would take too long for results and leaves too much to chance. Government officials can retire, and new leaders with different ideas can emerge. Not to mention Heine isn't getting any younger. He can't afford to wait. He wants to put the show on the road right now."

"You don't think Heine will try to extract a price?" Straub asked.

Bolan shook his head. "His psychology is fairly simple. My country and yours cares very much about what even one nuclear warhead would to do Germany's population. Heine couldn't care less. He isn't going to risk a change in the political climate by waiting. The sooner he strikes, the better for him."

"But what can he possibly gain?" Wezhardt asked, her eyes shining with fright. "Even the most ardent neo-Nazi wouldn't agree with killing thousands, perhaps hundreds of thousands of our own people and contaminating the fatherland!"

Straub ran the tip of his tongue over his very dry lips. "Remember, when Hitler realized that the war was lost, he pursued a scorched-earth policy. Three hundred thousand Germans perished when the Berlin U-Bahn, the subway, was flooded on his orders. He required German citizens to raze their own towns, farmers to destroy their stock, bridges to be blown up."

"What was it he said?" Bolan asked. "'Losses can never be too high'?"

"What's that got to do with anything?" Hyams demanded.

Taking a deep breath, Straub replied, "Herr Blanski said that Heine's psychology is simple. That it is, but it is also crazed. Heinrich Heine, with his devotion to occult principles, intends to make Germany and its people a blood sacrifice of truly monstrous proportions."

Bolan said grimly, "Like the demigod he believes he is, Heine wants to be sent with human sacrifices to his grave."

18

By six o' clock, Sven and Wulf had changed clothes and cars twice and were driving along the national expressway that covered Germany.

Sven was driving a late-model BMW and took an exit that led to the suburb of Spandau. Though the home of the infamous prison, it was also a section of abandoned manufacturing plants, schools and churches. The faces of many of the older buildings were still pockmarked with bullet scars from the house-to-house fighting that had taken place there more than a half century before.

Sven had several relatives in the area who could still point to the precise spots where invading Russian soldiers had been dropped in their tracks.

Both Sven and Wulf were still fairly young men, but they missed the glories of the Third Reich as though they had participated in them. During their long stints as West Berlin border guards, they had talked to a number of older officers who claimed to have been in the thick of things.

When they were forced out of their careers, they quickly discovered that they were pariahs; not even the police wanted them. Private security organizations weren't interested in them. When they were contacted by a mysterious group that had a need for their skills, they asked no questions. Wulf, Sven and many others like them simply joined it.

It was a schizophrenic relationship. Sven enjoyed his time in the clinic, since he and his comrades were provided with every comfort, even women. He didn't even object to being sent to Brazil, since he had never been out of Germany before.

But the old man, Heine, frightened and awed him at the same time. Sven had never heard of the Order of Thule, but he received the distinct impression of some massive, shadowy wheel that he served as a simple, expendable spoke.

Heine demanded complete, unquestioning obedience, and Sven cooperated. But now he was seriously questioning the wisdom of not only what Heine was doing, but what he was doing.

He had lost many comrades at the clinic. Only a few, less than fifteen, had managed to escape. He couldn't imagine what such a decimated force could accomplish. Any kind of frontal assault was out of the question.

But Heine had felt that any risks were acceptable to retrieve the black box from the Wust and Wimmer office. Though the mission had been successful, Sven had lost even more comrades, and a certain amount of faith to the cause and the man to whom he had pledged his loyalty.

He turned the BMW down a dark side street, away from the business section of Spandau. He traveled four blocks, parked, then he and Wulf got out. The night seemed peaceful. A cool breeze stirred the branches of a few trees along the street.

Sven carried the box inside a suitcase. The two men walked three blocks and came to a group of deserted buildings that sprawled across the space of a city block. A high barbed-wire fence encircled the lot, which contained a group of factory buildings formerly housing an automobile-manufacturing plant, but abandoned since 1944.

Posted signs warned trespassers off and gave notice that the property was in the hands of a real-estate company, which had been owned by Helmur Ganth.

Though Sven had only visited the place once, he knew the main building was but a false front concealing a fortress. It generated its own power and housed storerooms, living quarters and a garage containing a fleet of powerful, armor-plated vehicles of every type. Two helicopters stood fueled and ready beneath a rooftop bay.

God only knew how much money had been devoted to constructing the base over the years, and Sven had never been inclined to ask.

He and Wulf walked quickly along the opposite side of the street, parallel to the factory site. They paused when they reached the storefront of a small tobacco shop, which fronted the fenced-in main entrance of the factory. The lights were still shining behind the dust-streaked window.

The overweight proprietor sat behind a counter, glancing up dully from a German-language edition of *Playboy*. His face was covered by leathery warts. He gave a barely perceptible nod and grunted, "Wait," when the two men entered his shop.

He waddled around the counter to the door and turned a Closed sign around in the window. He jerked a thumb over his shoulder.

"Go," he said.

Sven and Wulf walked to the rear of the shop. They opened a door and continued along a short hallway, entered a small storeroom and walked directly to a shelf of cigarette cartons and cigar boxes.

Wulf, his hands free, reached under the shelf, seized an invisible handle and pushed to the left, then pulled straight back. That section of the wall moved outward. Behind it was a landing, and a flight of stairs leading down twenty feet to another door at the bottom.

Sven and Wulf entered, and, standing on the landing, Wulf tugged the wall panel back into place. When a latch clicked, a bulb over the door below lit up.

When Sven had first learned of his employer's fondness for hidden doors and secret passages, he had been amused, then enthralled. It all seemed like some kind of game. Now there was a sinister significance to all the precautions.

"This is all so much crap, like something out of some stupid movie," Wulf muttered.

With a surge of fear, Sven raised a finger to his lips and hushed him. "This place may be wired. He may hear you," he mouthed.

Wulf gave him a disgusted look with one raised eyebrow. His "So?" was deliberately loud.

Taking the finger from his lips, Sven made a gun from it and his thumb and pressed it to Wulf's forehead. Leaning forward, he whispered, "*Bang.* That's why 'so.'"

The disgusted look didn't vanish from Wulf's face, but he nodded in assent.

When they reached the bottom of the stairway, the door swung open automatically at their approach and closed after them. They turned sharply to the left, then right, then walked straight along a passage below street level.

In the dim light, they passed under the street and into the grounds occupied by the factory buildings. Another door loomed before them. This one was set in a concrete wall, reinforced with riveted steel cleats.

In the very center of the door was a small speaker grid. Sven spoke into it in clear tones, saying precisely, "Schaeffer. One. Two. Peenemünde."

There was the sound of solenoids clicking behind the door, then the whine of an electric motor as the door swung slowly inward, hinged on the right on oiled bearings.

Wulf and Sven passed through it, and the door closed behind them.

They walked along another corridor, entered a wooden door and walked up another short flight of stairs. The stairway opened up into a large common room, filled with cots, chairs and a couple of tables.

Only one man was in the room, lying on a cot. He wore only an undershirt, pulled up to his chest to make room for a blood-spotted bandage.

Sven walked over to him, murmuring, "Otto. How are you feeling?"

"Like I've been shot, how do you think I'm feeling?" Otto said weakly.

"Where are the others?"

"Standing guard duty. Leaving me here to die or get better." Otto tried to raise himself on his elbow. "Maybe dying would be better."

"How many of us made it back here?" Wulf asked.

"With you and Sven, it makes an even fifteen. Including me, that is."

"Damn," Wulf said in a fierce whisper. "We aren't even a decent gang, much less any kind of fighting force!"

"Where is he?" Sven asked, ignoring Wulf's remark.

"I don't know. I don't care," Otto croaked. "He's out of his mind, thinks he's the devil or God or something."

Otto's voice trailed off into a hacking rattle, and he collapsed back on the cot. Blood worked its way out of his mouth. His eyes closed.

Sven looked at him, realizing the bright red blood indicated a punctured lung, and he also caught a whiff of a perforated bowel. Otto wasn't dead yet, but he would be soon.

As he left the bedside, Wulf said softly, "We'll probably end up like that, you know. All this crap about a new and stronger Germany, money, making America kiss our ass is getting us killed off piecemeal."

"He has a plan," Sven said, equally quietly.

Wulf sneered. "Yeah, right."

They walked down a carpeted corridor and reached a black door made of polished walnut. Two mercenaries stood outside it, shouldering carbines. They nodded to Sven and Wulf.

"How long has he been here?" Sven asked one of them in a whisper.

"We got him here about two hours ago. He's visualizing, but he gave orders that we were to let you in as soon as you arrived. Just you, Sven."

Wulf sighed in relief and walked back down the corridor. Sven took a deep breath and then rapped on the door.

"Come," Heinrich Heine said.

Sven walked into a wide, square room that he had been in once before, and had hoped he would never be forced to enter again.

The only comparison Sven could make was to a shrine, but it was unlike any church or place of worship he'd ever ventured into.

The vast room was lined with rough-hewn granite blocks. In the center was a massive stone altar supported by three boulders. All around the walls were bronze plaques bearing the Reich eagle and Thulist lightning-bolt symbol. On granite pedestals rested a variety of regalia: swords, daggers, shields, jeweled crowns, a human skull, gem-encrusted crucifixes, a spear point and even a heavy diamond pendant. The room was dimly lit by torches flickering in wall brackets.

At the altar, standing, not sitting in his wheelchair, was Heine.

He was wearing a jet black ensemble that resembled an SS officer's uniform, but with its silver death's-head emblem worn like a badge.

A pair of bloodred sashes crossed his skinny chest like ammunition bandoliers. The sashes were decorated with symbols, swastikas, sunbursts and jagged marks Sven had heard called runes.

Heine's blue-veined hands were resting on a scattered collection of black-and-white photographs atop the altar. His eyes were closed, his head tilted back. His lips moved, but he made no sound.

Heine should have looked ridiculous, but he didn't.

Sven stood silently, feeling a dew of sweat break out on his upper lip. He didn't dare wipe it away. The weight of the telemetry box in the suitcase strained at his arm, but he didn't set it down.

Heine tipped his head forward, but he didn't open his eyes. "Sven."

"Yes, sir."

"Do you understand the purpose of visualization?"

"No, sir. Not really."

"Come here, Sven."

Sven slowly approached the altar. He saw the photographs were of concentration- and death-camp victims—men, women and children reduced to creatures barely recognizable as human beings, naked and stacked atop each other in mass graves like cordwood.

"Reality yields to the pressure of an iron will, visualizing a precise reality," Heine said. "An ancient technique that can turn physical conditions inside out. That explains Hitler's early successes. He had the power, then. But he lost it, and left Germany in ruins."

Heine opened his eyes. They were calm, not raging or bright. He seemed relaxed, confident, even fatherly. "I taught the techniques to him, Sven. I had the power then, and I have it now.

Destiny can be controlled, shaped, molded. That is what our undertaking is all about.''

Pressing the photographs with his fingertips, Heine said, ''I visualize a reality where all non-Aryans are reduced to the condition of these sacrifices. We can accomplish this, Sven, though our measures may seem extreme.''

Heine stared at him unblinkingly. ''Does that disturb you, my boy?''

''No, sir. It does not. Losses can never be too high.'' Sven meant what he said. For some reason, all his apprehension, his fear, was fading away.

''Good boy. I am relying on you. You accomplished your mission?''

Sven heaved the suitcase up, but he didn't rest it atop the altar. That seemed discourteous, if not blasphemous. ''Yes, sir. The American tried to stop us, and we lost five men, but your plan to confuse pursuit by having different vehicles along the escape route worked perfectly.''

Heine nodded. ''Sometimes the old tricks are the best. What of the American warrior?''

Sven shook his head. ''I don't know. He could not have followed us here, to our holy ground.''

Heine chuckled. ''This is only a replica of the original Thulian shrine on the sacred island of Rugen. That was a stronghold of the first Aryan race. I had this room built for initiations.''

Smiling at him fondly, Heine tapped his chest. ''The true holy ground is in here, Sven. In our Aryan hearts, in our Aryan blood.''

Sven smiled. ''I understand, sir.''

''I know you do. Assemble the others. We have plans to make, and we must move tomorrow.''

Sven turned to leave, but Heine called him back.

''If Otto hasn't yet died, please help him along. His constant complaints are a nuisance. I cannot be distracted.''

''You won't be, sir. I swear.''

HEINE WATCHED as Sven marched out of the room, head thrown back, shoulders square, a chest swelling with pride. He knew that

Sven had walked in consumed with doubts and fears, and was leaving with the conviction that he would die before he shirked his responsibility to the Aryan people.

His influence on Sven wasn't hypnotism. It was the control and direction of a subtle energy, training the powers of concentration until they could be focused like a laser. The driving force behind the technique was heightened emotion.

Hitler had possessed this ability in latent form until Heine found him, educated him and trained him to make conscious use of it. It was a power that persuaded an entire nation black was white.

Heine could recall many instances when Hitler's officers would at one and the same time accept a situation as hopeless, yet remain convinced their leader would find a solution.

But Hitler's raw egotism, combined with the powers awakened in him, drove him insane, and he dragged Germany into ruin.

He was Heine's greatest disappointment, and he accepted the responsibility of righting the Austrian's wrongs. Sacrificing him hadn't been enough.

The muffled crack of a gunshot reached Heine's ears, and he smiled. He had ordered Sven to kill Otto for two reasons: first, caring for a wounded man in such a critical situation was an unnecessary distraction. Second, he wanted to test the extent of his influence over the former border guard. Otto was his friend, and if Sven would kill a friend on command, then Heine's grip on him was strong.

And through Sven, that grip would tighten on the others, who he knew were uneasy and afraid.

Heine himself was afraid. He feared the American warrior would find some way to tip the scales of probabilities in his favor. The power of the Dag made that possible, and though the warrior couldn't focus his will through it, the ancient icon still spread its power over him like a protective cloak.

The door opened and the soldiers trooped in, eyeing their surroundings warily. A few bore bandages covering superficial wounds inflicted during the raid on the clinic, but most were in excellent shape, though physically and mentally drained.

That would make Heine's task much easier.

They stood in a ragged semicircle around the altar, and Heine stared at each man in turn, keeping his eyes on him until that man either glanced away or ducked his head.

"Greetings, warriors. Your work over the past few weeks has been gratifying. You have done well by your fatherland, and the shades of the ancient Aryan kings smile upon you with favor."

There were a few smiles, but Heine wasn't sure if they were amused or impressed. It didn't matter.

"This is only the beginning of your struggle. The power you will eventually control will be unlimited. But there is a little matter of seeing our undertaking through to fruition, first."

Heine paused. The men shifted uneasily. There was something calculated, ominous, about the man's sharp voice.

"Though we suffered a setback, it was only an inconvenience, not a tragedy. But there may be some of you who believe it is a tragedy and wish to dissolve our association. I urge those who hold to this belief to step forward and speak up."

No one did.

19

June 6

The battered little pickup was parked just off the gravel lane, hidden by thick bushes.

Mack Bolan sat at the wheel and tried to enjoy the warm air, rich with the smell of growing things. Part of his mind appreciated the beauty of a summer morning in the German countryside, but most of his attention was focused on hearing or sighting anything that seemed the slightest bit out of place.

The area within a five-mile radius of Site 611 was on full alert. The woods, the fields, the footpaths crawled with armed men; watch posts had been established in an ever widening radius around the missile site.

People with binoculars scanned the skies for approaching aircraft; secret-service specialists disguised as farmers, berry pickers and fishermen walked, picked and stooped all over the hills and meadows.

Bolan was wearing tinted glasses, and the brim of a hat was tilted to shade his face from the sun. He was wearing a lightweight tweed jacket and patched slacks.

Beneath the jacket was his combat harness. From it hung four V-40 minigrenades and six clips of ammunition—three for the Beretta in its shoulder rig, and three for the Desert Eagle riding high on his right hip. His war bag lay on the seat beside him.

A walkie-talkie hung from its strap on the rearview mirror.

In the bed of the truck, covered by a tarp, was the radiation detector. Only the antenna was visible. A thin wire crawled from the device through the oval window in the cab to a tiny amplifier in his right ear. Every watch post had a similar instrument.

Bolan had been sitting in the truck since dawn, checking in every ten minutes with other watch posts. Beyond cows, a few rabbits and an inquisitive hedgehog, nothing had been seen by anyone.

Hyams was stationed in the bunker of the site, coordinating and monitoring all the communications. He had spoken very little to Bolan since the night before, and hadn't seemed very interested in hearing about Darryl's betrayal or its implications. He was either too ashamed or paranoid to discuss it.

Bolan reviewed everything that had been agreed upon the previous night. He had studied maps of the vicinity, until he knew every way in and out of the area by heart.

A vehicle or aircraft would be the most efficient way of transmitting the code that would kill a lot of people, but Wezhardt claimed a portable electric generator was required to power up the emitter to the proper voltage. Just hooking it into the battery of a car or airplane wouldn't be sufficient.

Since they had no idea of the resources the Order could call upon, Bolan raised the possibility of multiple vehicles and multiple aircraft being employed as decoys.

According to Weisenburg, there was only one telemetry box, but by the time anyone figured out which car, truck, van, plane or chopper carried it, a large portion of eastern Germany could be radioactive slag.

Neither Hyams or Straub had disagreed, but they were concerned with maintaining a cloak of secrecy over the threat and the operation to thwart it.

Bolan understood the diplomatic concerns, but he had no patience with them. He had stalked the hellfire trail as a lone wolf for too long to worry about international incidents or hurt feelings. He remembered an old saying: "Defend me from my friends; I can take care of my enemies myself."

The passenger's door opened and Wezhardt climbed in. She was dressed as casually as he was. With a great deal of dignity, she pushed the roll of toilet paper under the seat.

"I hate nature," she announced.

Bolan didn't say anything. The walkie-talkie crackled with an order to check in. He complied.

Wezhardt glanced over at Bolan as he replaced the walkie-talkie on the mirror. "How can you be so bloody patient?"

"I'm not."

"You could have fooled me. We've been sitting here for hours, and you haven't moved."

"Sometimes the enemy brings the war to you. All you can do then is wait."

"You're military, aren't you?"

"I've already told you what I am, Ilona."

"Oh, right," she said, with a faint, mocking smile. "A sanitation expert pretending to be a physicist. A man who—"

Bolan suddenly stiffened and waved her into silence. He cocked his head to the left, out the window of the cab.

Removing the amplifier from his ear, he opened the door and stepped out, scanning the clear sky.

There was a speck on the horizon, and the chugging sound of vanes beating the air. The approaching helicopter was new and white, and it looked like it was going to pass right over their position.

Bolan reached in for the walkie-talkie, but it was already squawking. Wezhardt plugged the amplifier into her ear.

"I see it," Bolan said into the walkie-talkie. "It's a Messerschmitt, a two-seater. It's reducing altitude like it's looking for a place to land."

He kept his eyes on the chopper, and he saw the call letters and logo of a Berlin television station. He called in the description.

The voice at the watch post said, "Oh, shit! How'd they get wind of this?"

"They couldn't have."

The chopper chugged almost directly overhead. Because of the overhanging tree limbs, Bolan couldn't see who or how many sat in the cockpit. Over the booming beat of the blades, he heard a low, irregular sputter, and a sudden hesitation in the engine noise, as if it had lost some power.

Wezhardt snatched the amplifier out of her ear. "We've got a signal," she cried. "Oh, my God—!"

The helicopter banked, lowered and skimmed the crests of two hills, then sank out of sight.

"It's a decoy," Bolan snapped. "That chopper's too light to carry a generator, and we're at least four miles from the site."

Some of the panic went out of Wezhardt's face. "How can you be so sure?"

"I can't be, so I'm going to check it out. I won't waste my breath ordering you to stay behind. Do what you want."

Grabbing the war bag and slinging the walkie-talkie over a shoulder, Bolan set out at a run through the bushes.

When he heard the snapping of twigs behind him, he glanced back and saw her following him.

Bolan set a ground-eating lope, and he wasn't worried about whether Wezhardt could keep the pace. He pushed through the perimeter of the brush and was in fairly open pastureland, though the countryside was hilly.

The heat of the sun was becoming oppressive, but Bolan kept running. He looked back and saw that Wezhardt wasn't far behind, falling into the rhythm of the pace.

Bolan went up a slope swiftly, down the other side, splashed through a stream then hit a thicket of pine scrub that slowed him. He lost his footing for a moment and tripped, going down on one knee by a bush. Wezhardt caught up with him, panting.

They didn't speak, but pushed on through the thicket. Thorns and briars tore their clothes and scratched their faces and hands. They saw the helicopter sitting in a small hollow between two hillocks. The engine was off and the blades motionless. There was no one in or around it.

Bolan drew the Desert Eagle and scanned the area. The grass was high and thick and moved with the breeze, but he didn't see anyone. He reported in to the watch post and was told a unit was on its way and to sit tight.

He acknowledged the message, but didn't say he would comply with it. Whispering to Wezhardt to stay behind, he moved out into the hollow, the .44 held with both hands.

He crept up to the helicopter from behind and peered through the Plexiglas canopy into the cockpit. Both seats were empty.

Gesturing for Wezhardt to come forward, Bolan opened the hatch and examined the controls. There wasn't anything unusual about them.

"Maybe it's legitimate, and the pilot was forced to make an emergency landing and walked off to find help," she suggested.

"It would have been easier to radio for help," Bolan replied. "Besides, your radiation detector registered a microwave signal as it passed over, remember?"

Wezhardt nodded, as if a little annoyed by the reminder. She began working on the latches of the emergency maintenance hatch on the craft's fuselage.

"There's no sign of an emitter in the cockpit," she said. "So if there's one aboard, it has to be in here."

Bolan let her work on it. He kept his eyes and gun sweeping the area. He didn't turn around until he heard her say, "Right again."

She was pointing to the battery. A coaxial cable was attached to the positive terminus and ran to a small metal-walled box with perforated sides.

"There it is," she said, "hooked up to the battery. It's an emitter with a very limited effect radius, but strong enough to register on my instrument."

"You're right again and we're foxed again," Bolan said. "Weisenburg must have told Heine about these detectors you're so proud of."

Angrily she said, "Well, of course he would have. He's not a fool. Not only did he probably tell Heine about the detectors, he probably built a few in his time."

Bolan turned away, not wanting his temper to fray any further. Not even the most crazed Mob capo or the most deranged terrorist leader had ever displayed such a cheerful willingness to sacrifice men and material to gain an objective as Heinrich Heine. He grudgingly had to admit that the man *was* a brilliant military strategist, as well as one of the most evil men he had ever pitted himself against.

He called the watch post. "Call off the units. It was a diversionary tactic. There will probably be more. The chopper is unoccupied, and it doesn't have the telemetry box. I'm going to track the pilot. He has to have some destination in mind."

Bolan cut off the watch post's protests, reached in and yanked the power lead from the battery. He began circling the helicopter, his eyes on the ground.

"You're going to track the pilot?" Wezhardt asked. "Who do you think you are—Daniel Boone?"

"Go back to the truck, Ilona."

"Why should I?"

Bolan bent over grass that had been stamped down and was now rising back up. "One reason is that I was told you were to have minimal contact with the field operations. Primarily I want you to go back because someone has to man the detector."

Wezhardt wanted to argue, but she really couldn't. The American was right, and it was only a restless night and stinging briar scratches that made her so short with his manner. She watched him stand up and begin to walk toward another slope, pausing every few moments to stare at the ground, scan the terrain, then move on again.

"Be careful," she called to him.

Wezhardt fumed, walking in the direction she had come. She glanced back once and saw the man jogging toward the face of the slope.

Rather than force herself through the thorn-infested thicket again, Wezhardt detoured up a steep embankment, figuring to walk along its top until she reached open ground again.

She tramped along the crest of the embankment, looking at the wildflowers and enjoying the music of the songbirds. As a lifelong resident of the city, she rarely heard it. As she walked, she slowly got caught up in the warmth of the sun and the sense of tranquility.

Subsequently Wezhardt lost her way.

When she realized the embankment had dipped down and curved gently away from the direction she wanted to go, she didn't become upset or panicky. She stopped and looked around, shielding her eyes and tried to reorient herself.

A line of trees less than two hundred meters away bordered a green fenced-in pasture. Cows were grazing off to one side. Beyond the pasture was a two-story farmhouse and a long barn. She was too far away to see anyone, but she remembered Hyams mentioning a dairy farm in the vicinity. If nothing else, she would make for that and find the lane again.

It was a rougher walk than she estimated, full of foot-bruising stones, briars and muddy patches. Before she reached the line of trees at the edge of the pasture, she was regretting her decision.

She snagged her shirt and jeans in the barbed-wire fence when she slid between the strands, and before she straightened, she stepped in a very fresh, very thick puddle of manure.

Wezhardt cursed herself steadily as she crossed the pasture and climbed the fence on the opposite side. Following Blanski had been an impulsive, childish act, like the ingenue heroine in a teenage suspense novel.

Approaching the farmyard, she noted with appreciation the quaint style of the house, with its gabled roof, rooster-topped weather vane and old-fashioned lightning rod that had tiny iron cherubs welded to it.

She also noted the metal parabolic dish positioned at an eave.

True, television reception this far out in the hinterlands would be poor with just an antenna. Satellite dishes were quite common nowadays in Europe, especially in isolated villages where normal TV reception was blocked by mountains and valleys.

Chickens clucked and scratched in the yard, hunting between a tractor equipped with a six-disk plow and an old Volkswagen panel truck.

Wezhardt walked toward the back door, cupping her mouth with her hands. "Hello? I need directions back to the lane."

"How did you get here?" a voice snarled from behind her.

Wezhardt spun and saw a heavyset, thick-shouldered man in overalls emerging from the barn. He carried a three-tined pitchfork in one beefy but very clean hand.

The farmer glared at her darkly, not reacting to the smile she turned on him.

"I came across your pasture," she said, gesturing behind her.

"What the hell for?"

"I lost my way."

"Your way from what? There's nothing out there."

Wezhardt started to feel a tingle of fear and danger, so she told him a very sincere story about getting separated from her church group during a bird-watching expedition.

The farmer's flat face didn't change expression, but he slowly moved toward her, gazing at her intently. His eyes suddenly widened.

"Goddammit!" he cursed. "I don't believe it. *You!*"

With a surprising lightness of foot, the farmer leaped forward, thrusting the pitchfork like a spear.

Wezhardt barely managed to fall backward as a tine punctured her shirt and ripped a bleeding furrow just above her waist. She cried out in fear, in anger, in pain.

"You son of a bitch! Are you crazy?"

The farmer pressed forward and swept the pitchfork at her. Wezhardt ducked beneath it, and her fingers scooped up a handful of dirt that was rich with chicken droppings. She flung it upward, into the man's eyes.

As he spit, cursed and pawed at his face, Wezhardt kicked him between the legs. The farmer coughed out a strangled call for help and bent at the waist, dropping the pitchfork. Wezhardt turned and ran—straight into the muscular arms of a big man wearing a checked flannel shirt and faded jeans. His long blond hair was tied in a knot at the back of his head.

Wrestling her around, he hooked an arm up under her chin and bent her right wrist at an angle that brought a cry of pain from her.

"Dr. Wezhardt," he breathed into her ear, "you're much more attractive in the flesh than on video. Welcome to the Reich."

20

Over the years, Bolan had tracked human prey across terrain far more inhospitable than the German countryside. He had trailed the spoor of enemies through jungles, deserts and, more often than not, city streets.

Though his target was taking pains to cover his tracks by trying to keep to rocks and hard-packed earth, he might as well have been leaving a trail of bread crumbs for Bolan to follow.

He had figured out the timing; the pilot of the chopper had maybe a fifteen-minute head start, and no more than twenty. He had no idea where the man was going, but at least he was well on his way to someplace.

At ten-minute intervals, Bolan listened to the watch post frequency on the walkie-talkie. There were reports of feints on several fronts; a man in a truck with a microwave transmitter had driven blithely past an observation team. When chased down, he had meekly given himself up. An emitter transmitting a weak signal had been discovered less than two miles from the entrance road to Site 611.

None of the diversions could be ignored, even though Hyams's and Straub's people were scrambling all over the area. This kind of cat-and-mousing was a new form of terrorism in Bolan's experience.

Its sole purpose seemed to be generating fear. He was morally certain that Heine was somewhere close, enjoying it all immensely.

After about a half hour, Bolan reached the outer limits of the watch post's communication parameters, and he dropped the walkie-talkie into his war bag rather than having its awkward weight and shape hanging from a shoulder.

At the edge of a bog, Bolan stopped. The long reeds and marsh grass waved in the breeze. A few birds flapped up, and he heard the quack of ducks. Here and there, rising out of the shallow water, were grassy hillocks, like stepping-stones.

Bolan walked along the water's edge and found a place where the mud had been recently disturbed. It was a shallow indentation, already half-filled with dark water. He waded into the marsh at that point, carefully eyeing the reeds and cattails he pushed aside. He saw that several of the stalks had been broken.

When he reached the first of the overgrown hillocks, he noticed snapped-off stalks and uprooted weeds piled up over something, then stomped flat.

Kicking the stuff aside, he saw a folded white jumpsuit, the right sleeve bearing the same insignia as on the helicopter.

Bolan waded back into the marsh, heading for a low range of hills overlooking the bog. His prey had stripped off the jumpsuit for only one reason—he was too conspicuous in it, so he had changed to clothes that would make it easier for him to blend in with his surroundings. Changing clothes would have cost him some time, so the gap between Bolan and the hunted was narrowed.

Though he'd seen no one so far, Bolan assumed there had to be a few people around, farmers, fishermen or sheepherders. A man in a white jumpsuit would be noticed.

At the far edge of the marsh, Bolan found more tracks, and he followed them up the face of the hill. When he topped it, he saw a wide pasture spread out below. Grazing cows moved sluggishly through it. In the distance, he saw a barn and farmhouse. It had to be the dairy farm Hyams had described as the site's nearest neighbors.

A strip of woodland ran off to his left, bordering the farm property on its west side. Bolan made for the trees, assuming his prey would choose that route rather than exposing himself in the open expanse of pastureland.

The woods smelled fresh and clean after the heavy humidity of the bog. He found more and more signs of a man recently passing through, tracks and scuff marks, stepped-on tufts of grass, leaves dangling from broken stems.

The pilot appeared to be less concerned about throwing off pursuit, and the only reason for his confidence was that he was closing on his destination. The only possible safe haven was the dairy farm.

Rather than spend more time looking for signs of his quarry, Bolan increased his pace, heading through the woods in the direction of the farm. He reached a narrow footpath, angled away from it, dropped flat behind a tree and crawled forward until he reached a screen of shrubbery. Beyond the bushes, less than an eighth of a mile away, was the farmhouse and barn.

He pulled small, powerful binoculars from his war bag, and put them to his eyes.

Two men stood on the back steps of the farmhouse—one fair-haired, the other dark. Both were dressed in work clothes. He brought their faces into sharp focus. He recognized the blond man as the one who had escaped him at the Wust and Wimmer building.

Anticipation tingled through Bolan's blood. Step by step, he had followed the pilot to the main hardsite. Scanning the house, he saw something that made him unconsciously tense his muscles.

Protruding from the rear eave of the roof was a parabolic dish, at first glance nothing more frightening than a satellite television receiver. Bolan estimated it to be about five feet in diameter.

Another man emerged from the barn and spoke with the pair standing on the steps. He was wearing overalls and shouldering a pitchfork, but Bolan read his pedigree just the same.

Though there was no open flash of gun metal, Bolan knew it had to be there. He had no idea of the number of hardmen in the place, but it had to be increased by one. The pilot had led him on a circuitous route to the hardsite.

Under other circumstances, Bolan would have opted for a soft probe, to draw out the hardmen so he could get an estimate of the opposition. There was no time for that now, not even time to get back into communication range of the watch posts. Everything depended on stealth and strategy until he was sure of the killzone.

There was a soft crunch of leaves behind him. Bolan whirled, hand streaking for the Beretta.

ILONA WEZHARDT STRUGGLED, bit and kicked, but the big blond man dragged her into the house, through the kitchen, then pushed her up a narrow stairwell.

She tried to claw his eyes and put an elbow in his throat, but he outweighed her by at least a hundred pounds. He wrestled her up the steps, putting a knee against her rear and lifting.

He forced her up to the second floor and shoved her toward another flight of stairs, which led to a square opening in the ceiling. Wezhardt managed to sink her teeth deep into the man's wrist.

He cursed and spun her. "You mongrel bitch!"

He backhanded her across the face. The blow made a thousand multicolored stars flash before her eyes. She sagged in the man's grip, and she was roughly dragged up the steps, one hand tangled in her hair and the other holding her by the collar.

She was flung on the rough floorboards of a small attic room, a garret with only two windows, one at either end.

"What have we here, Sven?" a voice asked from the shadows.

"It's the American's whore," Sven replied. "He must really be desperate if he sends her on a suicide mission."

Wezhardt pushed herself into a sitting position and looked groggily around. An old man sat in a chair in front of one of the windows. He was backlit by the sunshine streaming in, and his features were indistinct, but she knew who he was, who he had to be.

"Heine," she muttered.

"Dr. Wezhardt," Heine said politely. "Since Sven tends to jump to conclusions, I don't accept his thesis of a suicide mission. So, what *are* you doing here?"

Wezhardt didn't reply. Sven prodded her in the side with a foot, right on the pitchfork wound. She cried out and struck at his leg with both fists.

"Enough!" Heine barked. "She is here, she is helpless, so

there is no need for further violence. At least for the moment. Go and bring up the first-aid kit.''

Sven hesitated, then left. Wezhardt stiffly climbed to her feet, one hand covering the bleeding cut in her side.

"I apologize for him," Heine said. "Sven can be a bit over-zealous and a little single-minded."

Wezhardt got a closer look at the man. Her first impression was of intensely penetrating blue eyes—intelligent eyes, all-seeing eyes, the eyes of a visionary. Or a demon.

"What have you done to the real owner of this place?" she demanded.

"Not a thing. You stand in his presence. I foreclosed on the mortgage of the tenants, which is my right. Though the Order's real-estate portfolio is not vast, it is diverse. We even own beach-front property in Miami. Rather ironic, is it not, owning the very buildings in which ancient Jews come to spend their waning years?"

Heine laughed softly, then said, "However, the question of what you are doing here has yet to be answered."

"We're on to you, Heine," Wezhardt said with an exaggerated calm. "You can't escape. The authorities are closing in even as we speak."

"Don't waste my time with such an obvious bluff, young woman. The authorities would not use you as a stalking horse, no matter how desperate their situation. No, I believe it is more likely you stumbled into my sphere, directed by the forces swirling around the American warrior and myself."

As he spoke, Wezhardt looked around the room. At the end nearest Heine was a small table. On it rested a portable computer terminal, not much larger than a laptop. It was connected by a pair of leads to a square, black metal box.

Her eyes followed a cable stretching from the box to the base of an input port in the wall. Her heart gave a great lurch when she saw the port was connected to the base of the satellite re-ceiver at the window. The dish itself was mounted on the exterior of the house.

Another cable, this one much thicker and coated with a heavier insulation, ran from the base of the receiver and disappeared down a hole drilled in the floor.

Heine had followed her visual inventory and smiled at the show of anxiety on her face.

"Yes," he said calmly. "That is the telemetry box built by Weisenburg, connected to a simple computer terminal. The dish itself is powered by a large generator in the cellar. Disabuse yourself of any doubt that the emitter doesn't have sufficient power to transmit the appropriate signals to the missile silo."

Wezhardt met his gaze, asking, "You haven't done it yet?"

"No."

"Why not?"

"Young woman, though your abilities and exotic looks intrigue me, you do not have the capacity to understand why I am doing anything."

Wezhardt backed away a step, breaking eye contact. She had the sense of a superhuman power about this man, as old as he was. He radiated an aura of a deep inner strength. The total effect was something chilling, as though she were in the company of an alien.

"You're an evil bastard," she said hoarsely.

Heine shook his head. "Good and evil have no real existence as anything but mental or societal concepts. Have you ever known a totally good or totally evil person? Of course not. Angels may not be my allies, but neither are they yours. At any rate, I do not deal in philosophical abstracts, but in necessities."

"Necessities," she echoed sarcastically. "What sort of necessities can you see in planning the deaths of so many people?"

Sven chose that moment to return, carrying a small white case. Heine gestured. "Lift up your shirt. Let Sven treat you. A cut like that could easily become infected out here."

Wezhardt hesitated, glancing from the old man to Sven, then raised the blood-soaked shirt to just beneath her breasts. Sven, with a surprisingly gentle touch, began swabbing the wound.

Heine spoke, in a low, patient, almost kindly tone.

"The forces that control the world are dangerously unbalanced. My former pupil began the slide, and others continued it. I do what I do to restore the balance before I leave this incarnation. When I return, in a new vessel, order will be restored to the world. It will be at peace.''

"A world of masters and slaves," Wezhardt said.

"You disapprove?"

"Goddamn right I disapprove. So would anyone who was sane.''

"Young woman, I am the sanest man you have ever met. The forces flowing through me are not what you could call sane, insane, good or evil. Those are human concepts.''

"Are you telling me you're not human?"

"Oh, the flesh I wear is certainly human enough, though it is failing me. I'm not concerned. I've had a long life in this incarnation, a full one, but I knew it couldn't last forever.''

Sven smeared a stinging antiseptic onto her wound, and she bit back a cry of pain.

"I don't know about incarnations," she said, "but I know people won't stand for your kind of world. It's been tried before and it never works.''

Heine chuckled. "Every government in existence wants my kind of world. Liberty, freedom, democracy are no more than labels to keep the sheep content. What do you think will happen after the missiles are launched? The course of world events will be changed forever. New laws of suppression will be enacted, and no one will object because they will think they are in place for their protection. The mass of humanity will be guided through various channels, and they won't even be aware of it. And even if a few do realize they are being manipulated, they won't care.''

"What's in all of this for you, Heine? What's your reward?"

"Do you have a thousand years for me to explain? No, so let me put it in a very simplistic fashion. I am arresting the tide, changing the flow of destiny. In my next incarnation, all the rules will be *my* rules.''

Wezhardt's mind reeled. The man was a raving psychotic— he had to be—but there was such a ring of unshakable certainty in his tone, his bearing, she felt blind terror filling her.

"All the people you'll kill to achieve this," she said, "how can that help you?''

"Sacrifices." Heine leaned forward. "What do you think the

purpose was of all the concentration camps, the motivation behind the so-called Final Solution? Blood and souls rendered to the forces I serve."

Sven bandaged the wound on her waist. Wezhardt was trembling now, clenching her fists, her nails biting into her palms.

"Then why wait?" she asked, pitching her voice low to disguise the quaver. "Get it over with."

Heine waved his hands through the air, as if moving them in time to some melody only he could hear. "The terror must rise, the fear must build to a crescendo. I feel it out there, pulsing in the wind, building like a pyramid. You feel it, too. When the capstone of terror is put into place, then—"

Heine reached out and dragged a forefinger along the computer keyboard like a pianist running through the scales.

"When it finally happens, it will be almost a relief. Also I must wait for the American warrior to return the Dag to me."

"What? You can't really expect him to do that!"

"I do indeed. I realize now the Dag was destined to go to him."

He tilted his head back, closed his eyes and sighed. "And it is his destiny to die with me."

Wezhardt stared at Heinrich Heine. She knew, without really knowing how she knew, that the old man was speaking the truth.

Addressing Sven, he said, "When the American arrives, do not molest him. Allow him to enter."

From below came a rumble and the high-pitched whine of a turbine warming up.

Sven smiled. "The generator is on-line, sir."

Heine nodded and made a dismissive gesture with one hand. "Take her away, Sven. Put her with the others."

21

The man with the gun was dressed in old, baggy trousers, a shapeless cotton work shirt and a gray cap. He was holding a small Titan pistol, deadly at such close range, leveled at Bolan's head. He was standing about three feet away.

"Come on, American," he said. "Go for it."

Slowly Bolan moved his hand away from the butt of the Beretta.

The man grinned. "You've got good sense."

His English was impeccable, touched with a slight Australian accent. "Stand up. Slowly. And I do mean slowly."

Bolan did as he was told, rising to his feet in stages. As he did, he turned his back to the man.

"Turn around."

Bolan didn't move.

"I said turn around, you bastard!"

The man took a step forward and grabbed the left shoulder of Bolan's coat. He allowed himself to be pulled in that direction, then he whirled.

The edge of his stiffened left hand slashed down hard on the clump of ganglia on the inner wrist of the man's gun hand. The man cried out in surprised pain.

He tried to turn away, to bring the little gun into play, but Bolan turned with him, locking the man's right wrist under his left arm and heaving up on it with all his upper-body strength.

The arm broke at the elbow with a wet crunching sound.

The pain was so sudden, so overwhelming, the man couldn't even scream.

As the Titan dropped from nerve-numbed fingers, Bolan maintained the pressure on the captured arm. He forced the man down on the ground, onto his back.

Disengaging the grip, Bolan pulled the Beretta in a lightning-fast draw. He had the silenced barrel on a direct line with the man's head, just in case he regained enough presence of mind to scream.

The man didn't. He gaped up at Bolan in terror, lips writhing over his teeth in silent agony. The soldier looked him over, saw that his shoes and pants were wet and realized he was the pilot he had been trailing for the past hour.

Though he'd carried a gun, he obviously wasn't an experienced hardman. Otherwise he never would have gotten close enough for Bolan to execute a standard frontal handgun disarm. He should have stuck with playing with his joystick.

"Tell me what I want to know," Bolan said quietly. "Just a few things, that's all."

Supporting his broken arm with his left hand, holding it out straight, the pilot's face was filmed with sweat. "Like what?"

"How many men are at the farm?"

The man looked away. "Come on, mate, you know I can't—"

The Beretta coughed, and a 9 mm parabellum round kicked up dirt between the man's thighs, barely a quarter of an inch from the crotch of his trousers.

"Tell me," Bolan demanded, "or next shot, you're a eunuch."

The pilot told. "Maybe a dozen, maybe a little more. Some guys have been deployed around the area."

"And the emitter?"

"I don't know, I just fly."

"Is Heine there?"

"I don't know that, either. I'm not paid to take a roll call."

Bolan walked around behind him. The man tried to follow him with his eyes.

"Face front," Bolan commanded.

The Beretta's sound suppressor came down sharply, denting the crown of the pilot's cap. He fell over sidewise, unconscious.

Bolan made a quick examination of his head, found no sign of a fracture, and stripped off the man's belt, shoes and socks.

He bound and gagged the pilot, then dragged him beneath a clump of bushes.

Glancing at his watch, Bolan wondered if the pilot was allotted a certain period of time to ditch the chopper and make his way to the farm, and if he didn't show up at that time, if a contingency plan would go into effect.

He doubted a search party would be sent out looking for the pilot, but the hardmen could very well assume he'd been captured and disclose the location of their base and make a pre-emptive move.

Peering through the binoculars again, he watched the movements of the men in the farmyard. Unlike the pilot, these men were disciplined and combat-worthy soldiers, equal to any he had encountered before.

Though they were pretending to be casual, they were watchful and wary. He considered changing clothes with the pilot and trying to bluff his way into the compound, but he instantly discarded the notion. The hardmen were too alert, too suspicious.

Scanning the house again, he saw movement between the front and rear doors. Two wide wooden covers slanted out from the foundation and formed a pair of trapdoors. It was an old-fashioned storm cellar, and a man was pushing one cover aside and climbing out.

A toolbox was in one hand and he shut the cover behind him, leaning over and latching it shut. Bolan moved the glasses to the right and studied the barn. It was a long, rambling building, several hundred yards from the house, but there appeared to be decent cover until within a few feet of a rear corner.

Taking off his jacket and hat, he opened the war bag and removed a tin of combat cosmetics. He applied green stripes to his face and hands, then moved off at an angle through the woods, quickly crossing the footpath and entering the undergrowth again.

He was certain guards had been posted, so his progress was slow and silent. It was another long run, against unknown odds, against time, against death.

Bolan made his way through the woods until he was directly opposite the back corner of the barn. He waited a long moment, straining his ears and eyes in search of hardmen that might come between him and his target. He heard and saw nothing, then eased himself up and around, and was inside the barn.

A long concrete-floored breezeway ran its entire length. Stalls were on either side, but only a few housed cows. They paid no attention to him as he walked through the barn, keeping his body to one side of the breezeway.

Reaching a wooden ladder that led to the hayloft, Bolan considered climbing it, then his eyes rested on a shape covered by a sheet of mildewed canvas, pushed up against the wall.

Bolan tugged away the canvas. Encased in a large transparent plastic bag were a man and a woman, pressed together face-to-face. The woman was middle-aged, with a gentle face. She wore a dirndl skirt and a deep blue blouse.

The man looked to be a few years older, dressed like a farmer. Both of them bore knife slashes across their throats.

Bolan didn't know who they were, but he was sure they were owners of the farm, simple, decent folk who had something the Order wanted, and it had been taken from them in one swift, ruthless move.

He had seen too many innocent dead, trapped in hellzones all over the world, to feel much anger or horror. But he was saddened by the waste, by the casual, almost contemptuous way these people's lives had been snuffed out.

Bolan's battle instincts were still on red alert, so when the man dropped from the hayloft, he wasn't caught completely off guard.

The soldier let himself collapse beneath the weight of the man, then twisted sideways. The thrust with the sharp tines of the pitchfork in the man's hand missed him.

He was the big, powerful man in overalls he'd glimpsed through the binoculars. The man hefted the pitchfork and made a stabbing motion again. Bolan didn't dare end it with the Beretta. Even a silenced shot might be heard in the quiet of the farmyard.

Bolan dived under the tines, catching the man at the knees and toppling him like a tree. He jumped on him, driving a knee to his stomach and raising the Beretta for a clubbing blow to the man's head.

The man's hand darted out with the speed of a striking snake and closed around Bolan's right wrist, immobilizing it. The German was strong, and he struggled with a savage ferocity. He opened his mouth to shout. Bolan didn't waste time trying to outmuscle him.

Stiffening his left hand, he curled the fingers inward toward the palm, locked his wrist and forearm and delivered a leopard's-paw strike to the tip of the man's nose.

His head snapped back, his nose smashed flat and spewing crimson. His eyes rolled up, showing only the whites, as bone chips were driven past the sinus cavities and into the brain's frontal lobes. He went limp beneath Bolan, faint gargling sounds issuing from his open mouth.

Patting the man down quickly, Bolan found no other weapon. He presumed an order had been issue to avoid gunfire, since it might be heard by any authorities in the area. Noise traveled far over the meadows and pastures.

Around the man's neck was a small walkie-talkie. Judging by its size, the range was extremely limited, probably just to the farmhouse.

Bolan doubted the man had the time to make a report before jumping him, but that didn't mean he didn't make regular check-in calls. The time for the check-in could be thirty seconds or thirty minutes away.

Dragging him by the straps of the overalls, Bolan laid the hardman next to the bodies of the middle-aged couple and spread out the canvas to cover him. Then he turned his attention back to the house.

He studied it from just inside the barn door and heard and saw nothing from within the house. Satisfied that the yard was unobserved, Bolan moved out. He crossed the expanse of the ground between the barn and the house in a semicrouch, sacrificing stealth for the greater speed of long strides.

He reached the cellar door, which was secured by an outside hasp and padlock. He leaned close to the door before touching the lock. He heard nothing on the other side.

With a hooked pick taken from the war bag, Bolan probed the lock until it opened with a faint click. He froze, listening again, then lifted one door panel and slid beneath it, onto a short flight of rough-hewn stone steps.

If someone was lurking down there with a gun, he knew he was presenting a perfect target, outlined by the brief flash of sunlight flooding the cellar. Nothing happened.

Bolan risked the needle beam from his penlight. All he saw was a typical farmhouse cellar: free-standing shelves holding jars of pickled vegetables, a few tools, an old washing machine and various odds and ends. He moved across the cellar, his feet making no noise on the hard-packed earth. A rickety wooden stairway stretched up to a closed door.

The soldier heard people moving above him, the muted murmur of male voices and the creak of floorboards. The penlight showed him the junction box on the wall, a cluster of electrical cables with frayed insulation running down from above, feeding into a metal sleeve. All the cables looked old.

He also saw a flexible conduit of bright, shiny aluminum snaking along the rafters, over to the wall, and terminating at a circuit box attached to the cast-iron casing of an electric generator.

The generator was bolted to a pair of two-by-fours, and they were sunk into a clean, whitish gray concrete slab. The generator looked brand-new.

Looking it over, Bolan saw it possessed considerable amperage. The lever on the fuse box was up, in the Off position. The generator wasn't connected to the main junction box. It was hooked to a separate line entirely, so it hadn't been installed simply for emergencies.

The door at the top of the stairs suddenly opened and a naked light bulb overhead blazed with light.

Bolan glided swiftly behind a shelf. Peering between dusty jars of preserves, he watched a squat, crew-cut man tramp down the steps, speaking to someone in a room above.

The man walked over to the generator and opened the panel to the fuse box. He worked a priming handle up and down for a few seconds, then, shutting the panel, he threw down the lever and the generator rumbled to life. The loud, high-pitched whine of the turbine filled the cellar. The jars on the shelves started to shimmy.

The man moved to the foot of the stairs, and he and someone Bolan couldn't see exchanged shouts. The man stood at the foot of the stairs, looking upward. Another shout from above elicited a thumbs-up reaction, and he turned back to the throbbing generator.

A jar fell from a high shelf. The sound of glass shattering was audible even over the steady whine. The man's head snapped around, his eyes widening as he glimpsed the dark figure crouching behind the shelf.

The light from the overhead bulb gleamed on polished gunmetal as he unleathered a pistol.

The Beretta spit out a pair of 9 mm slugs, punching twin paths through the man's chest, barely a finger's width apart. He went down heavily, striking the back of his head against the hard metal surface of the generator.

Bolan crossed the cellar quickly, examining the man in the rough work clothes. The Glock was still in his hand.

"Gunter!" a voice shouted from above.

Bolan had no choice but to gamble. Stepping to the generator, he nudged a numbered knob to a lower setting, and the rumbling whine decreased in volume.

"What's going on?" the voice demanded in German.

Bolan understood the simple query and, counting on the softening noise of the generator to muffle his voice, replied, "It was nothing."

His response evidently satisfied the man, because he heard footsteps going away from the cellar, then the opening and shutting of a door. Bolan started up the steps, touching the wooden risers with only the balls of his feet.

He walked into a spacious, rustic kitchen. The door leading to the outside was closed; he stepped over and locked it. He went to the window over the sink and parted the chintz curtains.

At first he saw no one, then a mercenary moved into his field of vision from around the corner of the house. He was holding a walkie-talkie to his ear and speaking over it.

The hardman had his back turned to him, so Bolan couldn't

hear what he was saying, but he appeared to be growing agitated. He stared at the barn and continued to speak into the walkie-talkie.

The man cast a glance toward the house, and Bolan moved back from the window a bit. He watched as the hardman pocketed the walkie-talkie, pulled a Glock from his waistband and began a quick walk toward the barn.

Bolan knew what was going to happen next.

The curtain was about to rise on the last act of the nightmare.

A clatter of feet descending the stairs from the second floor drew Bolan away from the window.

He heard two voices, a man's and a woman's. He recognized Wezhardt's voice, and rather than devoting time to wondering how she'd ended up here, Bolan ducked back into the cellar, standing on the top step and closing the door behind him. He left it open a crack.

The tall blond mercenary and Wezhardt appeared in the kitchen. The weed of suspicion growing in Bolan's mind wilted when he saw the hardman had Wezhardt's right arm crooked painfully behind her back. He manhandled her to the door and ordered her to open it.

Wezhardt had trouble unlocking it, and the mercenary applied more pressure to her arm, dragging a cry of pain and protest from her.

Bolan's finger tensed on the Beretta's trigger, but a shot now would endanger Wezhardt. The round that accounted for the hardman could easily pierce the woman, as well.

Wezhardt got the door open and was propelled through it, down the steps. She stumbled, nearly going to her knees, but the blond man yanked her to her feet by a hand tangled in her hair.

Bolan watched, teeth clenching in anger, as he stepped into the kitchen. The back door hung open, and he peered around the frame.

The hardman who'd been on the way to the barn stopped midway at a shout from the mercenary. The two exchanged words, then the man walked back and grabbed Wezhardt's left arm. They began dragging her to the barn.

Bolan thought of the dead couple locked in a cold embrace inside the plastic shroud, and he left the house in a sprint. He couldn't ignore the possibility that a watcher from another floor could see him, but he disregarded it. Reaching the tractor attached to the six-disk plow, he climbed into the saddle.

The two mercenaries had reached the barn entrance and were struggling with Wezhardt. She was kicking at one and shouting. The man put a hand over her mouth, and she was dragged out of sight.

Bolan turned the ignition key and pressed the starter button. The engine caught on the first try. Putting it into gear, he directed the tractor toward the barn.

The two hardmen appeared at the open barn door, gaping in astonishment. Both drew pistols from behind their backs, but they held their fire. As Bolan had figured, they were under orders to avoid gunplay.

Crouching behind the wheel, Bolan turned the disk plows on high speed, and the whirling motion set up a hum. Pressing a lever, he lifted the blades about a foot and a half from the ground and opened the throttle.

The tractor roared into the barn, and the pair of mercenaries raced ahead of it. The metal framework of the plow was so wide, the tractor had to be kept on a straight course. If bullets were flung Bolan's way, there was no leeway for evasive maneuvering.

However, its width prevented the hardmen from getting out of the tractor's path by putting their backs against the wall or the stall doors.

Bolan threaded the vehicle through the breezeway, and by the time the mercenaries had managed to run to the rear of the barn, they were disobeying the no-gunplay edict.

The blond man turned and aimed his pistol. Bolan ducked as low as he could, steering more by instinct than sight as he drove out the rear of the barn.

The sound of the Glock firing was less loud than the whang of a bullet ricocheting off the front of the tractor. Bolan jerked the wheel in the hardman's direction and raised his head and gun hand just enough to find and acquire a target.

He brought the blond man into the Beretta's sights, but the tractor jounced just as he squeezed the trigger. The bullet caught the mercenary high on the right shoulder. It wasn't a serious wound, or even incapacitating, but he staggered, legs tangling, and he fell into the tractor's path.

Bolan tried to navigate around him. The tractor's fat tires missed him by a fractional margin, but the plow swung wide on the coupling and the sharp steel disks caught him. He felt the tractor shudder as the blades struck flesh and bone.

A bullet bounced off the hood of the tractor, only a few inches from Bolan's face, metal slivers stinging his cheek. Yanking the wheel, he turned the tractor in the opposite direction from which the shot had come.

Manipulating the plow handle, he lowered the blades, and the whirling disks bit into the ground, sending up plumes of dust.

Bolan leaped from the saddle, rolled and got to his feet, keeping the tractor, now running wild, between him and the second gunman. He glimpsed him crouching about fifty feet away, peering through the shifting planes of dust.

He also glimpsed Wezhardt, racing full tilt from the barn, the pitchfork held in both hands.

The roar of the tractor's engine and the clatter of the plow covered the sound of her rushing approach. Without breaking stride, Wezhardt plunged the tines of the pitchfork into the mercenary's upper back, just above his shoulders.

The hardman screamed, fell forward, then struggled to his feet, his left hand reaching behind him. He looked like a pain-crazed insect, transfixed by a giant pin. With the gun in his right hand, he drew a bead on Wezhardt.

The silenced Beretta coughed out a round. The mercenary staggered backward, dropping the Glock, trying to stem the flow from a pulsing throat wound.

He fell, but he didn't hit the ground. The blunt end of the pitchfork's shaft dug into the soft earth, and the mercenary hung there, his body poised on the tines at a forty-five-degree angle.

The tractor continued on its wild course and smashed into a fence, then stalled.

Bolan glanced around for more opposition and saw none.

He found Wezhardt standing near the undergrowth. Fright was fresh in her eyes. He took her in his arms, but he couldn't afford the time to hold her until her trembling ceased.

"It's not over," he said.

He didn't need to say more. Wezhardt pushed herself away and began to talk, telling him about Heine in the attic room with the transmitter and telemetry box and the generator in the cellar. She had no idea of how many mercenaries might be around.

"Ordinarily I'd send you out of harm's way—"

Nostrils flaring, Wezhardt said, "You need my help."

He nodded. "I do. Heine might hit the launch-enabling transmission any second. He might have already done it."

"No. He's waiting for you."

Bolan's eyebrows rose.

"He's waiting for you to bring the Dag to him," she explained. She took a breath. "He's waiting for you to die with him."

"He's liable to have a long wait."

"He's given orders that you're not to be killed when you arrive. To do so would interfere with destiny."

"We can use that. All his men pulling sentry duty will probably be called back to base, if they're not on their way already."

Bolan plucked a Glock from the ground and handed it to her. Detaching a grenade from his combat harness, he gave her quick instructions on how to use it. He outlined his plan briefly and tersely.

Wezhardt's lips compressed in fear, but she gave a grim nod of understanding. She crouched out of sight, holding the grenade with both hands.

Bolan left her and walked through the barn. He was taking a big chance, relying on the help of a citizen, but it was her country and her future at stake. He was also assuming a risk by not trying to contact Hyams and Straub, but it was a necessary risk.

He would always act independently of the authorities when the circumstances demanded it. That was why he was chosen for this mission, and Hal Brognola knew it, even if the responsibility for its failure fell on his shoulders.

Bolan stopped at the open door long enough to put a full load into the Beretta before slipping it into the shoulder holster. He took two of the grenades from the harness, depressed the finger levers and pulled the safety pins.

Gripping them tightly in both hands, he walked out into the farmyard, striding for the back door of the house. He knew he was being watched. He was counting on it.

"Freeze!"

"Stop where you are!"

Two pairs of men, one to his left and one to his right, stood at the border of the yard. Glocks were in their fists, the barrels trained on him.

Bolan kept walking in measured, deliberate strides.

"Stop, you son of a bitch!"

"Get those hands up!"

The shouted commands carried notes of panic.

The men came closer, moving warily, trying to encircle him. When he was abreast of the VW panel truck, Bolan raised his hands, then opened them. The levers of the grenades fell.

All four men swore, yelled and stared to retreat.

Bolan tossed one of the V-40s toward the men on his right and the other beneath the truck. The double concussions hurled geysers of dirt into the air. Gravel and clods of earth rained to the ground.

The grenade detonating beneath the truck raised the rear end three feet and split the gas tank. The fuel caught fire and exploded. Tongues of fire lapped out; chunks of metal spun across the yard.

A wave of burning gasoline engulfed one of the men, and he screamed in terror and pain. He fell to the ground and rolled frantically, beating at the flames.

Bolan drew the Desert Eagle and the Beretta at the same time, crossed his arms over his chest and blasted through the smoke, dust and flame. He continued walking toward the house, but his eyes were constantly moving.

The grenades had accounted for one man, his bullets for two others. The man splashed with gasoline was still rolling wildly in the dirt.

Bolan reached the back steps. A man appeared in the open doorway, aiming a pistol with both hands.

"Drop it!" he shouted.

Bolan kept walking.

"Drop it!" the man shouted again. "Or I drop you!"

The Beretta sneezed out a single bullet, and the man in the doorway reeled backward into the kitchen.

Bolan walked up the steps and looked around the kitchen. The man lay on the floor near a garbage pail, leaking fluids, his eyes wide open and glassy.

The order Heine had given not to have him shot down could be pushed only so far. Whatever obedience the hardmen gave Heine wouldn't supersede their survival instinct. Only a man too stupid to live would stand making threats to an armed intruder that he wasn't allowed to carry through.

Bolan doubted the next mercenary he encountered would command him to drop his weapon first.

A dark man-shape appeared in the hallway off the kitchen, and the staccato beat of an autocarbine filled the house. Bolan rolled to the floor and to one side.

The steel-jacketed volley raked the kitchen, disintegrating glass, smashing woodwork, ripping wall boarding to splinters. The mercenary was good, tracking his target with a continuous stream of lead.

Bolan gave him a triple burst from the Beretta, which drilled through the man's gut and upward into his chest. He went down, firing the last few rounds into the ceiling. Climbing to his feet, Bolan stepped over the body and continued through the house, reaching a flight of stairs that led to the second floor.

With his back to the wall, Bolan cautiously climbed the steps, the Beretta leading the way. Several of the steps creaked beneath his weight. Before he set foot on the second floor, he went prone on the steps and simply listened.

He heard nothing for what felt like a very long time, then came the almost imperceptible rustle of cloth. A man was standing on the other side of a wall he would have to pass to get on the second floor. Bolan holstered the Beretta and took aim with the Desert Eagle, gauging where a man would stand in order to stage an ambush.

Bolan squeezed the trigger of the .44, and sent three 240-grain rounds blasting through the wall. He heard wood shredding and splitting as the bullets sought their target on the other side of the barrier.

By the time he heard the grunt of pain and surprise, he was up and moving. A man lay on his face, blood welling from three holes in his back, an autocarbine cradled in lifeless hands.

There was a second hardman in the room, and Bolan didn't see him until his right leg slashed up in a karate kick, the limb moving incredibly fast. The hardman missed his intended target, but he had a Fairbairn-Sykes combat knife backing his play. The blade darted at Bolan's vitals.

The Executioner countered the move, slamming the barrel of the pistol into his assailant's solar plexus and seizing the wrist of the knife hand and twisting.

The mercenary was ambidextrous. He let go of the stiletto in his right hand and caught it with his left, and began a thrust.

The Desert Eagle roared with a spurt of flame. The heavy slug caught the man in the center of the chest, the impact halting the forward motion of the knife. Bolan released him, and the man flopped wetly onto his back.

Easing back into the hallway, the soldier checked his watch. The time he'd allotted for Wezhardt to make her move was almost up. Action now was everything.

Padding through the hallway, he saw a short flight of steps reaching up to a closed door panel in the ceiling. Bolan put his foot on the first step. It creaked, and he waited for a reaction. It wasn't long in coming.

The panel opened about three inches. Someone poked a gun barrel through the opening and loosed a burst of rounds.

Bolan had ducked back toward a window, as the autofire chewed its way toward him. He didn't return the fire.

Fitting his fingers beneath the window sash, he slid it up. There was a small, shingled overhang below, and he climbed out, using a drainpipe as a handhold.

The edge of the roof was level with his chin, and he heaved

himself up, using only the strength in his legs and the levering power of one arm.

The roof slanted at a steep angle, so it was impossible to stand. He crawled toward the roofline, hoping the machine gun in the attic room would continue to chatter and mask the sound of his movements.

He topped the crest of the roof just as the gunfire ceased, and he stopped moving, bending to listen. He heard voices muttering from below, but he couldn't make out how many or what was being said.

Straddling the ridge, Bolan scooted forward, trying to keep his feet from grating against the shingles. When he reached the chimney, he stood. From his war bag he took a coil of rope and wrapped it around the base of the chimney, affixing it to the bricks with a small grappling hook.

Holding the slack in his left hand, he continued moving along the roofline. His progress felt agonizingly slow.

At the end of the roof, facing the front of the house, Bolan leaned forward, looking down at a window tucked between the eaves. An iron lightning rod rose from the juncture. He held on to it as he bent.

Though it was only a few feet below him, the window was small, barely large enough to admit a man of his size. By feel, he looped the rope's slack through a metal ring sewn into the leather at the back of his combat harness. He gave the line an experimental tug. It was secure around the chimney.

It was a dangerous maneuver. He could lose his grip and fall, or not be fast enough and get shot. But rather than stay perched on the roof and go through a litany of things that could go wrong, Bolan looped the rope around the lightning rod, flattened out and edged his body forward, allowing his legs to dangle.

He was making the assumption that the men in the garret below were on the alert for an attack from the second floor, and felt fairly safe from an assault from above or the outside.

Bolan moved carefully, his left hand gripping the lightning rod. Bracing his feet against the top frame of the window, he slowly eased his weight onto the rope.

The line jerked, and one of his feet slipped. For a moment, he kicked empty air. He found his footing again, and he inched farther out and down. Using his legs like springs, he pushed himself away from the front of the house. He adjusted the slack on the rope and dropped nearly a foot.

Swinging forward, both feet impacted flatly against the windowpane. It smashed inward with a loud clash and jangle. Through the flying splinters and shards of glass, Bolan fell to his knees inside a dimly lit room that ran the length of the house. A man stood near the far end, whirling at the racket of shattering glass. The autocarbine in his right hand stuttered.

Using the momentum of his fall, Bolan somersaulted beneath the stream of slugs, and when he came out of it, he was working the Desert Eagle. The noise of the Heckler & Koch was swallowed by the deeper, louder booms of the pistol.

Bolan felt a shock of impact against the meat of his right shoulder, and he knew a bullet had gouged a furrow through flesh and muscle. He willed himself to keep squeezing the .44's trigger.

The man with the carbine suddenly sprouted punctures in his face and head, and he careened backward violently. He slammed against the wall and fell forward, curled around the autocarbine. He never moved again.

Bolan got to his feet, feeling wet warmth slide down his arm, slicking the grip of the Desert Eagle.

A man was seated in a wheelchair at a computer console, his left hand resting lightly on the keyboard. Glancing at the dead gunman, he said, "Thank you. He needed to be executed for disobeying my orders not to shoot at you."

"Heine."

Heinrich Heine regarded him with a gracious, almost deferential smile.

"I'm told your name is Blanski," he said. "That is no name for such a fierce warrior."

Bolan approached him cautiously, gun held at arm's length, on a direct line with the man's hairless skull.

"Get away from that keyboard, Heine."

"At this point in our relationship," the old man said, "there is no harm in confiding your real name to me."

"What's in a name?"

Heine's mouth twitched in disappointment. "Still, I can see that you spring from superb Aryan stock."

"I won't tell you again. Get away from that board."

Heine laughed. "You don't have the stomach to shoot someone in my state."

"I don't, but if it's a choice between you or hundreds of thousands of people, I'll pull this trigger."

Heine kept his hand poised, vulturelike, over the keys. He gave Bolan a long, silent, speculative stare.

Bolan returned the stare, and he couldn't remember if he'd ever before seen such venomous eyes in a human being. He understood the terrible danger of this man.

He was no posturing bully, no deranged terrorist dreamer. Heinrich Heine was a dedicated man, exuding all the qualities of greatness that bred Alexanders, Napoleons, Caesars.

And Hitlers.

There was a brilliance about him, but it was warped all out of shape and bent to serve distorted ends. His mind and his imagination were devoted to hate, his sensitivity consecrated to serve twisted cruelty, reason turned to egomaniacal psychosis.

"The manner in which you've outmaneuvered me over the past few days is impressive," Heine declared. He could have been having a polite conversation in a drawing room. "I should have realized earlier that we were destined to share this moment, and I apologize for tasking you."

Distantly Bolan could hear the generator throbbing in the cellar. He looked at Heine's left hand. The old man noticed the eye action and smiled.

"Oh, yes. The sequence has already been input into the system. All I need do now is press the Enter key."

Bolan estimated it would take less than one second for the sequence to be fed from the computer to the telemetry box. Another second for the box to send the electronic data to the emitter and transmit the signal. The dish was already powered up, so another three seconds would be required for the microwave beam to travel three miles and talk to the computers on the missiles.

A total of five seconds would decide the course of history for hundreds of years to come.

"Drop your weapon," Heine said, his voice rising sharply. "Drop it at your feet and kick it away from you. *Now.*"

Bolan let the Desert Eagle fall to the floor.

"Now your satchel."

As Bolan slipped the strap of the war bag over his head, his hand dipped inside it and closed around a long smooth object. The bag dropped to the floor, but Bolan held the Dag in his hand.

He held it up, over his heart. Heine's body quivered as if he'd received an electric shock. He almost removed his hand from the keyboard, but he checked the motion.

"Give that to me." Heine's eyes shone bright.

"Like hell," Bolan said. "This is my property."

He turned his wrist, and Heine's eyes followed every motion of the Dag.

"My blood is on it. It's mine now."

Heine shot him a glare of pure hatred, but there was fear mixed in with it. He stretched out a trembling hand, leaning over the armrest of the wheelchair, but he kept his left hand on the keyboard. An aspirated stream of German hissed from between his lips.

Bolan didn't understand a word. He said, "It was given to me to safeguard. That's a trust I won't betray. Honor Is Loyalty, remember?"

Heine snarled, his eyes narrowing to slits. "Yes, I do."

His eyes fixed on Bolan's, his right hand dipped inside his coat and came out clutching a Walther P-38.

"You will give me the Dag," he said, speaking slowly and emphasizing each word. "Or I will kill you and wrest it from your dead hands."

"Why not do that in the first place?"

A glimmer of uncertainty flickered in Heine's eyes.

"You're afraid, aren't you?" Bolan asked. "You're afraid that if I have the Dag, there is a reason for it, and if you kill me, you might kill its power."

"You will give it to me, or I will transmit the signal."

"You'll do that anyway. Why should I make things easy for you?"

Lips peeled back from his gums, Heine spit, *"Schwein!"*

His knuckle whitened on the trigger of the Walther.

The sound of the explosion in the cellar wasn't overwhelmingly loud, but it was loud enough. Bolan felt the shock waves through the soles of his feet, and the concussion shook the foundation of the house. Loose objects in the garret fell over and clattered to the floor.

Heine punched the keyboard with a triumphant cry, then he did a wild-eyed double take. He hit the keys again, then he screamed.

The old man threw his head back and screamed. His eyes were wide with panic, with something more than panic. Without aiming, he fired the Walther.

Bolan rolled aside, at the same time hurling the Dag in a sweeping side arc of his right arm.

The relic was heavy, poorly balanced, but the point of the center blade made a crunching sound as it embedded itself in Heine's breastbone.

Heine stared down at the object impaling his chest. The Walther thudded to the floor. Shaking hands rose to grasp the hilt. He didn't try to pull it out; he simply held the Dag, fingers caressing and fondling the stone hilt. He lifted his face and looked at Bolan, a silent question in his eyes.

"Ilona Wezhardt," Bolan told him. "A good person, a good German. She threw a grenade into the cellar where you keep your generator and cut the power to the transmitter."

Heine's eyelids drooped. He chuckled, then grimaced in pain. Head bowed, he whispered something in English. Bolan leaned down to hear.

"What did you say?"

"I said that perhaps we will meet again, under different circumstances."

"Unlikely, Heine."

"In our next incarnations. Perhaps we'll even fight on the same side."

"Even more unlikely."

Heine didn't hear him. The demigod of Thule no longer looked like a man who commanded the forces of destiny.

He looked like a dead old man.

Bolan retrieved the Desert Eagle and before he left the attic room, he expended a round on the telemetry box, turning it into a mass of split metal and shattered silicon circuitry.

The house was on fire by the time Bolan reached the ground floor. The grenade had ignited something flammable in the cellar. Smoke lay in heavy sheets, and flames were licking up between the floorboards.

Detecting the metallic odor of propane, Bolan remembered the kitchen had a gas stove. A stray shot had to have severed the gas line. He quickly left by the front door.

Wezhardt was waiting for him in the yard. He cut off her questions and the noises of sympathy she made over his wound and hustled her away from the house. They had gotten about thirty yards when the gas line ignited. A thundering column of flame nearly fifty feet high mushroomed from the house. Rolling balls of fire billowed up into the blue sky, and burning debris was hurled in all directions.

Loud, ear-knocking explosions rocked the quiet countryside as ammunition let go somewhere in the wreckage.

Bolan looked at the monstrous, crackling pyre roaring into the heavens.

"That ought to attract somebody's attention," he said.

EPILOGUE

There wasn't much to do after that.

Verfassungschutz operatives hunted down the few mercenaries still in the fields around Site 611. There was very little shooting, though several had to be clubbed unconscious with gun butts. Most of the mercenaries surrendered.

Within ninety minutes, all of them had been apprehended and were talking. The identities and locations of all Thule contacts and supply dumps were turned over to the German intelligence service.

Raiding parties poured out of Verfassungschutz bureaus all over western Germany. In due course, the innocent dupes, driven by greed rather than politics, would be sorted out from the truly guilty. In the interim, anyone with any connections to the Order of Thule was suspect.

By sundown, the crisis appeared over.

At the farm, the flames had been doused, and men in oxygen masks and back tanks were kicking through the blackened, smoking debris. There was very little left of the house. Most of it was scattered across several acres.

Mack Bolan and Ilona Wezhardt watched the search operation, leaning against a Land Rover. Both of them were quiet. Bolan's shoulder wound had been treated by a medic and no longer throbbed.

It was superficial, more unsightly than critical. The bullet had plowed a painful furrow through a few layers of skin and bruised the muscle, but the wound would heal quickly.

That was more than Bolan could say for the reunited Germany.

A soot-streaked Straub approached them, stripping off his oxygen mask.

"I believe we've found Heine's remains," he said. "And least we think so. There's very little left as a frame of reference for identification."

"And the Dag?" Bolan asked.

He shook his head. "No trace yet. It was probably pulverized by the explosions."

"We can only hope so," Bolan said.

Straub eyed Bolan. "You were right. I was working from the wrong viewpoint. Perhaps I didn't want to admit to myself that the evil of bygone days hadn't died of old age."

"Maybe it did," Wezhardt said. "But it was resurrected, when the time was right."

Straub didn't reply to that. He went back to directing the search operation. He was extremely distressed, and Bolan didn't blame him. It probably wasn't the first time fascists had jeopardized his organization and his job security.

A dark green sedan pulled up in the yard. Hyams climbed out, looking jubilant.

"We've got the enabling codes at the site changed," he said. "A new set of precautionary measures is in the works. Something like this will never happen again, by God."

"As long as those weapons exist, something like it will happen," Bolan argued. "Maybe not in our lifetimes, but it will happen again. The only way to stop it is to remove the temptation. Don't just lock the cookie jar, but smash the jar and the cookies in them into crumbs."

Hyams looked sour. "You're an optimistic bastard, Blanski."

"I manage."

Hyams forced a smile to his face. "Thanks to you, I'm going to be extremely busy for the next couple of weeks. We've got to sort all this out and file all the intelligence. The Order of Thule has contacts and conduits all over the damn place. Exposing it is a real coup."

"For who?"

As if he hadn't heard, Hyams went on. "The Joint Chiefs have notified the White House that they are very pleased with the way we resolved this matter. I'm passing on the congratulations to you. If that makes any kind of difference.''

"It doesn't.''

"I imagine you'll be receiving an official commendation.''

"I don't think so, Major. I'm not eligible.''

Hyams scowled and gestured to the sedan. "My driver will take you to the airport. You have a jet waiting, so don't let us keep you.''

Bolan turned away from him and walked toward the smoldering debris. He stood and studied it from a distance. Wezhardt joined him.

"So it's over?'' she asked.

"For you, yes. For your country, I don't know.''

"What about you? It's never truly over for you, is it?''

When Bolan didn't answer, she said softly, "You're wondering what the hell it's all about.''

"Yeah.''

"But you always pick up and go on, don't you? To the next battle, to the next killing field, to tilt at another windmill.''

She said no more, but pressed up against him and leaned her head against his chest. Slowly Bolan put an arm around her and stroked her hair. He turned Wezhardt to him and leaned down to kiss her tenderly on the lips, cupping her face between his hands.

They stood there in a long embrace, oblivious to the swirling smoke and the men moving around them.

Mack Bolan lived for the moments between the hellgrounds, but he knew others always beckoned and always would so long as he lived.

That was why he was called the Executioner, and he would be called that until some day he strode into a hellzone that was too hot for him to cool down. And even then, that name would be his epitaph.

The Executioner would always give as good as he got.

James Axler

OUTLANDERS™

ICEBLOOD

Kane and his companions race to find a piece of the
Chintamanti Stone, which they believe to have power
over the collective mind of the evil Archons. Their
journey sees them foiled by a Russian mystic named
Zakat in Manhattan, and there is another dangerous
encounter waiting for them in the Kun Lun mountains
of China.

One man's quest for power unleashes a cataclysm in
America's wastelands.

The dawn of the
Fourth Reich...

THE Destroyer™

#114 Failing Marks
The Fatherland Files Book III

Created by
WARREN MURPHY
and RICHARD SAPIR

From the mountains of Argentina the losers of World War II are
making plans for the Fourth Reich. But when the Destroyer's brain
is downloaded, he almost puts an end to the idea. Adolf Kluge
plans to save the dream with a centuries-old treasure. But then, the
Master of Sinanju may have different plans....

The third in The Fatherland Files, a miniseries based on a secret
fascist organization's attempts to regain the glory of the Third Reich.

Available in February 1999 at your favorite retail outlet.

In the badlands,
there is only survival....

JAMES AXLER

DEATH LANDS®

Crucible of Time

A connection to his past awaits Ryan Cawdor as the group takes a mat-trans jump to the remnants of California. Brother Joshua Wolfe is the leader of the Children of the Rock—a cult that has left a trail of barbarism and hate across the ravaged California countryside. Far from welcoming the group with open arms, the cult forces them into a deadly battle-ritual—which is only their first taste of combat....